Prisoners: Fast
Misery Anc

Mary Cholmondeley

Alpha Editions

This edition published in 2024

ISBN 9789362518958

Design and Setting By
Alpha Editions
www.alphaedis.com
Email - info@alphaedis.com

Contents

CHAPTER I

Grim Fate was tender, contemplating you,
And fairies brought their offerings at your birth; You take the rose-leaf pathway as your due,
Your rightful meed the choicest gifts of earth.

—ARTHUR C. LEGGE.

Fay stood on her balcony, and looked over the ilexes of her villa at Frascati; out across the grey-green of the Campagna to the little compressed city which goes by the great name of Rome.

How small it looked, what a huddled speck with a bubble dome, to be represented by so stupendous a name!

She gazed at it without seeing it. Her eyes turned towards it mechanically because it contained somewhere within its narrow precincts the man of whom she was thinking, of whom she was always thinking.

It was easy to see that Fay—the Duchess of Colle Alto—was an Englishwoman, in spite of her historic Italian name.

She had the look of perfect though not robust health, the reflection over her whole being of a childhood spent much in the open air. She was twenty-three, but her sweet fair face, with its delicate irregular features, was immature, childish. It gave no impression of experience, or thought, or of having met life. She was obviously not of those who criticise or judge themselves. In how many faces we see the conflict, or the remains of conflict with a dual nature. Fay, as she was called by her family, seemed all of a piece with herself. Her unharassed countenance showed it, especially when, as at this moment, she looked harassed. Anxiety was evidently a foreign element. It sat ill upon her smooth face, as if it might slide off at any moment. Fay's violet eyes were her greatest charm. She looked at you with a deprecating, timid, limpid gaze, in which no guile existed, any more than steadfastness, any more than unselfishness, any more than courage.

Fay had come into the world anxious to please. She had never shown any particular wish to give pleasure. If she had been missed out of her somewhat oppressed and struggling home when she married, it is probable that the sense of her absence was tinged by relief.

She had never intended to marry the Duke of Colle Alto. It is difficult to say why that sedate distinguished personage married her.

Fay's face had a very sweet and endearing promise in it which drew men's eyes after her. I don't know what it meant, and they did not know either, but they instinctively lessened the distance between themselves and it. A very thin string will tow a very heavy body if there is no resistance, and the pace is slow. The duke looked at Fay, who was at that moment being taken out for her first season by her grandmother, Lady Bellairs. Fay tried to please him, as was her wont with all except men with beards. She liked to have him in attendance. Her violet eyes lighted up with genuine pleasure when he came to see her.

It is perhaps difficult for the legions of women who do not please easily, and for the handful whose interests lie outside themselves, and who are not desirous of pleasing indiscriminately, it is difficult for either to realise the passionate desire to please which possesses and saps the life of some of their sisters. Admiration with them is not a luxury, any more than a hot-water bottle is a luxury to the aged, or a foot rest to a gouty foot. It is a necessity of life. After a becoming interval, the interstices of which had been filled with flowers, the duke proposed to Lady Bellairs for Fay's hand. Fay did not wish to marry him. He was not in the least her ideal. Neither did she wish to remain unmarried, neither did she wish to part with her grave, distinguished suitor who was an ornament to herself. And she was distinctly averse to living any longer in the paternal home, lost in a remote crease in a Hampshire down. Poor women have only too frequently to deal with these complicated situations, with which blundering, egotistic male minds are seldom in perfect sympathy.

Fay had never willingly relinquished any of the men who had cared for her, and some had cared much. These last had as a rule torn themselves away from her, leaving hearts, or other fragments of themselves, behind, and were not to be cajoled back again, even by one of her little gilt-edged notes. But the duke did not break away. He had selected her, she pleased him, he desired to marry an Englishwoman. He had the approval of Lady Bellairs.

The day came when Fay was suddenly and adroitly confronted with the fact that she must marry him, or lose him.

Many confirmed bachelors who openly regret that they have never come across a woman to whom they cared to tie themselves for life might be in a position to descant on the inability of wives to enter into their husbands' inmost feelings, if only they—the bachelors—had known on a past occasion how to act with sudden promptitude on the top of patience.

The duke played the waiting game, and then hit hard. He had coolly allowed himself to be trifled with, until the moment arrived when it did not suit him to be trifled with any longer.

The marriage had not proved a marked success, nor an entire failure. The duke was an irreproachable husband, but, like many men who marry when they are no longer young, he aged suddenly after marriage. He quickly became bald and stout. His tact except in these two particulars remained flawless. He never allowed his deep chagrin to appear when, three years after his marriage, he still remained without a son to continue his historic name.

He was polite to his wife at all times, mildly sarcastic as to her extravagance. Fay was not exorbitantly extravagant; but then the duke was not exorbitantly rich. One of Fay's arts, as unconscious as that of a kitten, was to imply past unhappiness, spoken of with a cheerful resignation which greatly endeared her to others—and to herself. The duke had understood that she had not had a very happy home, and he had honestly endeavoured to make her new home happy. In the early days of his marriage he made many small experiments in the hope of pleasing the pretty creature who had thrown in her lot with his. Possibly also there may have been other subtle, patient attempts to win somewhat from her of another nature. Possibly there may have been veiled disappointments, and noiseless retreats under cover of night.

However these things may have been, after the first year Fay made the discovery that she was unhappily married. The duke was kind, in kindness he never failed; but he was easily jealous—at least she thought so; and he appeared quite unable to see in their true light her amicable little flirtations with his delightful compatriots. After one or two annoying incidents, in which the compatriots had shown several distinctly un-English characteristics, the duke became, in his wife's eyes, tiresome, strict, a burden. Perhaps, also, she felt the Englishwoman's surprise at the inadequate belief in a woman's power of guarding her own virtue, which remains in some nations an hereditary masculine instinct. She felt that she could take care of herself, which was, in reality, just what she could not do, as her imperturbable, watchful husband was well aware.

But was he aware of the subject of her thoughts at this moment? It was more than probable that he was. But Fay had not the faintest suspicion that he had guessed anything.

One of her many charms was a certain youthful innocence of mind, which imputed no evil to others, which never suspected that others would impute it to her. Her husband was wearisome. He looked coldly on her if she smiled on young men, and she had to smile at them when they smiled at her. But, she reasoned, of course all the time he really knew that he could trust her entirely. There was no harm in Fay's nature, no venom, there were no dark places, no strong passions, with their awful possibilities for good and evil. She had already given much pain in her short life, but inadvertently. She was of that large class of whom it may truly be said when evil comes, that they are more sinned against than sinning. They always somehow gravitate into the places where people *are* sinned against, just as some people never attend a cricket-match without receiving a ball on their persons.

And now trouble had come upon her. She had at last fallen in love. I would not venture to assert that she had fallen in very deep, that the "breakers of the boundless deep" had engulfed her. Some of us make shipwreck in a teacup tempest, and when our serenity is restored—there is nothing calmer than a teacup after its storm—our experience serves, after a decent interval, as an agreeable fringe to our confidential conversation.

Anyhow, Fay had fallen in love. I feel bound to add that for some time before that event happened life had become intolerably dull. The advent to Rome of her distant connection, Michael Carstairs, had been at this juncture a source of delight to her. She had, before her marriage, flirted with him a very little—not as much as she could have wished; but Lady Bellairs, who was fond of him, had promptly intervened, and the young man had disappeared into his examinations. That was four years ago.

In reality Fay had half-forgotten him; but when she saw him suddenly, pale, handsome, distinguished, across a ballroom in Rome, and, after a moment's uncertainty, realised who he was, she felt the same pleasurable surprise, soft as the fall of dew, which pervades the feminine heart when, in looking into an unused drawer, it inadvertently haps upon a length of new ribbon, bought, carefully put away, and forgotten.

Fay went gently up to Michael, conscious of her beauty and her wonderful jewels, and held out her hand with a little deprecating smile.

"And so we meet again at last," she said.

He turned red and white.

"At last," he said with difficulty.

She looked more closely at him. The dreamy, poetic face had changed during those four years. She became dimly aware that he had not only grown from a youth into a man, but that some other transformation had been painfully wrought in him.

Instinctively her beaming face became grave to match his. She was slow to see what others were feeling, but quick to reflect their mood. She sighed gently, vaguely stirred, in spite of herself, by something—she knew not what—in her companion's face.

"It is four years since I saw you," she said.

And from her lowered voice it seemed as if her life were rooted in memory alone.

"Four years," said Michael, who, promising young diplomat as he was, appeared only able to repeat parrot-wise her last words after her.

A pause.

"Do you know my husband?"

"I do not."

"May I introduce him to you?"

Fay made a little sign, and the duke approached, superb, decorated, dignified, with the polished pallor as if the skin were a little too tight, which is the Charybdis of many who have avoided the Scylla of wrinkles.

The elder Italian and the grave, fair, young Englishman bowed to each other, were made known to each other.

That night as the duke drove home with his wife he said to her in his admirable English:

"Your young cousin is an enthusiast, a dreamer, a sensitive, what your Tennyson calls a Sir Galahad. In Italy we make of such men a priest, a cardinal. He is not an *homme d'affaires*. It was not well to put him into diplomacy. One may make a religion of art. One may even for a time make a religion of a woman. But of the English diplomacy one does not make a religion."

Fay lay awake that night. From a disused pigeon-hole in her mind she drew out and unfolded to its short length that attractive remnant, that half-forgotten episode of her teens. She remembered everything—I mean everything she wished to remember. Michael's face had recalled it all, those exquisite days which he had taken so much more seriously than she had, the sudden ruthless intervention of Lady Bellairs, the end of the daydream. Fay, whose attention had been adroitly diverted to other channels, had never wondered how he took their separation at the time. Now that she saw him again she was aware that he had taken it—to heart.

During that sleepless night Fay persuaded herself that Michael had not been alone in his suffering. She also had felt the parting with equal poignancy.

They met again a few days later by chance in an old cloistered, deserted garden. How often she had walked in that garden as she was doing now with English friends! His presence gave the place its true significance. They met as those who have between them the bond of a common sorrow.

"And what have you been doing all these four years?" she asked him, as they wandered somewhat apart.

"I have been working."

"You never came to say good-bye before you went to that place in Germany to study."

"I was told I had better not come."

"I suppose grandmamma told you that."

"She did, most kindly and wisely."

A pause.

She was leaning in the still May sunshine against an old grey tomb of carved stone. Two angels with spread wings upheld the defaced inscription. Above it, over it, round it, like desire impotently defying death, a flood of red roses clambered and clung. Were they trying to wake some votary who slept below? A great twisted sentinel cypress kept its own dark counsel. Against its shadow Fay's figure in her white gossamer gown showed more ethereal and exquisite even than in memory. She seemed at one with this wonderful, passionate southern spring, which trembled between rapture and anguish. The red roses and the white irises were everywhere. Even the unkept grass in which her light feet were set was wild with white daisies.

"Do you remember our last walk on the down that day in spring?" she said suddenly.

She had forgotten it until last night.

"I remember it."

"It was May then. It is May again now."

He did not answer. The roses left off calling to the dead, and suddenly enfolded the two young grave creatures leaning against the tomb, in a gust of hot perfume.

"Do you remember," Fay's voice was tremulous, "how you gave me a bit of pink may?"

"I remember."

"I was looking at it yesterday. It is not very pink now."

It was true. In all shallow meanings, and when she had not had time to get her mind into a tangle, Fay was perfectly truthful. She had yesterday been turning over the contents of a little cedar box in which she kept her childish possessions, and she had found in an envelope a brown unsightly ghost of what had once been a may-blossom on a Hampshire down. She had remembered the vivid sunshine, the wheeling seagull, the soft south wind blowing in from the sea. Michael had kissed her under the thin dappled shade of the flowering tree, and she had kissed him back.

Michael's eyes turned for a long moment to the yellow weather-stained arches of the cloister, and then he looked full at Fay with a certain peculiar detached glance which had first made her endeavour to attract him. There is a look in a man's face which women like Fay cannot endure, because it means independence of them.

"I thought," he said, with the grave simplicity which apparently was unchangeable in him whatever else might change, "that it was only I who remembered. It has always been a comfort to me that any unhappiness which my want of forethought, my—my culpable selfishness may have caused, was borne by myself alone."

"I was unhappy too," she said, speaking as simply as he. She looked up at him suddenly as she said it. There was a wet glint in her deep violet eyes. She believed absolutely at that moment that she had been as unhappy as he for four years. There was no suspicion in her mind that she was not genuine. Only the sincere ever doubt their sincerity. Fay never doubted hers. She felt what she said, and the sweet eyes turned on Michael had the transparent fixity of a child's.

They walked unsteadily back to the others and spoke no more to each other that day. Conscience pricked Fay that night.

"Leave him alone," it said. "You have both suffered. Let the dead past bury its dead."

Fay's conscience was a wonderfully adaptable one with a tendency to poetic quotation. It showed considerable tact in adopting her point of view. Nevertheless from that generally fallacious standpoint it often gave her quite respectable advice. "Leave him alone," said the hoodwinked monitor. "You are married and Andrea is easily jealous. Michael is sensitive, and has been deeply in love with you. Don't stir him up to fall in love with you again. *Leave him alone.*"

The young British matron waxed indignant. Was she, Fay, the kind of woman to forget her duty to her husband? Was Michael the kind of man to make love to a married woman? Such an idea was preposterous, unjust to both of them. And people would begin to talk at once if she and her cousin

(Michael was only a distant connection) were studiously to avoid each other, if they could not exchange a few words simply like old friends. No one had suggested an attitude of rigid avoidance; but throughout life Fay had always convinced herself of the advisability of a certain wished-for course by conjuring up, only to discard it, the extreme and most obviously senseless opposite of that course—as the only alternative.

She imagined her husband saying: "Why won't you ask Mr. Carstairs to dinner? He is your cousin and he is charming. What can the reason be that you so earnestly refuse to meet him?" And then Andrea, who always "got ideas into his head," would begin to suspect that there had been "something" between them.

No. No. It would be far wiser to meet naturally now and then, and to treat Michael like an old friend. Fay had a somewhat muffled conception of what an old friend might be. After deep thought she came to the conclusion that it was her duty to ask Michael frequently to the house. When Fay once recognised a duty she performed it without delay.

She met with an unexpected obstacle in the way of its adequate performance. The obstacle was Michael.

The young man came once, and then again after an interval of several months, but apparently nothing would induce him to frequent the house.

Fay did not recognise her boyish eager lover in the grave sedate man, old of his age, who had replaced him. His dignified and quite unobtrusive resistance, which had not indifference at its core, added an intense, a feverish, interest to Fay's life. She saw that he still cared for her, and that he did not intend to wound himself a second time. He had had enough. She put out all her little transparent arts during the months that followed. The duke watched.

She had implied to her husband with a smile that she had not been very happy at home. She implied to Michael with a smile that it was not the duke's fault, but that she was not very happy in her married life, that he did not care much about her, and that they had but few tastes in common. Each lived their own life on amicable terms, but somewhat apart from each other. She owned that she had hoped for something rather different in marriage. She had, it seemed, started life with a very exalted ideal of married life, which the duke's

coarse thumb
And finger failed to plumb.

Michael remained outwardly obdurate, but inwardly he weakened. His tender adoration and respect for Fay, wounded and mutilated though they had been, had nevertheless survived what in many minds must have proved their death-blow. He still believed implicitly all she said.

But to him her marriage was the impassable barrier, a barrier as enfranchisable as the brown earth on a coffin lid.

After many months Fay at last vaguely realised his attitude towards her. She told herself that she respected it, that it was just what she wished, was in fact the result of her own tactfully expressed wishes. She seemed to remember things she had said which would have led him to behave just as he had done. And then she turned heaven and earth to regain her personal ascendency over him. She never would have regained it if an accident had not befallen her. She fell in love with him during the process.

The day came, an evil day for Michael, when he could no longer doubt it, when he was not permitted to remain in doubt. Who shall say what waves of boundless devotion, what passionate impulses of protection, of compassion, of intense longing to shield her from the fire which had devastated his own youth, passed in succession over him as he looked at the delicate little creature who was to him the only real woman in the world—all the rest were counterfeits—and who now, as he believed, loved him as he had long loved her.

Michael was one of the few men who bear through life the common masculine burden of a profound ignorance of women, coupled with an undeviating loyalty towards them. He supposed she was suffering as he had suffered, that it was with her now beside the fountain, under the ilexes of her Italian garden, as it had been with him during these five intolerable years.

How Fay wept! What a passion of tears, till her small flower-like face was bereft of all beauty, of everything except a hideous contraction of grief!

He stood near her, not touching her, in anguish far deeper than hers. At last he took her clenched hand in his.

"Do not grieve so," he said brokenly. "It is not our fault. It is greater than either of us. It has come upon us against our wills. We have both struggled. You don't know how I have struggled, Fay, day and night since I came to Rome. But I have been in fault. I ought never to have come, for I knew you were living near Rome. But I did not know it had touched you, and for myself I had hoped—I thought—that it was past—in as far as it could pass—that I was accustomed to it. Listen, Fay, and do not cry so bitterly. I will leave Rome at once. I will not see you again. My poor darling, we have come to a hard place in life, but we can do the only thing left to us—our duty."

Fay's heart contracted, and she suddenly ceased sobbing. She had never thought of this horrible possibility that he would leave her.

She drew the hand that clasped hers to her lips and held it tightly against her breast.

"Don't leave me," she stammered, trembling from head to foot, from sheer terror at the thought; "I will be good. I will do what is right. We are not like other people. We can trust each other. But I can't live without seeing you sometimes, I could not bear it."

He withdrew his hand. They looked wildly into each other's eyes. His convulsed face paled and paled. Even as he stood before her she knew she was losing him, that something was tearing him from her. It was as certain that he was going from her as if she were standing by his deathbed.

He kissed her suddenly.

"I shall not come back," he said. And the next moment he was gone.

CHAPTER II

Nous passons notre vie à nous forger des chaînes, et à nous plaindre de les porter.

—VALTOUR.

For a long time Fay had stood on her balcony looking out towards Rome, while the remembrance of the last few months pressed in upon her.

It was a week since she had seen Michael, since he had said, "I shall not come back."

And in the meanwhile she had heard that he had resigned his appointment, and was leaving Rome at once. She had never imagined that he would act so quickly, with such determination. She had vaguely supposed that he would send in his resignation, and then remain on. In novels in a situation like theirs the man never really went away, or if he did he came back. Fay knew very little of Michael, but nevertheless she instinctively felt and quailed before the conviction that he really was leaving her for ever, that he would reconstruct a life for himself somewhere in which she could not reach him, in which she would have no part or lot. He might suffer during the process, but he would do it. His yea was yea, and his nay, nay. She should see him no more. Some day, not for a long time perhaps, but some day, she should hear of his marriage.

Suddenly, without a moment's warning, her own life rose up before her, distorted, horrible, unendurable. The ilexes, solemn in the sunset, showed like foul shapes of disgust and nausea. The quiet Campagna with its distant faintly outlined Sabine hills was rotten to the core.

The duke passed across a glade at a little distance, and, looking up, smiled gravely at her, with a slight courteous gesture of his brown hand.

She smiled mechanically in response and shrank back into her room. Her husband had suddenly become a thing to shudder at, repulsive as a reptile, intolerable. Her life with him, without Michael, stretched before her like a loathsome disease, a leprosy, which in the interminable years would gradually eat her away, a death by inches.

The first throes of a frustrated passion at the stake have probably seldom failed to engender a fierce rebellion against the laws which light the faggots round it.

The fire had licked Fay. She fled blindfold from it, not knowing whither, only away from that pain, over any precipice, into any slough.

"I cannot live without him," she sobbed to herself. "This is not just a common love affair like other people's. It is everything, my whole life! It is not as if we were bad people! We are both upright! We always have been! We have both done our best, but—I can't go on. What is reputation worth, the world's opinion of me?—*nothing.*"

It was not worth more to Fay at that moment than it has ever been worth to any other poor mortal since the world's opinion first clashed with love.

To follow love shows itself time and time again alike to the pure and to the worldly as the only real life, the only path. But if we disbelieve in it, and framing our lives on other lines become voluntarily bedridden into selfishness and luxury, can we—when that in which we have not believed comes to pass—can we suddenly rise and follow Love up his mountain passes? We try to rise when he calls us from our sick beds. We even go feverishly a little way with him. But unless we have learnt the beginnings of courage and self-surrender before we set out, we seem to turn giddy, and lose our footing. Certain precipices there are where only the pure and strong in heart may pass, at the foot of which are the piled bones of many passionate pilgrims.

Were Fay's delicate little bones, so subtly covered in soft white flesh, to be added to that putrefying heap? But can we blame anyone, be they who they may, placed howsoever they may be, who when first they undergo a real emotion try however feebly to rise to meet it?

Fay was not wholly wise, not wholly sincere, but she made an attempt to meet it. It was not to be expected that the attempt would be quite wise or quite sincere either. Still it was the best she could do. She would sacrifice herself for love. She would go away with Michael. No one would ever speak to her again, but she did not care.

Involuntarily she unclasped a diamond Saint-Esprit from her throat which the duke had given her, and laid it on her writing-table. She should never wear it again. She no longer had the right to wear it. It was a unique jewel. But what did she care for jewels now! They had served to pass the time in the sort of waking dream in which she had lived till Michael came. But she was awake now. She looked at herself in the glass long and fixedly. Yes, she was beautiful. How dreadful it must be for plain women when they loved! They must know that men could not really care for them. They might, of course, respect and esteem them, and wish in a lukewarm way to marry them, but they could never really love them. She, Fay, carried with her the talisman.

A horrible doubt seized her, just when she was becoming calm. Supposing Michael would not! Oh! but he *would* if he cared as she did. The sacrifice was all on the woman's side. No one thought much the worse of men when they did these things. And Michael was so good, so honourable that he would certainly never desert her. They would become legal husband and wife directly Andrea divorced her.

From underneath these matted commonplaces, Fay's muffled conscience strove to reach her with its weak voice.

"Stop, stop!" it said. "You will injure him. You will tie a noose round his neck. You will spoil his life. And Andrea! He has been kind in a way. And your marriage vows! And your own people at home! And Magdalen, the sister who loves you. Remember her! Stop, stop! Let Michael go. You were obliged to relinquish him once. Let him go again now."

Fay believed she went through a second conflict. Perhaps there lurked at the back of her mind the image of Michael's set face—set away from her; and that image helped her at last to say to herself, "Yes. It is right. I will let him go."

But did she really mean it? For while she said over and over again, "Yes, yes; we must part," she decided that it was necessary to see him just once again, to bid him a last farewell, to strengthen him to live without her. She could not reason it out, but she knew that it was absolutely essential to the welfare of both that they should see each other just once more before they parted—*for ever*. The parting no longer loomed so awful in her mind if there was to be a meeting before it took place. She almost forgot it directly her mind could find a staying point on the thought of that one last sacred interview, of all she should say, of all they would both feel.

But how to see him! He had said he would not come back. He left Rome in a few days. She should see him officially on Thursday, when he was in attendance on his chief. But what was the use of that? He would hardly exchange a word with her. She might decide to see *him* alone; but what if he refused to see *her*? Instinctively Fay knew that he would so refuse.

"We must part." Just so. But how to hold him? How to draw him to her just once more? That was the crux.

In novels if a woman needs the help of the chivalrous man ever kneeling in the background, she sends him a ring. Fay looked earnestly at her rings. But Michael might not understand if she sent him one, and if the duke intercepted it he would certainly entirely misconstrue the situation.

Fay sat down at her writing-table, and got out her note-paper. Truth compels me to state that it was of blue linen, that it had a little gilt coronet on it, and that it was scented.

She thought a long time. At least she bit the little silver owl at the end of her pen for a long time. She tore up several sheets. At last she wrote in her large, slanting, dashing handwriting:

"*I know that we must part. You are right and I wish it too. It is all like a terrible dream, and what will the awakening be?*" (Fay did not quite know what she meant by this, but it impressed her deeply as she wrote it, and a tear dropped on "the awakening" and made it look like "reckoning." She was not of those, however, who having once written one word ever think it can be mistaken for another; and really reckoning did quite as well as awakening.) "*But I must see you once before you go. I have something of urgent importance to say to you.*" (It was not clear to Fay what the matter of importance was. But has not everyone in love laboured daily under a burden as big as Christian's, of subjects which demand instant discussion, or the bearer may fall into a state of melancholia? Fay was convinced as she wrote that there was something she ached to say to him: and also the point was to say something that would bring him.) "*Don't fail me. You have never failed me yet. You left me before when it was right we should part. Did I try to keep you then? Did I say one word to hold you back?*" (Fay's heart swelled as she wrote those words. She saw, bathed in a new light, her own courage and uprightness in the past. She realised her extraordinary strength of character. She had not faltered then.) "*I did not falter then. I will not do so now, though this time is harder than the first.*" (It certainly was.) "*You have to come to my little party on Thursday with your chief. I cannot speak to you then. I am closely watched. When the others have gone come back through the gardens. The door by the fountain will be unlocked, and come up the balcony steps to my sitting-room. The balcony window will be open. You know that I should not ask you to do this unless it was urgent. Will you fail me at the last? For we shall never meet again, Michael!*"

Fay closed the note, directed it, pinned it into the lace of her inmost vest—the wife of an Italian distrusts pockets and postal arrangements—and then wept her heart out, her vain, selfish little heart, which for the first time in her life was not wholly vain, nor wholly selfish. Perhaps it was not her fault if she was cruel. It takes many steadfast years, many prayers, many acts of humble service before we may hope to reach the place where we are content to bear alone the brunt of that pang, and to guard the one we love even from ourselves.

CHAPTER III

There will no man do for your sake, I think,
What I would have done for the least word said. I had wrung life dry for your lips to drink,
Broken it up for your daily bread.

—A. C. SWINBURNE.

A witty bishop was once heard to remark that one of the difficulties of his social life lay in the fact that all women of forty were exactly alike, and it was impossible to recall their individual label, to which archdeacon, or canon, or form of spinster good works, they belonged. It would be dangerous, irreverent, to pry further into the recesses of the episcopal, or even of the suffragan, mind. There are snowy peaks where we lay helpers should fear to tread. But it may be stated, without laying ourselves open to a suspicion of wishing to undermine the Church, that when the woman of forty in her turn acidly announces, as she not infrequently does, that all young men seem to her exactly alike, she is in a parlous condition.

Yet many women had said that Michael was exactly like every other young man. And to all except the very few who knew him well he certainly did appear to be—not an individual at all—but only an indistinguished unit of a vast army.

His obvious good looks were like the good looks of others. He looked well bred, but to look that is as common in a certain class as it is rare in another. He had the spare, wiry figure, tall and lightly built, square in the shoulders, and thin in the flank; he had the clear weather-beaten complexion, the clean, nervous, capable hand, and the self-effacing manner, which we associate with myriads of well-born, machine-trained, perfectly groomed, expensively educated, uneducated Englishmen. Our public schools turn them out by the thousand. The "lost legion" is made up of them. The unburied bones of the pioneers of new colonies are mostly theirs. They die of thirst in "the never never country," under a tree, leaving their initials cut in its trunk; they fall by hundreds in our wars. They are born leaders where acumen and craft are not needed. Large game was made for them, and they for it. They are the vermin destroyers of the universe. They throw life from them with both hands, they play the game of life with a levity which they never showed in the business of cricket and football.

They are essentially not of the stuff of which those dull persons, the thinkers, the politicians, the educationalists, are made. No profession knows them except the army. They have no opinions worth hearing. Only the women who are to marry them listen to them. They are sometimes squeezed into Parliament and are borne with there like children. About one in a hundred of them can earn his own living, and then it is as a land agent.

They make adorable country squires, and picturesque, simple-minded, painstaking men of rank. They know by a sort of hereditary instinct how to deal with a labouring man, and a horse, and how to break in a dog. They give themselves no airs. We have *millions* of men like this, and it is doubtful whether the nation finds much use for them, except at coronations, where they look beautiful; or on county councils, where they can hold an opinion without the preliminary fatigue of forming it; and on the bloodstained fringes of our empire, where they serenely meet their dreadful deaths.

In the ranks of that vast army I descry Michael, and I wonder what it is in him that makes me able to descry him at all. He is like thousands of other men. In what is he unlike?

I think it must be something in his expression. Of many ugly men it has been said with truth that one never observes their ugliness. Something in the character redeems it. With Michael's undeniable good looks it was the same. One did not notice them. They were not admired, except, possibly, for the first moment, or across a room. His rather insignificant grey eyes were the only thing one remembered him by, the only part of him which seemed to represent him.

It was as if out of the narrow window of a fortress *our friend* for a moment looked out; that "friend of our infinite dreams" who in dreams, but, alas! never by day, comes softly to us across the white fields of youth; who, later on, in dreams but never by day, overtakes us with unbearable happiness in his hand in which to steep our exhaustion on the hillside; who when our hair is grey comes to us still in dreams but never by day, down the darkening valley, to tell us that our worn out romantic hopes are but the alphabet of his language.

Such a look there was in Michael's eyes, and what it meant who shall say? Once and again at long intervals we pass in the thoroughfare of life young faces which have the same expression, as if they saw beyond, as if they looked past their own youth across to an immortal youth, from their own life to an unquenchable, upwelling spring of life. When Michael spoke, which was little, his words verged on the commonplace. He explained the obvious with modest directness. He had thought out and made his own a small selection of platitudes. It is at first a shock to some of us when we discover that a beautiful spiritual nature is linked with a tranquil commonplace mind and narrow abilities.

When Michael's eyes rested on anything his still glance seemed to pass through it, into its essence. An inscrutable Fate had willed that his eyes should not rest on any woman save Fay.

Was her little hand to rend his illusions from him; or did he perhaps see her as she was, as her husband, her shrewd old grandmother, her sister even, had never seen her? Fay had revealed to Michael that of which many men who write glibly of passion die in ignorance, the wonder and awe of love, clothed in a woman's form, walking the earth. And in a reverent and grateful loyalty Michael would have laid down his life for her, as gladly as Dante would have done for "his lady." But Michael would have laid down his in silence, as one casts off a glove. He had never read the "New Life." It is improbable that it would have made any impression on him if he had read it. He never associated words or books or poetry with feelings. What he felt he held sacred. He was unconsciously by nature that which others of the artistic temperament consciously are in a lesser degree, and are doomed to try to express. Michael never wanted to express anything, had no impulse of self-revelation, no interest in his own mental experiences.

While Fay was turning over her little *bric-a-brac* assortment of feelings, her toy renunciations, her imitation convictions, Michael was slowly making the great renunciation without even taking himself into his confidence. To go away. To see her no more. This was death by inches. As he sat hour after hour in his little room behind the Embassy it seemed to him as if, by some frightful exertion of his will, he were wading with incredible slowness out to sea, over endless flats in inch-deep water, which after an interminable journey would be deep enough to drown him at last.

The nausea and horror of this slow death were upon him. Nevertheless, he meant to move towards it. And where Michael's eye was fixed there his foot followed. He was not of those who rend themselves by violent conflict. If he had ever been asked to give his reason for any action of his life, from the greatest to the smallest, he would have looked at the questioner in mild surprise, and would have said: "It was the only thing to do."

To him vacillation and doubt were unknown. A certain wisdom could never be his, for he saw no alternatives. He never balanced two courses of action against each other.

"There were no two ways about it," he said to his godfather, the Bishop of Lostford, respecting a decision where there were several alternatives, which he had endeavoured to set before Michael with impartiality. But Michael saw only one course, and took it.

And now again he only saw one course, and he meant to take it. He sickened under it, but his mind was made up. Fay's letter which duly reached him only made him suffer. It did not alter his determination to go. Certainly, he would see her again, if she desired it so intensely, and had something vitally important to tell him, though he disliked the suggestion of a clandestine meeting. Still it was Fay's suggestion, and Fay could do no wrong. But he knew that nothing she could do or say, nothing new that she could spring upon him would have power to shake his decision to leave Rome on Friday. *It was the only thing to do.*

CHAPTER IV

L'on fait plus souvent des trahisons par faiblesse que par un dessein formé de trahir.

—LA ROCHEFOUCAULD.

Fay's evening-party was a success. Her parties generally were. It was a small gathering, for as it was May but few of the residents had come down to the villas. Some of the guests had motored out from Rome. My impression is that Fay enjoyed the evening. She certainly enjoyed the brilliancy which excitement had momentarily added to her beauty.

All the time she was saying to herself, "If people only knew. What a contrast between what these people think and what I really am. Perhaps this is the last time I shall have a party here. Perhaps I shall not be here to-morrow. Perhaps Michael will insist on taking me away with him, from this death in life, this hell on earth."

What large imposing words! How well they sounded! Yes, in a way Fay was enjoying herself.

Often during the evening she saw the grave, kindly eyes of the duke upon her. Once he came up to her, and paid her a little exquisite compliment. Her disgust and hatred of him were immediately forgotten. She smiled back at him. She did not love him of course. A man like that did not know what love was. But Fay had never yet felt harshly towards any man who admired her. The husband who did not understand her watched her with something of the indulgent, protecting expression which we see on the face of the owner of an enchanting puppy, which is ready to gallop on india rubber legs after any pair of boots which appears on its low horizon.

The guests had ebbed away by degrees. Lord John Alington, a tall, bald, boring Englishman, and one or two others, remained behind, arranging some expedition with the duke.

Michael's chief had long since gone. Michael did not depart with him, but took his leave a few moments later. Michael's departure from Rome the following day on urgent affairs was generally known. The duke had watched him bid Fay a mechanical farewell, and had then expressed an urbane regret at his departure. The thin, pinched face of the young man appealed to the elder one. The duke had liked him from the first.

"It is time he went," he said to himself as he watched Michael leave the room. As Michael left it Fay's excitement dropped from her, and she became conscious of an enormous fatigue. A few minutes later she dragged herself up the great pictured staircase to her little boudoir overlooking the garden, and sank down exhausted on a couch. Her pretty Italian maid was waiting for her in the adjoining bedroom, and came to her, and began to unfasten her jewels.

Fay dismissed her for the night, saying she was not going to bed yet. She often stayed up late reading. She was of those who say that they have no time for reading in the day, and who like to look up (or rather, to say afterwards they looked up) to find the solemn moon peering in at them.

To-night there was no solemn or otherwise disposed moon.

Fay's heart suddenly began to beat so wildly that it seemed as if she would suffocate. What violent emotion was this which was flooding her, sweeping away all landmarks, covering, as by one great inrolling tidal wave, all the familiar country of her heart? Whither was she being swept in the midst of this overwhelming roaring torrent? Out to sea? To some swift destruction? Where? Where?

She clutched the arm of the sofa and trembled. She had known so many small emotions. What was this? And like a second wave on the top of the first a sea of recklessness broke over and engulfed her. *What next?* She did not know. She did not care. Michael, his face and hand. These were the only realities. In another moment she should see him, feel him, hold him, never, never let him go again.

In the intense stillness a whisper came up through the orange blossom below her balcony:

"Fay."

She was on the balcony in a moment. The scent of the orange blossom had become alive and confused everything.

"Come up," she said almost inaudibly.

"I cannot."

"You must. I must speak to you."

"Come down here then. I am not coming up."

She ran down, and felt rather than saw Michael's presence at the foot of the little stair.

He was breathing hard. He did not move towards her.

"You sent for me, so I came," he said. "Tell me quickly what I can do for you, how I can serve you. I cannot remain here more than a moment. I endanger your safety as it is."

It was all so different from what she had expected, from what she had pictured to herself. He was so determined and stern; and it had never struck her as possible that he would not come up to her room, that the interview would be so short.

"I can't speak here," she said, angry tears smarting in her eyes.

"You can and must. Tell me quickly, dearest, why you sent for me. You said it was all-important. I am here, I will do your bidding, if you will only say what it is."

"Take me with you," she gasped inaudibly.

She had not meant to say that. She was merely the mouthpiece of something vast, of some blind destructive force that was rending her. She swayed against the railings, clinging to them with both hands.

Even as she spoke her voiceless whisper was drowned in a sound but very little louder. There was a distant stir, a movement as of waking bees in the house.

He had not heard her. He was listening intently.

"Go back instantly and shut the window," he said, and in a moment she felt he was gone.

She crept feebly up the stairs to her room and sank down again on the couch, broken, half dead.

"I shall see him no more. I shall see him no more," she said to herself, twisting her hands. What a travesty, what a mockery that one hurried moment had been! What a parting that was no parting! He had no heart. He did not really love her.

Through her stupor she felt rather than heard a movement in the house. She stole out of her room to the head of the grand staircase. Nearly all the lights had been put out. Close to a lamp in the saloon below, the duke and Lord John were standing, looking at a map. "The Grotta Ferrata road is the best," the duke was saying. And as he spoke a servant came in quickly, and whispered to the duke, who left the saloon with him.

Fay fled back to her own room. Something was happening. But what? Could it have any connection with herself and Michael? No, that seemed impossible. And Michael must by now have left the gardens, by the unlocked door by which he had come in.

Fay drew the reading lamp nearer to her, and opened the book of devotions which Magdalen, her far off sister in England, had sent her. Her eyes wandered over the page, her mind taking no heed.

"*For it is the most pain that the soul may have, to turn from God any time by sin.*"

There certainly was a sort of subdued stir in the house. A nameless fear was invading Fay's heart. The book shook in her hand. What *could* be happening? And if it was, as it must be, something quite apart from her and Michael, what did it matter, why be afraid?

"*For sin is vile, and so greatly to be hated that it may be likened to no pain which is not sin. And to me was showed no harder hell than sin.*"

A low tap came at the window. Fay started violently, and the book dropped on the floor.

The tap was repeated. She went to the window, and saw Michael's face through the glass.

She opened the glass door, and he came in. His clothes were smeared and torn, and there was blood upon his hand.

"Something has happened," he said. "I don't know what it is, but the garden is surrounded, and there is someone watching at the door I came in at. I have tried all the other ways. I have tried to climb the wall, but there was glass at the top. I can't get out. And they are searching the gardens with lanterns."

Even as he spoke they saw lights moving among the ilexes.

"They can't know," she said faintly.

"It does not seem possible. They are probably looking for someone else, but I can't be found here at this hour without raising suspicion. Is there any way out through the house from here?"

"Only down the grand staircase."

"I must risk it. Show me the way."

They went together down the almost dark corridor. Fay's heart sickened at the thought that a belated servant might see them. But all was quiet. At the head of the staircase they both peered over the balustrade. At its foot in a narrow circle of light stood the duke and Lord John, and a man with a tri-coloured sash. Even as they looked, the three turned and began slowly to mount the staircase.

Fay and Michael were back in her boudoir in a moment.

"There is a way out here," he said, indicating the door into her bedroom.

"It leads into my bedroom, and then through to Andrea's rooms. There is no passage, and he has a dog in his room. It would bark."

"I must go back to the garden again," he said, and instantly moved to the window. Both saw two *carabinieri* standing with a lantern at the foot of the balcony steps.

"If you go down now," said Fay hoarsely, "my reputation goes with you."

He looked at her.

It was as if his whole life were focussed on one burning point; how to save her from suspicion. If he could have shrivelled into ashes at her feet he would have done it. She saw her frightful predicament, and almost hated him.

The animal panic of being trapped caught them both simultaneously. He overcame it instantly, while she shook helplessly as in a palsy.

He went swiftly back to the door leading to the staircase, and glanced through it.

"They are coming along the corridor," he said. "They will certainly come in here."

"Stand behind the screen," she gasped. "I will say no one has been here, and they will pass through into the other room. As soon as they have left the room go quickly out by the staircase."

He looked round him once, and then walked behind a tall screen of Italian leather which stood at the head of a divan.

Fay took up her book from the floor, but her numb fingers refused to hold it. She put it on the edge of the table near her, under the lamp, hid her shaking hands in the folds of her long white chiffon gown, and fixed her eyes upon the page.

The words of the dead saint swam before her eyes:

"*Yea, He loveth us now as well while we are here, as He shall do while we are there afore His blessed face. But for failing of love on our part, therefore is all our travail.*"

There were subdued footsteps outside, a tap, the duke's voice.

"May I come in?"

"Come in," she said, but she heard no words.

She made a superhuman effort.

"Come in," she said again, and this time to her relief she heard the words distinctly.

The duke entered and held the door half closed.

"I feared to disturb you, my child," he said, "but it is unavoidable that I disturb you. It is a relief to find that you are not yet in bed and asleep. A very grave, a very sad event has happened which necessitates the presence of the police commissioner. Calm yourself, my Francesca, and my good friend the *delegato* will explain."

The official in the sash came in. Lord John stood in the doorway.

"Duchess," said the official, "I grieve to say that one of your guests of this evening, the Marchese di Maltagliala, has been assassinated in the garden, or possibly in the road, and his dead body was dragged into the garden afterwards. He was found just inside the east garden door, which by some mischance had been left unlocked."

A deathlike silence followed the *delegato's* words.

"A DEATHLIKE SILENCE FOLLOWED THE DELEGATO'S WORDS"

Fay turned her bloodless face towards him, and her eyes never left him. She felt Michael listening behind the screen.

"There was hardly an instant," continued the official, with a touch of professional pride, "before the alarm was given. By a fortunate chance I myself happened to be near. The garden was instantly surrounded. It is being searched now. It seems hardly possible that the assassin can have escaped. I entreat your pardon for intruding this painful subject on the sensitive mind of a lady, and breaking in on your privacy."

"I should think he has escaped by now," said Fay hoarsely.

"It is possible, but improbable," said the official. Then he turned to the duke. "This is, I understand from you, the only way into the house from the garden?"

"The only way that might possibly still be open," said the duke. "The doors on the ground floor are both locked, as we have seen."

"We greatly feared," continued the duke, turning to his wife, "that the murderer if he were still in the garden, finding it was being searched, might terrify you by rushing in here."

"No one has been in here," said Fay automatically.

"Have you been in this room ever since you left the saloon?" said her husband.

"Yes. I have been reading here ever since."

"Then it is impossible that anyone should have escaped into the house through this room," said the duke. "The duchess must have seen him. It is no longer necessary to search the house."

The *delegato* hesitated. He opened the glass door and spoke to the men with the lantern.

"They are convinced that it is not possible he is concealed in the garden," he said. "Perhaps if the duchess were deeply engaged in study he might have serpentinely glided through into the next room without her perceiving him. It is, I understand, the duchess's private apartment. It might be as well—where does the duchess's apartment lead into?"

"Into my rooms," said the duke, "and my dog is there. He would have given the alarm long ago if any stranger had passed through my room. If he is silent no one has been near him."

There was a pause.

Fay learned what suspense means.

The *delegato* twirled his moustaches.

He was evidently reluctant to give up the remotest chance, and yet reluctant to inconvenience the duke further.

"It is just possible," he said, "that the assassin may have taken refuge in here before the duchess came back to her apartment. My duties are grave, duchess. Have I your permission?"

Fay bowed.

The duke, still urbane, but evidently finding the situation unduly prolonged, led the way into Fay's bedroom.

This story would never have been written if Lord John had not remained standing in the doorway.

Did Michael know he was there? He had not so far spoken, or given any sign of his presence.

"Won't you go into my room, Lord John, and help in the capture," she said distinctly; and as she spoke she was aware that she was only just in time.

But Lord John would not go in, thanks. Lord John preferred to advance heavily in her direction, and to sit down by her on the couch, telling her not to look so terrified, that he would take care of her.

She stared wildly at him, livid and helpless.

A door was softly opened, and was instantly followed by the furious barking of a dog.

"Go and help them," said Fay to Lord John.

But Lord John did not move. Like all bores he was conscious of his own attractive personality. He only settled his eyeglass more firmly in his pale eye.

"You never spoke to me all evening," he said, with jocular emphasis. "What have I done to deserve such severity?"

In another moment the duke and the official returned, followed by Sancho, a large Bridlington terrier, still bristling and snarling at the official.

Fay called the dog to her, and held it forcibly, pretending to caress it.

"No one has gone by that way," said the *delegato* to the duke. "The dog proves that."

"Sancho proves it," said the duke gravely.

As he spoke he paused as if suddenly arrested. His eyes were fixed on a small Florentine mirror which hung over Fay's writing-table in the angle of the wall. The duke's face changed, as a man's face might change, who, conscious of no enemy, feels himself stabbed from behind in the dark. Then he came forward, and said with a firm voice:

"We will now go once more into the gardens. Lord John, you will accompany us."

Lord John got heavily to his feet.

"Take Sancho with you," said Fay, holding the dog with difficulty, who was obviously excited and suspicious, its mobile nostrils working, its eyes glued to the screen.

The duke opened the glass door, and Sancho, his attention turned, rushed out into the night, barking furiously.

"You need have no further fear," said the duke to Fay, looking into her eyes. "The assassin has certainly escaped."

"No doubt," said Fay.

"Unless he is hiding behind the screen all the time," said Lord John, with his customary facetiousness. "It is about the only place in the room he could hide in, except of course the wastepaper basket."

The *delegato*, who was not apparently a man who quickly seized the humorous side of a remark, at once stepped back from the window, and glanced at the wastepaper basket.

"I may as well look behind the screen," he said, and went towards it.

But before he could reach it the screen moved, and Michael came out from behind it.

The four people in the room gazed at him spell-bound, speechless; Lord John reeled against the wall. The duke alone retained his self-possession.

Michael advanced into the middle of the room, and for a moment his eyes met Fay's. Who shall say what he read in their terror-stricken depths?

Then he turned to the duke and said:

"I ask pardon of you, duke, and of the duchess, my cousin, for the inconvenience I have caused you. I confess to the murder of the Marchese di Maltagliala, and sought refuge in the garden. When the garden was surrounded I sought refuge here. I did not tell the duchess what I had done, but I implored her to let me take shelter here, and to promise not to give me up. She ought at once to have given me up. She yielded to the dictates of humanity and suffered me to hide in this room. Duchess, I thank you for your noble, your self-sacrificing but unavailing desire to shield a guilty man."

Michael went up to her, took her cold hand and kissed it. Then he turned again to the duke.

"I offer you my apologies for this intrusion," he said, and the two men bowed to each other.

"And now, signor," he said in Italian to the amazed official, "I am at your service."

CHAPTER V

Qui sait tout souffrir peut tout oser.

—VAUVENARGUES.

Michael was imprisoned for the night in a cell attached to the Court of Mandamento, and the next day was sent to Rome to await his trial at the *assise.*

Early on the second day after he reached Rome the duke came to him. The two men looked fixedly at each other. They exchanged no form of greeting.

The duke made a little sign with his hand, and the warder withdrew outside the cell door, which he left ajar.

Then the duke sat down by Michael.

"I should have come yesterday," he said in English, "but it took time to gain permission, and also"—he nodded towards the door—"to arrange."

"For God's sake give me details," said Michael.

The duke gave them in a low voice. He described in a careful sequence the exact position of the dead body, the wound, caused by stabbing in the back, the strong inference that the murdered man had been attacked in the road, and then dragged just inside the Colle Alto garden door.

"I don't see any reason why he should have gone outside the garden," said Michael.

"Neither do I. But the garden door was unlocked. It had been locked as usual, my gardener swears, and the key left in the lock on the inside. Who then opened it, if for some reason the marchese did not open it himself?"

Michael did not answer.

"I saw the body before it was moved," continued the duke. "It was still warm. I incline to think the marchese was murdered actually inside the garden, and that he fell on his face where he stood, and was dragged behind the hydrangeas. But the *delegato* thought differently. You will remember, Carstairs, that the dead man had been dragged by the feet."

"Did I put him on the right side or the left of the door as you go in?"

"On the left."

"On his face?"

"Yes."

There was a pause.

"You had no quarrel with the marchese, I presume?" said the duke significantly.

"On the contrary," said Michael; "it is not known, but I had."

"Just so. Just so. About a woman?"

Michael winced.

"About a horse," he said.

"No," said the duke, with decision. "Think again. Your memory does not serve you. It was about a woman. Was it not a dancing-girl?"

"I am not like that," said Michael, colouring.

"It is of no account what you are like, or what you are not like. What matters is that which is quickly believed. A quarrel about a woman is always believed, especially by women who think all turns on them. Were you not in Paris at Easter?"

"I was."

"Was not the marchese in Paris at Easter?"

"He was. I saw him once at the Opera with the old Duke of Castelfranco."

"Just so. A quarrel about a dancing-girl at Paris at Easter. That was how it was."

"You are right," said Michael, regaining his composure with an effort. "I owed him a grudge. You will be careful to mention this to no one?"

"I will mention it only to one or two women on whom I can rely," said the duke; "and to them only in the strictest confidence."

Michael nodded.

Silence fell between them, and he wondered why the duke did not go. The warder shifted his feet in the passage.

Presently the duke began to speak in a low, even voice.

"I owe you an apology," he said. "I saw you standing behind the screen, reflected in a little mirror, and for one moment I thought you had done me a great injury. It was only for a moment. I regained myself quickly. I would have saved you if I could. But I owe you an apology for a suspicion unworthy of either of us."

"It was natural," said Michael. He was greatly drawn to this man.

"I may in some matters be deceived," continued the duke, "for in my time I have deceived others, and have not been found out. I don't know why you were in my wife's rooms that night. Nevertheless, I clearly know two things: one, that you did not murder the marchese, and the other, that there was nothing wrong between you and my wife. With you her honour was safe. You and I are combining now to guard only her reputation before the world."

Michael did not answer. He nodded again.

"At the price," continued the duke, "probably of your best years."

"I am content to pay the price," said Michael. "It was the only thing to do." Then he coloured like a girl, and raised his eyes to the duke's. "I went to her that night to say good-bye," he said. "That was why the garden door was unlocked. I love her. I have loved her for years."

It seemed as if everything between the two men had become transparent.

"I know it," said the duke. "She also, the duchess, is in love with you."

Michael drew back perceptibly. His manner changed.

"A little—not much," continued the duke. "I watched her, when you gave up yourself. She could have saved you. She could save you still—by a word. But she will not speak it. She appeared to love me a little once. I was not deceived. I knew. She loves you a little now. Why do you deceive yourself, my friend? There is only one person for whom she has a permanent and deep affection—for her very charming self."

The words fell into the silence of the bare room. Michael's thin hands, tightly clenched, shook a little.

The duke bent towards him.

"Is she worth it?" he said, with sudden passion.

No answer. Michael hid his face in his hands.

"Is she worth it?" said the duke again.

Michael looked up suddenly at the duke, and the elder man winced at the expression in his face. He looked through the duke, through his veiled despair and disillusion, beyond him.

"Yes, she is worth it," he said. "You do not understand her because you only love her in part. I meant to serve her by leaving Rome, but now I can't leave it. What I can do for her I will. It is no sacrifice—I am glad to do it—

to have the chance. I have always wished—to serve her—to put my hands under her feet."

The sudden radiance in Michael's face passed. He looked down embarrassed, annoyed with himself.

"There remains then but one other person to be considered," said the duke, looking closely at him. "The beautiful heroine, the young lover, these are now accommodated. All is *en régle*. But that dull elderly person who takes the *rôle* of husband on these occasions! Is there not a husband somewhere? What of him? Will he indeed fold his arms as on the stage? Will he indeed stand by as serenely as you suppose and suffer an innocent man to make this sacrifice for the sake of his—honour?"

"He will, only because he must," said Michael, catching his breath. "I had thought of that. He can do nothing. Have I not accused myself? And his honour is also hers. They stand and fall together."

"'IS SHE WORTH IT?' HE SAID WITH SUDDEN PASSION"

"They stand and fall together," said the duke slowly. "Yes, that is true. And he is old. He is finished. He is the head of a great house. His honour is perhaps the only thing that still means anything to him. Nevertheless, it is strange to me that you think he would consent to keep it at so great a cost, the cost perhaps of twenty years. That were impossible.... He could not permit *that.* But—one little year—at most. That perhaps his conscience might permit. One little year! You are young. Supposing he has within him," he laid his hand on his heart, "that of which his wife does not know, which means that his release is *sure.* Do you understand? Supposing it must come soon—very soon—her release—and yours. Perhaps then——" There was a long pause. "Perhaps then his conscience might suffer him to keep silence."

Michael's hand made a slight movement. The duke took it in his, and held it firmly.

"Listen," he said at last. "Once when I was young, twenty years ago, I loved. I too would fain have served a woman, would have put my hands under her feet. There is always one such a woman in life, but only one. She was to me the world. But I could only trouble her life. She was married. She had children. I knew I ought to go. I meant to go. She prayed me to go. I promised her to go—nevertheless I stayed. And at last—inasmuch as she loved me very much—I broke up her home, her life, her honour, she was separated from her children. She lost all, and then when all was gone she died. The only thing which I could keep from her was poverty, which would have been nothing to her. She never reproached me. There is no reproach in love. But—she died in disgrace, and alone. From the first to the last it was her white hands under my feet. That was how I served the one woman I have deeply loved, the one creature who deeply loved me." The duke's voice had become almost inaudible. "You have done better than I," he said.

Then he kissed Michael on the forehead, and went out.

They never met again.

CHAPTER VI

The year slid like a corpse afloat.—D. G. ROSSETTI.

And how did it fare with Fay during the days that followed Michael's arrest?

Much sympathy was felt for her. Lord John, wallowing in the delicious novelty of finding eager listeners, went about extolling her courage and unselfishness to the skies. Her conduct was considered perfectly natural and womanly. No man condemned her for trying to shield her cousin from the consequences of his crime. Women said they would have done the same, and envied her her romantic situation.

And Fay, shut up in her darkened room in her romantic situation—she who adored romantic situations—what were Fay's thoughts?

There is a travail of soul which toils with hard crying up the dark valley of decision, and brings forth in anguish the life entrusted to it. Perhaps it is the great renunciation. Perhaps it is only the loyal inevitable deed which is struggling to come forth, to be allowed to live for our healing and comfort.

But there is another travail of soul, barren, unavailing, which flings itself down, and tosses in impotent misery from side to side, from mood to mood, as in a sickly trance.

Such was Fay's.

Her decision not to speak had been made in the ment when she had let Michael accuse himself, and she kept silence. But that she did not know. She thought it was still to make.

"I must speak. I must speak," she said to herself all through the endless day after Michael's arrest, all through the endless night, until the dawn came up behind the ilexes, the tranquil dawn that knew all, and found her shuddering and wild-eyed.

"I must speak. I cannot let Michael suffer for me, even to save my reputation."

Her reputation! How little she had cared for it twenty-four hours ago, when passion clutched the reins!

But now—— The public shame of it—the divorce which in her eyes must ensue—Andrea! Her courteous, sedate, inexorable husband, whose will she could not bend, whom she could not cajole, whose mind was a closed book to her; a book which had lain by her hand for three years, which she had never had the curiosity to open!—Fay feared her husband, as we all fear what we do not understand. He would divorce her—and then—— And Magdalen at home—and——

A flood of suffocating emotion swept over her, full of ugly swimming and crawling reptiles, and invertebrate horrors, the inevitable scavengers of the sea of selfish passion.

Fay shrank back for very life. She could not pass through that flood and live. Nevertheless she felt herself pushed towards it.

"But I have no choice. I *must* speak. He is innocent. He is doing this to shield me because he loves me. But I also love him, far, far more than he loves me, and I will prove it."

Fay went in imagination through a fearful and melodramatic scene, in which she revealed everything before a public tribunal. She saw her husband's face darken against her, her lover's lighten as she saved him. She saw her slender figure standing alone, bearing the whole shock, serene, unshaken. The vision moved her to tears.

Was it a prophetic vision?

It was quite light now, and she crept to her husband's room. She had not seen him during the previous day. He had been out the whole of it. She felt drawn towards him by calamity, by the loneliness of her misery.

The duke was not asleep. He was lying in bed with his hands clasped behind his head. His sallow face, worn by a sleepless night, and perhaps by a wounding memory, was turned towards the light, and the new day dealt harshly with it. There were heavy lines under the eyes. The eyes looked steadily in front of him, plunged deep in a past which had something of the irrevocable tenderness of the dawn in it, the holy reflection of an inalienable love.

He did not stir as his wife came in. His eyes only moved, resting upon her for a moment, focussing her with difficulty, as if withdrawn from something at a great distance, and then they turned once more to the window.

A pale primrose light had risen above the blue tangled mist of ilexes and olives. The cypresses stood half-veiled in mist, half-sharply clear against the stainless pallor of the upper sky.

"I am so miserable, Andrea."

He did not speak.

"I cannot sleep."

Still no answer.

"I am convinced that Michael is innocent."

"It goes without saying."

"Then they can't convict him, can they?"

"They will convict him," said the duke, and for a moment he bent his eyes upon her. "Has he not accused himself?"

"They won't—hang him?"

The duke shrugged his shoulders. He did not think fit to enlighten his wife's ignorance of the fact that in Italy there is no capital punishment.

"But if he has not done it, and we know he has not," faltered Fay.

"He is perhaps shielding someone," said the duke, "the real murderer."

"I don't see how that could be."

"He may have his reasons. The real murderer is perhaps a friend—or a—woman. Your cousin is a romantic. It is always better for a romantic if he had not been born. But generally a female millstone is in readiness to tie itself round him, and cast him into the sea. The world is not fitted to him. It is to egotistic persons like you and me, my Francesca, to whom the world is most admirably adapted."

"I don't see how the murderer could be a woman. Women don't murder men on the high road."

"No, not on the high road. You are in the right. How dusty, how dirty is the high road! But I have known, not once nor twice, women to murder men very quietly. Oh! so gently and cleanly—to let them die. I am much older than you, but you will perhaps also live to see a woman do this, Francesca. And now retire to your room, and let me counsel you to take some rest. Your beauty needs it."

She burst into tears.

"How little you care!" she said between her sobs, "how heartless you are! I will never believe they will convict him. He is innocent, and his innocence will come to light."

"I think the light will not be suffered to fall upon it," said the duke.

Afterwards, years afterwards, Fay remembered that conversation with wonder that its significance had escaped her. But at the time she could see nothing, feel nothing except her own anguish.

She left her husband's room. There was no help or sympathy in him. She went back to her own room and flung herself face downwards on her bed. Let no one think she did not suffer.

A faint ray of comfort presently came to her at the thought that Michael's innocence might after all come to light. It might be proved in spite of himself.

She would pray incessantly that the real murderer might give himself up, or that suspicion should fall on him, and he should be dragged to justice. And then, if—*after all*—Michael were convicted and his life endangered, then she *must* speak. But—not till then. Not now when all might yet go well without her confession.... And it was not as if she were guilty of unfaithfulness. She had not done anything wrong beyond imprudence. Yes, she had certainly been imprudent; that she saw. But she had done nothing *wrong*. It could not be right to confess to what in public opinion amounted to unfaithfulness on her part, and dishonourable conduct on his, when it was not so. They were both innocent. It would be telling a lie to let anyone think either of them could be guilty of such a sordid crime. It looked sordid now. Why should she drag down his name with hers into the mud—unless it were absolutely necessary.... And she must remember how distressed Michael would be if she said a word, if she flung her good name from her, which he had risked all to save. Some semblance of calm returned to her, as she thus reached the only conclusion which the bias of her mind would permit. The stream ran docilely in the little groove cut out for it.

During the days and weeks that followed Fay shut herself up, and prayed incessantly for Michael.

She prayed all through the interminable interval before the trial.

"If it goes against him, I will speak," she said.

Yet all the time Michael who loved her knew that she would not speak. Her husband who could have loved her, and who watched her struggle with compassion, knew that she would not speak. Only Fay who did not know herself believed that she would speak.

The day came when the duke gravely informed her that Michael was found guilty of murder.

Fay's prayers it seemed had not availed. She prayed no more. There was no help in God. Probably there was no God to pray to. Her sister Magdalen seemed to think there was. But how could she tell? Besides, Magdalen had such a calm temperament, and nothing had ever happened to make her unhappy, or to shake her faith. It was different for Magdalen.

Evidently there was no justice anywhere, only a blind chance. "The truth will out," Fay had said to herself over and over again. She had tried to have faith. But the truth had not come out. She was being pushed, pushed over the edge of the precipice. Oh, why had Michael fallen in love with her when they were boy and girl! She remembered with horror and disgust those early days, that exquisite dawn of young passion in the time of primroses. It had brought her to *this*—to this horrible place of tears and shame and shuddering—to these wretched days and hideous nights. Oh, why, why, had he loved her! Why had she let herself love him!

Suddenly she said to herself, "They may reprieve him yet. If his sentence is not commuted to imprisonment I will speak, so help me God I will."

It could never be known whether she would have kept that oath, for the next day she heard that Michael had been sentenced to fifteen years' imprisonment. Why had Andrea been so cruel as to let her imagine for a whole horrible night that Michael's would be a death sentence, when in Italy it seemed there was no capital punishment as in England? It was just like Andrea to torture her needlessly! When the sentence reached her Fay drew breath. The horrible catastrophe had been averted. To a man of Michael's temperament the living grave to which he was consigned was infinitely worse than death. But what was Michael's temperament to Fay? She shut her eyes to the cell of an Italian prison. Michael would live, and in time the truth would come to light, and he would be released.

She impressed this conviction with tears on his half-brother Wentworth Maine, the kind, silent elder brother, Michael's greatest friend, who had come out to Italy to be near him, and who heard sentence given against him with a set face, and an unshaken belief in his innocence. Even to Wentworth Michael had said nothing, could be induced to say no word. He confessed to the murder. That was all.

Wentworth, who had never seen Fay before, as she had married just before he came to live at his uncle's place in Hampshire near Fay's home, saw the marks of grief in her lovely face, and was unconsciously drawn towards her. He was shy as only men can be; but he almost forgot it in her sympathetic presence. She came into his isolated, secluded life at the moment when the barriers of his instinctive timidity and apathy were broken down by his first real trouble. And he was grateful to her for having done her best to save Michael.

"I shall never forget that," he said, when he came to bid her good-bye. "There are very few women who would have had the courage and unselfishness to act as you did."

Fay winced and paled, and he took his leave, bearing away with him a grave admiration for this delicate, sensitive creature, so full of tender compassion for him and Michael.

He made no attempt to see her again when he returned to Italy some months later to visit Michael in prison. To visit Fay on that occasion would have taken him somewhat out of his way, and Wentworth never went out of his way, not out of principle, but because such a course never occurred to him. He would have liked to see her, in order to tell her about Michael's condition, and also to deliver in person a message which Michael had sent to Fay by him. But when he realised that a detour would be necessary in order to accomplish this, he wrote to Fay to tell her with deep regret that it was impossible for him to see her, gave her Michael's message, and returned to England by the way he came. Nevertheless, he often thought of her, for she was inextricably associated with the unspeakable trouble of his life, his brother's living death.

When all was over, and the last sod had—so to speak—been cast upon that living grave, Fay tried to take up her life again. But she could not. She had lost heart. She dared not be alone. She shunned society. At her earnest request her sister Magdalen came out to her for a time, from the home in England, into which she was wedged so tightly. But even Magdalen's calm presence brought no calm with it, and the deepening friendship between her sister and her husband only irritated Fay. Everything irritated Fay. She was ill at ease, restless, feebly sarcastic, impatient.

There is a peace which passes understanding, and there is an unpeace which passes understanding also. Fay did not know, would not know, why she was so troubled, so weary of life, so destitute of comfort.

Had she met the great opportunity of her life, the turning point, and missed it? I do not think so. It was not for her.

A year later the duke died.

He made a dignified exit. An attack of vertigo to which he was liable came on when he was on horseback. He was thrown and dragged, and only survived a few days as by a miracle. His wife, who had seen little of him during the last year, saw still less of him during the days of his short illness. But when the end was close at hand he sent for her, and asked her to remain in a distant recess of his room during the painful hours.

"It will be a happier memory for you," he said gently to her between the paroxysms of suffering, "to think that you were there."

And so propped high in a great carved bedstead in the octagonal room where the Colle Altos were born, and where, when they could choose, they died, the duke lay awaiting the end.

He had received extreme unction. The chanting choir had gone. The priest had closed his pale fingers upon the crucifix, when he desired to be left alone with his wife.

She drew near timidly and stood beside his bed.

He bent his tranquil, kindly eyes upon her.

"Good-bye, my Francesca," he said. "May God and his angels protect you, and give you peace."

A belated compunction seized her.

"I wish I had been a better wife to you, Andrea," she said brokenly, laying her hand on his.

He made the ghost of a courteous, deprecating gesture, and raised her hand to his lips. The effort exhausted him. He closed his eyes and his hand fell out of hers.

Through the open window came a sudden waft of hot carnations, a long drawn breath of the rapturous Italian spring.

It reached the duke. He stirred slightly, and opened his eyes once more. Once more they fell on Fay, and it seemed to her as if with the last touch of his cold lips upon her hand their relation of husband and wife had ceased. Even at that moment she realised with a sinking sense of impotence how slight her hold on him from first to last had been. Clearly he had already forgotten it, passed beyond it, would never remember it again.

"It is spring," he said, looking full at her with tender fixity, and for a moment she thought his mind was wandering. "Spring once more. The sun shines. He does not see them, the spring and the sunshine. Since a year he does not see them. Francesca, how much longer will you keep your cousin Michael in prison?"

And thereupon the duke closed his eyes on this world, and went upon his way.

CHAPTER VII

A bachelor's an unfinished thing ... He wants somebody to listen to his talk.

—EDEN PHILLPOTTS.

Reader, do you know Barford, in Hampshire? If you don't, I can tell you how to get to it. You take train from Victoria, and you get out at Saundersfoot. There is nothing at Saundersfoot, except a wilderness of lodgings and a tin station and a high wind. It need not detain an active mind beyond the necessary moment of enquiring by which road it may be most quickly left. I cannot tell you who Saunders was, nor why the watering-place was called after his foot. But if you walk steadily away from it for five miles inland, along the white chalky road between the downs, you will arrive at the little village of Barford.

There is only one road, so you cannot miss your way. Little twisty lanes fretted with sheep-tracks drop down into it now and then from the broad-shouldered downs on either side, but take no notice of them. If you persevere, you will in due course see the village of Barford lying in front of you, which, at a little distance, looks as if it had been carelessly swept into a crease between the downs, while a few cottages and houses on the hillside seem to have adhered to the ground, and remained stuck where they were when the sweeping took place.

After you have passed the pond and the post office, and before you reach the school, you will see a lodge, and an old Italian iron gateway, flanked by a set of white wooden knobs planted in the ground on either side, held together by chains. The white knobs are apparently there in order to upset carriages as they drive in or out. But very few carriages have driven in or out during the last two years, except those of the owner of Barford Manor, Wentworth Maine. Wentworth, since he inherited the place from his uncle five years ago, had always led a somewhat secluded life. But during the last two years, ever since his half-brother, Michael, had been sentenced and imprisoned in Italy, Wentworth had withdrawn himself even more from the society of his neighbours. He continued to shoot and hunt, and to do his duties as a magistrate and as a supporter of the Conservative party, but his thin, refined face had a certain worn, pinched look, which spoke of long tracts of solitary unhappiness. And the habit of solitude was growing on him.

The old Manor House, standing in its high-walled gardens, its sunny low rooms looking out across the down, seemed wrapped in an atmosphere of ancient peace, which consorted as ill with the present impression of the place as does old Gobelin tapestry with a careful modern patch upon its surface. The patch, however, adroitly copied, is seen to be an innovation.

The old house, which had known so much, had sheltered so much, had kept counsel so long, seemed to resent the artificial peace that its present owner had somewhat laboriously constructed round himself, within its mellow, ivied walls.

There is a fictitious tranquillity which is always on the verge of being broken, which depends largely on uninterrupted hours, on confidential, velvet-shod servants, on a brooding dove in a cedar, on the absence of the inharmonious or jarring elements which pervade daily life.

Such an imitation peace, coy as a fickle mistress, Wentworth cherished. Was it worth all the trouble he took to preserve it, when the real thing lay at his very door?

On this February morning, as he sat looking out across the down, white in the pale sunshine, the current of his life ran low. He had returned the night before from one of his periodical journeys to Italy to visit Michael in his cell. He was tired with the clang and hurry of the long journey, depressed almost to despair by the renewed realisation of his brother's fate. Two years—close on two years, had Michael been in prison.

In Wentworth's faithful heart that wound never healed. To-day it bled afresh. He bit his lip, and his face quivered.

Wentworth was not as handsome as Michael, but, nevertheless, he was distinctly good to look at, and the half-brothers, in spite of the fifteen years' difference between their ages, bore a certain superficial resemblance to each other. Wentworth was of middle height, lightly and leanly built, with a high bridge on a rather thin nose, and with narrow, clean grey eyes under light eyelashes. He looked as if he had been made up of different shades of one colour. His light brown hair had a little grey in it, his delicately cut face and nervous hands were both tanned, by persistent exposure to all kinds of weather, to nearly the same shade of indeterminate brown as his hair.

You could not look at Wentworth without seeing that he was a man who had never even glanced at the ignoble side of life, for whose fastidious, sensitive nature sensual lures had no attraction, a man who could not lie, who could not stoop, whose mind was as clean as his hand, and, for an Englishman, that is saying a good deal. He was manly in a physical sense.

He rode straight, he shot well. He could endure bodily strain with indifference, though he was not robustly built. He was sane, even-tempered, liable to petty resentments, mildly and resolutely selfish, except where Michael was concerned, a conscientious and just master—at least, just in intention—a patient and respectful son where patience and respect had not been easy.

The strain of scholar and student in him was about evenly mixed with that of the country gentleman. The result was a certain innate sense of superiority which he was not in the least aware that he showed. He had no idea that he was considered "fine," and "thinking a good deal of himself," by the more bucolic of his country neighbours. No one could say that Wentworth was childlike, but perhaps he was a little childish. He certainly had a *naïf* and unshakable belief that the impressions he had formed as to his own character were shared by others. He supposed it was recognised by his neighbours that they had a thinker in their midst, and always tacitly occupied the ground which he imagined had been conceded to him on that account.

His mother, a beautiful, foolish, whimsical, hard-riding heiress, the last of a long line, had married the youngest son—the one brilliant, cultivated member—of a family as ancient, as uneducated, and as prosaic as her own. Wentworth was the result of that union. His father had died before his talents were fully recognised: that is to say, just when it was beginning to be perceived that he was a genius only in his own class, and that there were hordes of educated men in the middle classes who could beat him at every point on his own ground, except in carriage and appearance, and whom no one regarded as specially gifted. Still, in his own county, among his own friends, and in a society where education and culture eke out a precarious, interloping existence, and are regarded with distrustful curiosity, Lord Wilfrid Maine lived and died, and was mourned as a genius.

After many years of uneasy, imprudent widowhood, the widow of the great man had made a disastrous second marriage, and had died at Michael's birth.

No one had disputed with Wentworth over the possession of Michael. Wentworth, a sedate, self-centred young man of three-and-twenty, of independent means, mainly occupied in transcribing the nullity of his days in a voluminous diary, had taken charge of him virtually from his first holidays, during which Michael's father had achieved the somewhat tedious task of drinking himself to death. Michael's father had appointed Wentworth as his son's guardian. If it had been a jealous affection on Wentworth's part, it had also been a deep one. And it had been returned with a single-hearted devotion on Michael's part which had gradually knit together the hearts of the older and the younger man, as it seemed indissolubly. No one had come between them. Once or twice Wentworth had become uneasy, suspicious of Michael's affection for his tutor at Eton, distrustful of the intimacies Michael formed with boys, and, later on, with men of his own age. Wentworth had nipped a few of these incipient friendships in the bud. He vaguely felt that each case, judged by its own merits, was undesirable. Some of these friendships he had not been able to nip. These he ignored; among that number was Michael's affection for his godfather, the Bishop of Lostford. Michael's boyish passion for Fay, Wentworth had never divined. It had come about during the last year of his great uncle's life at Barford, which was within a few miles of Priesthope, Fay's home. Michael had spent many weeks at Barford with the old man, who was devoted to him. Everyone had expected that he would make Michael his heir, but when he died soon afterwards, it was found he had left the place, in a will dated many years back, to Wentworth. If Michael had never mentioned his first painful contact with life to Wentworth, it was perhaps partly because he instinctively felt that the confidence would be coldly received, partly also because Michael was a man of few words, to whom speech had never taken the shape of relief.

There had no doubt been wretched moments in Wentworth's devotion to Michael, but nevertheless it had been the best thing so far in his somewhat colourless existence, with its hesitating essays in other directions, its half-hearted withdrawals, its pigeon-holed emotions. He had not been half-hearted about Michael. It is perhaps natural that we should love very deeply those who have had the power to release us momentarily from the airless prison of our own egotism. How often it is a child's hand which first opens that iron door, and draws us forth into the sunshine! With Wentworth it had been so. The pure air of the moorland, the scent of the heather and the sea seem indissolubly mingled with the remembrance of those whom we have loved. For did we not in their company walk abroad into a new world, breathe a new air, while Self, the dingy turnkey, for once slept at his post?

One of the reasons of his devotion to Michael was that Michael's character did not apparently or perceptibly alter. He was very much the same person in his striped convict's blouse as he had been in his Eton jacket. But it is doubtful whether Wentworth had ever realised of what materials that character consisted. Wentworth was of those who never get the best out of men and women, who never divine and meet, but only come into surprised uncomfortable contact with their deeper emotions. Michael's passion of service for Fay would have been a great shock to Wentworth had he suspected it. It remained for the duke to perceive the latent power in Michael, and to be taken instantly into his confidence on the matter, while Wentworth, unwitting, had remained for life outside his brother's mind.

Some men and women are half conscious that they are thus left out, are companions only of "the outer court" of the lives of others. But Wentworth never suspected this, partly because he regarded as friendship a degree of intimacy which most men and all women regard as acquaintanceship. He did not know there was anything more. Those from whom others need much, learn perforce, whether they will or no, to what heights, to what depths human nature can climb and—fall. But Wentworth was not a person on whom others made large demands. But if his love for Michael had been his one tangible happiness, it had become now his one real pain.

Contrary to all his habits, he sat on, hour after hour, motionless, inert, watching the cloud shadows pass across the down. He tried to rouse himself. He told himself that he must settle back into his old occupations. He must get forward with his history of Sussex, and write up his diary. He must come to some decision about the allotment scheme on his property in Saundersfoot. He must go over and help Colonel Bellairs not to make a fool of himself about the disputed right of way across his property where it joined Wentworth's own land. Colonel Bellairs always bungled into business matters of the simplest nature as a bumble bee bungles into a spider's web. For Colonel Bellairs to touch business of any kind was immediately to become hopelessly and inextricably involved in it, with much furious buzzing. His mere presence entangled the plainest matter into a confused cocoon, with himself struggling in the middle.

Wentworth must save the old autocrat from putting himself in the wrong, when he was so plainly in the right. Wentworth must at any rate, if he could do nothing else this morning, read his letters, which had accumulated during his short absence.

Without moving from his chair he turned over, with a groan, the pile of envelopes waiting for him at his elbow. Invitations, bills, tenants' complaints, an unexpected dividend. It was all one to him. The Bishop of Lostford—so his secretary wrote—accepted Wentworth's invitation to dine and sleep at Barford that night, after holding a confirmation at Saundersfoot. Wentworth had forgotten he had asked him. Very well, he must remember to order a room to be got ready. That was all. A subscription earnestly solicited by the daughter of a neighbouring clergyman for a parish library. Why could he not be left in peace? Oh! what was the use of anything—of life, health, money, intellect, if existence was always to be like this, if every day was to be like this, only like this? This weary, dry-as-dust grind, this making a handful of bricks out of a cartload of straw, this distaste and fatigue, and sense of being duped by satisfaction, which was only another form of dissatisfaction, after all. What was the use of living exactly as you liked, *if you did not like it?* Oh, Michael! Michael!

Michael! He forgot that he had often been nearly as miserable as this when Michael had been free and happy. Not quite, but nearly. Now he attributed the whole of his recurrent wretchedness, which was largely temperamental, to his distress about his brother's fate.

That wound, never healed, bled afresh. Who felt for him in his trouble? Who, among all his friends, cared, or understood? No one. That was the way of the world.

Fay's sweet, forlorn face, snowdrop pale under its long black veil, rose suddenly before him, as he had seen it some weeks ago, when he had met her walking in the woods near her father's house. She had gone back to her old home after the duke's death. She, at least, had grieved for him and Michael with an intensity which he had never forgotten. Even in her widowed desolation she had remembered Michael, and always asked after him when Wentworth went over to Priesthope. And Wentworth was often there, for one reason or another. Michael, too, had asked after her, and had sent her a message by his brother. Should he go over to-day and deliver it in person? Among his letters was a scrawling, illegible note, already several days old, from Colonel Bellairs, Fay's father, about the right of way. The matter, it seemed, was more urgent than Wentworth had realised. Any matter pertaining to Colonel Bellairs was always, in the opinion of the latter, of momentous urgency.

Colonel Bellairs asked Wentworth to come over to luncheon the first day he could, and to walk over the debatable ground with him.

Wentworth looked at his watch, started up and rang the bell, and ordered his cob Conrad to be brought round at once.

CHAPTER VIII

Le plus grand élément des mauvaises actions secrètes, des lâchetés inconnues, est peut-être un honheur incomplet.

—BALZAC.

When Fay, in her panic-stricken widowhood, had fled back to her old home in Hampshire, she found all very much as she had left it, except that her father's hair was damply dyed, her sister Magdalen's frankly grey, and the pigtail of Bessie, the youngest daughter, was now an imposing bronze coil in the nape of her neck.

But if little else was radically changed in the old home except the hair of the family, nevertheless, the whole place had somehow declined and shrunk in Fay's eyes during the three years of her marriage. The dear old gabled Tudor house, with its twisted chimneys, looked much the same from the outside, but within, in spite of its wealth of old pictures and cabinets and china, it had contracted the dim, melancholy aspect which is the result of prolonged scarcity of money. Nothing had been spent on the place for years. Magdalen seemed to have faded together with the curtains, and the darned carpets, and the bleached chintzes.

Colonel Bellairs alone, a handsome man of sixty, had remained remarkably young for his age. The balance, however, was made even by the fact that those who lived with him grew old before their time. It had been so with his wife. It was obviously so with his eldest daughter. Many men as superficially affectionate as Colonel Bellairs, and at heart as callous, as exacting and as inconsiderate, have made endurable husbands. But Colonel Bellairs was not only irresolute and vacillating and incapable of even the most necessary decisions, but he was an inveterate enemy of all decision on the part of others, inimical to all suggested arrangements or plans for household convenience. The words "spring cleaning" could never be mentioned in his presence. The thing itself could only be achieved by stealth. A month at the seaside for the sake of the children was a subject that could not be approached. All small feminine social arrangements, dependent for their accomplishment on the use of the horses, were mown down like grass. Colonel Bellairs hated what he called "living by clockwork."

You may read, if you care to do so, in the faces of many gentle-tempered and apparently prosperous married women, an enormous fatigue. Wicked, blood-curdling husbands do not bring this look into women's faces. It is men like Colonel Bellairs who hold the recipe for calling it into existence.

Mrs. Bellairs, a beautiful woman, with high spirits, but not high-spirited, became more and more silent and apathetic year by year, yielded more and more and more, yielded at last without expostulation equally at every point, when she should have yielded and when she should have stood firm, yielded at last even where her children's health and well-being were concerned.

Apathy and health are seldom housemates for long together. Mrs. Bellairs gradually declined from her chair to her sofa. She made no effort to live after her youngest daughter was born. She could have done so if she had wished it, but she seemed to have no wish on the subject, or on any other subject. There is an Arabian proverb which seems to embody in it all the melancholy of the desert, and Mrs. Bellairs exemplified it. "It is better to sit than to stand. It is better to lie than to sit. It is better to sleep than to lie. It is better to die than to sleep."

Fay had been glad enough, as we have seen, to escape from home by marriage. No such way of escape had apparently presented itself for the elder sister. As Magdalen and Fay sat together on the terrace in front of the house, the contrast between the sisters was more marked than the ten years' difference of age seemed to warrant.

Magdalen was a tall, thin woman of thirty-five, who looked older than her age. She had evidently been extremely pretty once. Perhaps she might even have been young once. But it must have been a long time ago. She was a faded, distinguished-looking person, with a slight stoop, and a worn, delicately-featured face, and humorous, tranquil eyes. Her thick hair was grey. She looked as if she had borne for many years the brunt of continued ill health, or the ill health of others, as if she had been obliged to lift heavy weights too young. Perhaps she had. Everything about her personality seemed fragile except her peace of mind. You could not look at Magdalen without seeing that she was a happy creature.

But very few did look at her when Fay was beside her. Fay's beauty had increased in some ways and diminished in others during the year of her widowhood. She had become slightly thinner and paler, but not to the extent when beauty suffers wrong. A very young face can bear a worn look, and even have its charm enhanced thereby. The mark of suffering on Fay's childlike face and in her deep violet eyes had brought with it an expression which might easily be mistaken for spirituality, especially by those—and they are very many—to whom a pallid and attenuated aspect are the outward signs of spirituality.

That she was miserable was obvious. *But why was she so restless?* Magdalen had often silently asked herself that question during the past year. Even Bessie, the youngest sister, had noticed Fay's continual restlessness and had commented on it, had advised her sister to embark on a course of reading, and to endeavour to interest herself in work for others.

She had also, with the untempered candour of eighteen, suggested to Fay that she should cease to make a slave of Magdalen. It is hardly necessary to add that Fay and Bessie did not materially increase the sum of each other's happiness.

As Magdalen and Fay were sitting together in the sun the door into the garden opened, and Bessie stalked slowly towards them across the grass, in a short cycling skirt.

"It surely is not necessary to be quite so badly dressed as Bessie," said Fay with instant irritation. "If she must wear one of those hideous short skirts, it might at any rate be well cut. I have told her so often enough."

Since Bessie had been guilty of the enormity of suggesting a course of reading, Fay had made many sarcastic comments on Bessie's direful clothes.

"I must advise her to take dress more seriously," said Magdalen absently. She was depressed by a faint misgiving about Bessie. Bessie was to have lunched to-day with congenial archæological friends, intelligent owners of interesting fossils. Nevertheless, when Wentworth's cob Conrad was seen courteously allowing himself to be conducted to the stable she instantly decided to lunch at home, and to visit her friends when they were not expecting her, in the afternoon. *It could make no difference to them*, she had told Magdalen, who shook her head over that well-known phrase, which Colonel Bellairs had long since established as "a household word." Bessie was not to be moved by Magdalen's disapproval, however. She retired to her chamber, donned a certain enamel brooch which she only wore on Sundays, and appeared at luncheon.

It was not a particularly cheerful meal. Wentworth was silent and depressed. Colonel Bellairs did not for an instant cease to speak about the right of way during the whole of luncheon, even when his back was turned while he was bending over a ham on the sideboard. And the moment luncheon was over he had marched Wentworth off to the scene of the dispute.

Magdalen was vaguely uneasy at the tiny incident of Bessie's change of plan, and was glad it had escaped Fay's notice. Most things about Bessie did escape Fay's notice except her clothes. Bessie was not at eighteen an ingratiating person. No one had ever called her the sunbeam of the home. She had preserved throughout her solemn childhood and flinty youth a sort of resentful protest against the attitude of her family at her advent, namely, that she was not wanted. Her mother had died at her birth, and for several years afterwards her father had studiously ignored her presence in the house, not without a sense of melancholy satisfaction at this proof of his devotion to her mother.

"No, no. It may be unreasonable. It may be foolish," he was wont to say to friends who had not accused him of unreasonableness, "but don't ask me to be fond of that child. I can't look at her without remembering what her birth cost me."

Bessie was a fine, strong young woman, with a perfectly impassive handsome face—no Bellairs could achieve plainness—and the manner of one who moves among fellow creatures who do not come up to the standard of conduct which she has selected as the lowest permissible to herself and others. Bessie had not so far evinced a preference for anyone in her own family circle, or outside it. Her affections consisted so far of a distinct dislike of and contempt for her father. She had accorded to Fay a solemn compassion when first the latter returned to Priesthope. Indeed, the estrangement between the sisters, brought about by the suggested course of reading, had been the unfortunate result of a cogitating pity on Bessie's part for the lamentable want of regulation of Fay's mind.

Bessie liked Magdalen, though she disapproved of her manner of life as weak and illogical. You could not love Bessie any more than you could love an ironclad. She bore the same resemblance to a woman that an iron building does to a house. She was not in reality harder than tin or granite or asphalt, or her father; but it would not be an over-statement to suggest that she lacked softness.

She advanced with precision to the bench on which her sisters were sitting.

"I am now going to cycle to the Carters'," she said to Magdalen. "I forgot to mention till this moment that I met Aunt Mary this morning at the Wind Farm, and that she gave me a letter for father, and said that she and Aunt Aggie were lunching with the Copes."

"Poor Copes!" ejaculated Fay.

"And would both come on here afterwards to an early tea," continued Bessie, taking no notice of the interruption. "Aunt Mary desired that you would not have hot scones for tea, as Aunt Aggie is always depressed after them. She said there was no objection to them cold, and buttered, but not hot."

"I shall have tea in my own room then," once more broke in Fay. "I can't stand Aunt Mary. She is always preaching at me."

"It is a pity that Fay is disinclined to share the undoubted burden of entertaining our relatives," said Bessie, addressing herself exclusively to Magdalen, "as I do not feel able to defer my visit to the Carters any longer."

Magdalen struggled hard against a smile, and kept it under.

"Possibly the aunts are coming over to consult father about a private matter," she said. "The letter beforehand to prepare his mind looks like it. So it would be best if you and Fay were not there. The aunts' affairs generally require the deepest secrecy."

"And then father lets it all out at dinner before the servants," said Bessie over her shoulder as she departed.

When she was out of hearing Fay said with exasperation, "You are not wise to give way so much to Bessie, Magdalen. She is selfishness itself. Why did not you insist on her staying and helping with the aunts? She never considers you."

Magdalen was silent.

"I hate sitting here with the house staring at me," said Fay. "I can't think why you are so fond of this bench. Let us go into the beech avenue."

For a long time past Magdalen had noticed that Fay always wanted to be somewhere she was not.

They went in silence through the little wood that bounded the gardens, and passed into the great, bare, grey aisle of the beech avenue.

In a past generation a wide drive had led through this avenue to the house. It had been the south approach to Priesthope. But in these impoverished days, the road, with its sweep of turf on either side, had been neglected, and was now little more than a mossy cart-rut, with a fallen tree across it.

The two sisters sat down on a crooked arm of the fallen tree.

It was a soft, tranquil afternoon, flooded with meek February sunshine. Far away between the green-grey trunks of the trees, the sea glinted like a silver ribbon. Everything was very still, with the stillness set deep in peace of one who loves and awaits in awe love's next word. The earth lay in the sunshine, and listened for the whisper of spring. Faint birdnotes threaded the high windless spaces near the tree-tops.

"Look!" said Magdalen, "the first crocus."

What is there, what can there be in the first yellow crocus peering against the brown earth, that can reach with instant healing, like a child's "soft absolving touch," the inflamed, aching, unrest of the spirit? It does not seek to comfort us. Then how does comfort reach through with the crocus; as if the whole under-world were peace and joy, and were breaking through the thin sod to enfold us?

Fay looked at the flame-pure, upturned face of the little forerunner, absently at first, and then with growing absorption, until two large tears slowly welled up into her eyes and blotted it out. She shivered, and crept a little closer to her sister. She felt alienated from she knew not what, dreadfully cold and alone in the sunshine, with her cheek against her sister's shoulder. Though she did not realise it, something long frost-bound in her mind was yielding, shifting, breaking up. The first miserable shudder of the thaw was upon her.

She glanced up at Magdalen, who was looking into the heart of the crocus, and a sudden anger seized her at the still rapture of her sister's face. The contrast between her own gnawing misery and Magdalen's serenity cut her like a knife. What right had Magdalen to be so happy? Why should she have been exempted from all trouble? What had she done that anguish could never reach her? Fay's love for Magdalen, and at this time Magdalen was the only person for whom she had any affection—had all the violent recoils, the mutinous anger, the sudden desire to wound on the one side, all the tender patience and grieved understanding on the other which are the outcome of a real attachment between a bond woman and a free one.

The one craved, the other relinquished; the one was consumed with unrest, the other had reached some inner stronghold of peace. The one was imprisoned in self, the other was freed, released. The one made demands, the other was willing to serve. It seems as if only the free can serve.

"I am very miserable," said Fay suddenly. She was pushed once more by the same blind impulse that had taken her to her husband's room the night after Michael's arrest.

She used almost the same words. And as the duke had made no answer then, so Magdalen made none now. She had not lived in the same house with Fay for nearly a year for nothing.

Magdalen's silence acted as a goad.

"You think, and father thinks," continued Fay, her voice shaking, "you are all blinder one than the other, that it's Andrea I'm grieving for. It's not."

"I know that," said Magdalen. "You never cared much about him. I have often wondered what it could be that was distressing you so deeply."

Fay winced. Magdalen had noticed something, after all.

"I have sometimes feared,"—continued Magdalen with the deliberation of one who has long since made up her mind not to speak until the opening comes, and not to be silent when it does come—"I have sometimes feared that your heart was locked up in an Italian prison."

"My heart!" said Fay, and her visible astonishment at a not very astonishing inference was not lost on Magdalen. "My heart!" she laughed bitterly. "Do you really suppose after all I've suffered, all I've gone through, that I'm so silly as to be in love with anyone in prison or out of it? I suppose you mean poor dear Michael. I hate men, and their selfish, stupid, blundering ways."

Fay had often alluded to the larger sex *en bloc* as blunderers since the night she had told Michael to stand behind the screen.

"There are two blunderers coming towards us now," said Magdalen, as the distant figures of Colonel Bellairs and Wentworth appeared in the beech avenue.

Both women experienced a distinct sense of relief.

Colonel Bellairs had many qualities as a parent which made him a kind of forcing-house for the development of virtue in those of his own family. He was as guano spread over the roots of the patience of others; as a pruning hook to their selfishness. But he had one great compensating quality as a father. He never for one moment thought that any man, however young, visited the house except for the refreshment and solace of his own society. He never encouraged anyone to come with a view to becoming acquainted with his daughters. His own problematic re-marriage, often discussed in all its pros and cons with Magdalen, was the only possible alliance that ever occupied his thoughts. In this respect he was an ideal parent in his daughters' eyes, an inhumanly selfish one according to his two sisters, Lady Blore and Miss Bellairs, at this moment stepping out towards Priesthope from the north lodge.

"'YOU ARE ALL BLINDER ONE THAN THE OTHER, THAT IT'S ANDREA I'M GRIEVING FOR'"

Wentworth had almost given up hope of a word with Fay until he saw her sitting with Magdalen in the avenue. The world would be a much harder place than it already is for women to live in if men concealed their feelings. A reverent and assiduous study of the nobler sex leads the student to believe that they imagine they conceal them. But it is women who early in life are taught to acquire this art, at any rate when they are bored. Half the happy married women of our acquaintance would be the widows of determined suicides if women allowed it to appear when they were bored as quickly as men do.

Wentworth had no idea that he was not an impassable barrier of reserve. He often said of himself: "I am a very reserved man, I know. It is a fault of character. I regret it, but I can't help it. I have not the art of chatting about my deepest feelings at five o'clock tea as a man must do who lays himself out to be popular with women. What I feel it is my nature to conceal."

His reserve on this occasion was concentrated in his face, which remained unmoved. But the lofty impassiveness on which he prided himself did not reach down to his legs. Those members, which had been dragging themselves in a sort of feeble semi-paralysis in the wake of the ruthless Colonel Bellairs, now straightened themselves, and gave signs of returning energy. Magdalen from a distance noted the change. Wentworth for the first time was interested in what Colonel Bellairs was saying. His own voice, which had become almost extinct, revived. There was also a hint of spring in the air. Not being a person of much self-knowledge, he mentioned that fact to Colonel Bellairs.

Colonel Bellairs looked at him with the suspicion which appears to be the one light shadow that lies across the sunny life of the bore.

"I said so half an hour ago," he remarked severely, "when we were inspecting my new manure tanks, and you said you did not notice it."

"You were right all the same," said the younger man.

What an interest would be added to life if it were possible to ascertain how many thousands of times people like Colonel Bellairs are limply assured that they are in the right! The mistake of statistics is that they are always compiled on such dull subjects. Who cares to know how many infants are born, and how many deaf mutes exist? But we should devour statistics, we should read nothing else if only they dealt with matters of real interest: if they recorded how often Mr. Simpson, the decadent poet, had said he was "a child of nature," how often, if ever, the Duchess of Inveraven and Mr. Brown, the junior curate at Salvage-on-Sea, had owned they had been in the wrong; whether it was true that an Archbishop had ever really said "I am sorry" without an "if" after it, and, if so, on what occasion; and whether any novelist exists who has not affirmed at least five hundred times that criticism is a lost art.

"Is the right-of-way dispute progressing?" said Magdalen to her father as the two men came up and stopped in front of them.

Colonel Bellairs implied that it would shortly be arranged, as his intellect was being applied to the subject.

Wentworth said emphatically, for about the thirtieth time, that the right of a footpath, or church path across the domain was well established and could not be set aside; but that whether it was also a bridle path was the moot point; and whether Colonel Bellairs was justified in his recent erection of a five-barred stile.

(I may as well add here, for fear the subject should escape my mind later on, that at the time of these pages going to press the dispute, often on the verge of a settlement, had reached a further and acuter stage, being complicated by Colonel Bellairs' sudden denial even of a church path, to the legal existence of which he had previously agreed in writing.)

Wentworth trod upon the crocus and said he must be going home.

"We will walk back to the house with you," said Magdalen, and she led the way with her father.

"I wish you would tell your Aunt Mary," he said to Magdalen as they walked on, "that I will not have her servants wandering in Lindley wood. Jones tells me they were there again last Sunday with a dog, that accursed little yapping wool mat of Aunt Aggie's! I simply won't stand it. I would rather you told her. It would come better from you."

"I will tell her."

Colonel Bellairs was beginning late in life to lean on Magdalen. She was fond of him in a way, and never yielded to him. *On ne peut s'appuyer que contre ce qui résiste.* Though Colonel Bellairs did not know it, he was always wanting to *s'appuyer*. He had found in his daughter something solid to lean against, which he had never found in his wife, who had not resisted him.

"Oh! and look here, Magdalen. I had a letter from your Aunt Mary this morning, a long rigmarole. She says she is following her letter, and is coming to have a serious talk with me. Hang it all! Can't a man have a moment's peace?"

Colonel Bellairs tore out of an inner pocket a bulky letter in a bold, upright hand, marked *Private*, at the top.

"I wish to the devil she would mind her own business, and let me manage mine," he said pettishly, thrusting the letter at Magdalen.

"I don't like to read it, as it is marked 'Private.'"

"Read it. Read it," said Colonel Bellairs irritably.

Magdalen read the voluminous epistle tranquilly from beginning to end as she and her father walked slowly back to the house.

It was an able production, built up on a solid foundation. It dealt with Colonel Bellairs' "obvious duty" with regard to the man to whom Magdalen had been momentarily engaged fifteen years before, and who, owing to two deaths in the Boer war, had unexpectedly succeeded to an earldom.

"Well! well!" said Colonel Bellairs at intervals, more interested than he wished to appear. "What do you think of it? We noticed in the papers a week ago that he had succeeded his cousin."

"Wait a minute, father. I have only come to my lacerated affections."

"How slow you are! Your Aunt Mary does pound away. She has a touch as light as a coal-sack. The wonder to me is how she ever captured poor old Blore."

"Perhaps she did it by letter. She writes uncommonly well. 'Magdalen's joyless homelife of incessant, unselfish service.' That is very well put, isn't it? And so is this: 'It is your duty now to inform him that you withdraw all opposition to the renewal of the engagement, and to invite him to Priesthope.' Really, Aunt Mary sticks at nothing. I warn you solemnly, father, this is only the thin end of the wedge. Unless you stand firm now, she'll want to choose our new stair carpet for us next. Really, I think at her age she might take a little holiday, and leave the Almighty in charge."

"Is that all you've got to say?" said Colonel Bellairs, somewhat surprised. "Do you wish me to ask him to the house or do you not? I don't object to him. I never did, except as a son-in-law, when he had no visible means of subsistence."

"And no intention of making any."

"Just so. But I always rather liked him, and, and—time slips by"—(it had indeed), "and I can't make much provision for you, in fact, almost none, and I may marry again; in fact, it is more than likely I shall shortly marry again." Colonel Bellairs was for a moment plunged in introspection. "So perhaps, on the whole, it would be more generous on my part to ignore the past and ask him to the house."

"After forbidding him to come to it?"

Colonel Bellairs began to lose his temper.

"I shall ask whom I think fit if I choose to do so. I am master in this house. If he does not care to come, he can stay away."

"Ask him, in that case."

"You agree that on the whole that would be best."

"Not at all. I think it extremely undignified on your part, and that it is a pity that you should be so swayed by Aunt Mary as to go by her judgment instead of your own. You never thought of asking him till she tried to coerce you into it."

"I am not going to be coerced by any woman, much less by that man in petticoats," said Colonel Bellairs wrathfully. "But she will be here directly. H'm! What on earth am I to say to her if I *don't* ask him?... She will be here directly."

They had reached Colonel Bellairs' study by now, and he sat down heavily in his old leather arm-chair. Magdalen was standing on the hearthrug near him with the letter in her hand. She held it over the fire, he nodded, and she dropped it in.

"Perhaps, Magdalen," said her father with dignity, "it would be just as well if I kept clear of the whole affair. Women manage these little things best among themselves. I would rather not be dragged in. Anything on that subject, any discussion, or interchange of opinion would come best from *you*, eh?"

"I think so, father."

Colonel Bellairs watched his sister's letter burn, with the fixed eye of one about to drop off into an habitual nap.

The asphyxiating atmosphere of a man's room, where a window is never opened except to let in a dog, or to shout at a gardener, and where years of stale tobacco brood in every nook and curtain, enveloped its occupant with a delicious sense of snug repose, and exerted its usual soporific charm.

"Took Mary a long time to write," he said, with a sleepy chuckle, as the last vestige disappeared of the laboriously constructed missive which Lady Blore had sat up half the previous night, with gold-rimmed pince-nez on Roman nose to copy out by her bedroom candle, and had sent to pave the way before her strong destructive feet.

The footman came in.

"Lady Blore and Miss Bellairs are in the drawing-room."

"Just pull the blinds half-way down before you go," said Colonel Bellairs to Magdalen, "and remember other people have got letters to write as well as her, and I'm not to be disturbed on any account."

CHAPTER IX

On garde longtemps son premier amant quand on n'en prend point de second.

—LA ROCHEFOUCAULD.

The two aunts meanwhile were sitting waiting in the drawing-room.

When Mrs. Bellairs died, which event, according to Aunt Aggie, had been brought about by a persistent refusal to wear on her chest a small square of flannel, (quite a small square) sprinkled with camphorated oil, and according to Aunt Mary by a total misconception of the Bellairs' character; when this event happened, the two aunts became what they called supports to their brother's motherless children.

They were far from being broken reeds which pierce the hands of those who lean on them.

No one had ever leaned on Aunt Mary or Aunt Aggie. Aunt Mary might perhaps be likened to one of those stout beams which have a tendency to push ruthlessly through the tottering outer wall which they are supposed to prop, into the inner chamber of the tenement which has the misfortune to be the object of their good offices.

She had contracted, not in her first youth, a matrimonial alliance—it could hardly be called a marriage—with a general, distinguished in India and obscure everywhere else, who had built a villa called "The Towers" a few miles from Priesthope. The marriage had taken place after years of half-gratified reluctance on his part and indomitable crude persistence on hers. In short it was what is generally called "a long attachment," and proves beyond dispute, what is already proven to the hilt, that the sterner sex prefer to have their affairs of the heart arranged for them; that once lost sight of they are mislaid, once let loose on parole they never return, once captured they endeavour to escape; that even when finally married nothing short of the amputation of all external interests will detain them within the sacred precincts of THE HOME.

Aunt Mary had had trouble with her general, but though she was no tactician, she was herself a general. His engagement to her had only been the first of the crushing defeats which she had inflicted upon him. Now at last at The Towers a deathlike peace reigned. Sir John, severely tried by rheumatism and advancing years, had, so to speak, given up his sword.

His wife's magnanimity had provided him with what she considered suitable amusements and occupations. He was told that he took an interest in breeding pigs, and he, who had once ruled a province rather larger than England, might now be seen on fine mornings tottering out, tilted forward on his stick, making the tour of the farmyard, and hanging over the low wall of his model pigstyes.

In Magdalen's recollections, Aunt Mary had always looked exactly the same, the same strong, tall, robust, large-featured, handsome woman, with black hair, and round, black, unwinking eyes, who invariably dressed in black and wore a bonnet. Even under the cedar at The Towers Aunt Mary wore a bonnet. When she employed herself in a majestic gardening the sun was shaded from her Roman nose by a black satin parasol.

There are some men and women whom it is monstrous to suppose ever were children, ever young, ever different from what they are now. Whatever laws of human nature may rule the birth of others, they, at any rate, like the phœnix, sprang full grown, middle aged, in a frock coat, or a bugled silk gown, from some charred heap of unconsenting parental ashes.

Aunt Mary was no doubt one of these.

Near her, on the edge of her chair, perhaps not so entirely on the edge of it as at first appeared, sat Aunt Aggie. Aunt Aggie looked as if she had been coloured by some mistake from a palette prepared to depict a London fog.

Her eyes were greyish yellow, like her eyelashes, like her hair,—at least her front hair,—like her eyebrows, and her complexion. She was short and stout. She called slender people skeletons. Her gown, which was invariably of some greyish, drabbish, neutral-tinted material, always cocked up a little in front to show two large, flat, soft-looking feet.

Aunt Aggie began quite narrow at the top. Her forehead was the thin edge of the wedge, and she widened slowly as she neared the ground; the first indication of a settlement showing in the lobes of her ears, then in her cheeks, and then in her drab-apparelled person. Her whole aspect gave the impression of a great self-importance, early realised and made part of life, but kept in abeyance by the society of Aunt Mary and by a religious conviction that others also had their place, a sort of back seat, in the Divine consciousness.

It would not be fair to Aunt Aggie to omit to mention, especially as she continually made veiled allusions to the subject herself, that she also had known the tender passion. There had been an entanglement in her youth with a High Church archdeacon. But we all know how indefinite, how inconclusive, how meagre in practical results archidiaconal conferences are apt to be! After one of them it was discovered that the entanglement was all on Aunt Aggie's side. The archdeacon remained unenmeshed. Under severe pressure from Lady Blore, then an indomitable bride of forty, flushed by recent victory, he even went so far as to say that his only bride was the Church. It was after this disheartening statement that Aunt Aggie found herself drawn towards an evangelical and purer form of religion. The Archdeacon subsequently married, or rather became guilty of ecclesiastical bigamy. But Aunt Aggie throughout life retained pessimistic views respecting the celibacy of the clergy.

Aunt Mary bestowed a strong businesslike peck, emphasized by contact with the point of a stone-cold nose, on Magdalen's cheek. Aunt Aggie greeted her niece with small inarticulate cluckings of affection. Have you ever kissed a tepid poached egg? Then you know what it is to salute Aunt Aggie's cheek.

"Where are Fay and Bessie?" enquired Aunt Mary instantly. When the aunts announced their coming, which was invariably at an hour's notice, they always expected to find the whole family, including Colonel Bellairs, waiting indoors to receive them. This expectation was never realised, but the annoyance that invariably followed had retained through many years the dew of its youth.

"Bessie and Fay are out. I am expecting them back every moment."

"They will probably be later than usual to-day," said Aunt Mary grimly, with the half-conscious intuition of those whom others avoid. Did she know that with the exception of Sir John, whose vanity had led him to take refuge in a *cul-de-sac*, her fellow creatures rushed out by back doors, threw themselves out of windows, hid behind haystacks, had letters to write, were ordered by their doctors to rest, whenever she appeared? Did she know? One thing was certain. Magdalen was one of the very few persons who had never avoided her, who at times openly sought her society. And Aunt Mary, though she would have been ashamed to own it, loved Magdalen. She intended that Magdalen should live with her some day at the Towers, as an unpaid companion, when Sir John and Aunt Aggie had entered into peace.

"And your father," continued Aunt Mary. "Did he get my letter? I intend to have a serious conversation with him after tea."

"Father has this moment come in, and he asked me to tell you that he had business letters which he is obliged to write."

"I know what *that* means."

"Oh! Mary!" interpolated Aunt Aggie eagerly. "You forget that Algernon always, from the time he was a young man, left his letters to the last moment. All the Bellairs do."

The Bellairs had other unique family characteristics, as peculiar to themselves as their choice of time for grappling with their correspondence, which Aunt Aggie was never tired of quoting. "Bellairs are always late for breakfast. It is no kind of use finding fault with Bessie about it. I was just the same at her age."

Aunt Aggie went through life under the belief that she was a peacemaker, which delicate task she fulfilled by making in an impassioned manner small statements which seldom contained a new or healing view of existing difficulties. She often spoke of herself as a "buffer" between contending forces. Sir John Blore had been known to remark that he could not fathom what Aggie meant by that expression, as it certainly was not appropriate to the domestic circle at The Towers, consisting, as it did, of one rheumatic Anglo-Indian worm, and one able-bodied blackbird.

"I intend to see your father after tea," repeated Aunt Mary, taking no notice of her sister's remark.

"Father is much worried about the right of way," continued Magdalen. "He showed me your most kind letter about myself, and——"

"Showed it to *you*!" said Aunt Mary, becoming purple. "It was not intended for any eye except your father's."

"Confidence between a father and his child," began Aunt Aggie, clasping her stout little hands, and looking eagerly from her sister to her niece.

Magdalen went on tranquilly. "It only told me what I knew before, Aunt Mary, that you have my welfare at heart. Father said that he thought it would be best if you and I talked the matter over. I agreed with him. It would be easier for me to discuss it with you. It would not be for the first time."

It would not indeed!

"Aggie," said Aunt Mary instantly, "you expressed a wish on your way here to see Bessie's fossils. You will go to the schoolroom and investigate them."

"I think they are kept locked," said Aunt Aggie faintly. She longed to stay. She had guessed the subject of the letter. She took in a love affair the fevered interest with which the unmarried approach the subject.

"They are unlocked," said Aunt Mary with decision.

Aunt Aggie swallowed the remains of her tea, and holding a little bitten bun in her hand slid out of the room. She never openly opposed her sister, with whom she lived part of the year when she let her cottage at Saundersfoot to relations in need of sea air.

An unmistakable aspect of concentration deepened in Aunt Mary's fine countenance.

"Magdalen," she said at once, "in the presence of that weak sentimentalist my lips are closed. But now that we are alone, and as it is your wish to reopen the subject, it is my duty to inform myself whether anything has transpired about Everard Constable—Lord Lossiemouth, as I suppose he now is."

"Nothing," said Magdalen with a calmness that was almost cheerful. If she was as sensitive as she looked she had a marvellous power of concealing it. She never shrank. She was apparently never wounded. She seldom showed that any subject jarred on her. It is affirmed that animals develop certain organs to meet the exigencies of their environment. A sole's eye (or is it a sand-dab's?) travels up round its head regardless of appearances when it finds it is more wanted there than on the lower side. We often see a similar distortion in the mental features of the wives of literary men. So perhaps also Magdalen had adapted herself to the Bellairs' environment, with which it was obvious that she had almost nothing in common except her name.

Aunt Mary loved Magdalen in a way, yet she never spared her the discussion of that long-ago attachment of her youth, violently mismanaged by Colonel Bellairs. The rose of Aunt Mary's real affection had a little scent, but it was set round with thorns.

"He has behaved disgracefully," she said, looking with anger and disappointment at her niece's faded face.

"We have discussed that before," said Magdalen tranquilly. "I, as you know, do not blame him. But it is all a hundred years ago, and better forgotten."

"He was poor then. No one ever thought he would succeed with two lives between. But it is different now that he is wealthy and in a position to marry."

"He has never been in a position to marry me," said Magdalen, "because he never cared enough for me to make an effort on my behalf. That was not his fault. He mistook a romantic admiration for love, and naturally found it would not work. How could it? It was not necessary to turn heaven and earth to gain me. But it *was* necessary to turn a few small stones. He could not turn them."

"Well, at any rate, he asked you, and you accepted him."

"A hundred years ago."

"And you have waited for him ever since."

"Not at all. I am not waiting for him or for anyone."

"You would have married Mr. Grenfell if it had not been for Everard."

"Perhaps I should have married Everard if it had not been for Everard," said Magdalen.

It seemed as if nothing could shake her dispassionate view of the matter.

"Your feelings were certainly engaged, Magdalen. There is no use in denying that."

"Have I ever denied it?"

Aunt Mary was silent for a moment, but her under lip was ominously thrust out. She was not thinking of what Magdalen had said. If she had ever listened to the remarks of others when they differed from her, she would not have become Lady Blore. She was only silent because she was rallying her forces.

"A woman's hands become talons when they try to hold on to a man when he wants to get away," said Magdalen gently.

Aunt Mary turned on her niece an opaque eye that saw nothing beyond the owner's views.

"Something ought to be done," she said with emphasis. "After all, your father dismissed him. I shall advise your father to write to him, and if he does not—I shall write to him myself."

"I hope you will not do that," said Magdalen. "Do you remember what a subject for gossip it was at the time? When father became angry with Everard he told everyone, and it became a sort of loud turmoil. The servants knew, the parish knew, the whole county knew that I had had a disappointment. I have remained ever since in the eyes of the neighbours a sort of blighted creature, a victim of the heartlessness of man. A new edition of that old story now that my hair is grey would be, I think, a little out of place. I had hoped——"

The door was suddenly thrown open, and Bessie marched into the room with Aunt Aggie hanging nervously at her heels.

"I came back as quickly as I could from the Carters' in order not to miss you," said Bessie to Aunt Mary in her stentorian voice, and she presented a glowing rose cheek to be kissed.

Magdalen shot a grateful glance at her sister, and the conversation became general.

After the aunts had departed, Bessie said to Magdalen on their way upstairs to dress, "I found when I reached the Carters' that they had gone out with Professor Ridgway to see the Roman camp. Only old Mrs. Carter was at home, and she was rather chilly, and said they had expected me to luncheon. They had had a little party to meet the Professor. I saw that my conduct called for an apology. I made one."

"I am glad of that."

"I see now that it would have been wiser to have gone over for luncheon as arranged. I also thought how selfish it was of Fay not to help you with the aunts. And then I perceived that there were not two pins to choose between us, as I had been just as bad myself, so I hurried back as quickly as I could."

"I was most grateful to you when I saw you come in. And Aunt Mary was pleased too. She never shows it much; but she was."

"It is of secondary importance whether she was pleased or not. My object in returning was twofold: to help you, and also for the sake of my own character. I begin to see that unless I am careful I shall become as selfish as father."

Magdalen did not answer.

"The aunts never do things like other people," continued Bessie. "I found Aunt Aggie standing, eating a bun, just outside the drawing-room door. She was quite flurried when I came up, and said she wanted to see my fossils, but would rather look at them another day."

CHAPTER X

La vie est un instrument dont on commence toujours par jouer faux.

Wentworth and Fay did not follow Colonel Bellairs and Magdalen back to the house. When they reached the end of the avenue they turned back silently by mutual consent, and retraced their steps down it.

Presently they reached the trunk of the tree where Fay had been sitting with Magdalen.

Fay sank down upon it once more, white and exhausted. He sat down at a little distance from her.

"How is Michael?" she said at last, twisting her ungloved hands together.

"I came to tell you about him; I only got back last night. I knew you would wish to hear."

"How is he?"

"He has been ill. He has had double pneumonia. It started with hæmorrhage, and some of the blood got into the lungs, and caused pneumonia. He is better now, nearly well, in fact. The prison doctor seemed a sensible man, and he spoke as if he were interested in Michael. From what he said I gathered that he did not think Michael would survive another winter there. The prison[1] stands in a sort of marsh. It is a very good place to prevent prisoners escaping, but not a good place for them to keep alive in. The doctor is pressing to have Michael moved. He thinks he might do better at the 'colonia agricola,' where the labour is more agricultural; or that even work in the iron mines of Portoferriao would try his constitution less than the swamp where he now is."

[1] The prison described has no counterpart in real life.

"Was he still in chains?"

"No. And the doctor said there was some talk of abolishing them altogether. If not, he will be obliged to go back to them now he is better. He is looking forward to the sea lavender coming out. He says the place is beautiful beyond words when it is in flower: whole tracts and tracts of grey lilac blossom in the shallows, and hordes of wild birds. He asked me to tell you that you were to think of him as living in fairyland."

Fay winced as if struck.

"You gave him my message?" she stammered.

"Of course I did. And he said I was to tell you not to grieve for him, for he was well and happy."

"Happy!" echoed Fay.

"Yes, happy. He said he had committed a great sin, but that he hoped and believed that he was now expiating it, and that it would be forgiven."

"I am absolutely certain," said Fay in a suffocated voice, "that Michael did not murder the Marchese di Maltagliala."

"That is impossible," said Wentworth.

"Then what great sin can he be expiating?"

Even as Fay asked the question she knew the answer. Michael believed he was expiating the sin of loving another man's wife. In his mind that was probably on a par with the murder he had not committed.

"I asked him that," said Wentworth, "but he would not say. He would only repeat that his punishment was just."

Two large tears ran down Fay's cheeks.

"It is unjust, unjust, unjust!" she gasped. "Why does God allow these dreadful things?"

There was a long silence.

For a time Wentworth had forgotten Fay. He saw again the great yellow building standing in a waste of waters. He saw again the thin, prematurely aged face of his brother, the shaved head, the coarse, striped convict dress, the arid light from the narrow barred window. He saw again Michael's grave smile, and heard the tranquil voice, "This place is beautiful in autumn. Mind you come next when the sea lavender is out."

The remembrance of that meeting cut sharper than the actual pain of it at the moment. He had gone through with it with a sort of stolid endurance, letting Michael see but a tithe of what he felt. But the remembrance was anguish unalloyed. For a time he could neither speak nor see.

A yellow butterfly that had waked too soon floated towards them on a wavering trial trip. Close at hand a snowdrop drooped "its serious head." The butterfly knew its own, and lit on the meek, nunlike flower, opening and shutting its new wings in the pallid sunshine. It had perhaps dreamed, as it lay in its chrysalis, "that life had been more sweet." Was this chill sunshine that could not quicken his wings, was this grim desert that held no goal for butterfly feet, was this one snowdrop—*all*? Was this indeed the summer of his dreams, in the sure and certain hope of which he had spun his cocoon, and laid him down in faith?

Fay looked at it in anguish not less than Wentworth's, whose dimmed eyes saw it not at all. She never watched a poised butterfly open and shut its wings without thinking of Michael. The flight of a seagull across the down cut her like a lash. He had been free once. He who so loved the down, the sea, the floating cloud, had been free once.

When Wentworth had winked his steady grey eyes back to their normal state, he looked furtively at Fay. She was weeping silently. He had seen Fay in tears before, but never without emotion. With a somewhat halting utterance he told her of certain small alleviations of Michael's lot. The permission, urgently asked, had at last been granted that English books might be sent him from time to time. The lonely, aching smart of Wentworth's morning hours was vaguely soothed and comforted by Fay's gentle presence.

She appeared to listen to him, but in reality she heard nothing. She sat looking straight in front of her, a tear slipping from time to time down her white cheek. Except on one or two occasions Fay had that rarest charm of looking beautiful in tears. She became paler than ever, never red and disfigured and convulsed, with the prosaic cold in the head that accompanies the emotions of less fortunate women.

"How old is Michael?" she asked suddenly in the midst of a painstaking account of certain leniencies as to diet, certain macaronis and soups which the doctor had insisted on for Michael.

"He is twenty-seven."

"And how long has he been in prison?"

"Nearly two years."

"And he has thirteen more," said Fay, looking at Wentworth with wide eyes blank with horror.

"No," said Wentworth, his voice shaking a little. "No, Michael will not live long in that swamp, not many years, I think."

"But they will move him to a better climate."

"He does not want to be moved. I should not, either, in his case."

Fay's hands fell to her sides.

"When my mother died," said Wentworth, "I promised her to be good to Michael. There was no need for me to promise to be good to him. I always liked him better than anyone else. I taught him to ride and to shoot. He got his gun up sharp from the first. It's easy to do things for anyone you like. But what is hard is when the time comes"—Wentworth stopped, and then went on—"when the time comes that you can't do anything more for the person you care for most."

Silence.

The yellow butterfly was still feebly trying to open and shut his wings. The low sun had abandoned him to the encroaching frost, and was touching the bare overarching branches to palest gold, "so subtly fair, so gorgeous dim"; so far beyond the reach of tiny wings.

"I don't think," said Wentworth, "I would stick at anything. I don't know of anything I would not do, anything I would not give up, to get him back his freedom. But it's no use, I can do nothing for him."

"Oh! Why does not the real murderer confess?" said Fay with a sob, wringing her hands. "How can he go on, year after year, letting an innocent man wear out his life in prison, bearing the punishment of his horrible crime?"

That mysterious murderer occupied a large place in Fay's thoughts. She hated him with a deadly hatred. He was responsible for everything. That one crooked channel of thought that persistently turned aside all blame onto an unknown offender, had at last given a certain crookedness, a sort of twist, to the whole subject in Fay's mind.

"I begged Michael again for the twentieth time to tell me anything that could act as a clue to discovering the real criminal," said Wentworth. "I told him I would spend my last shilling in bringing him to justice, but he only shook his head. I told him that some of his friends felt certain that he knew who the murderer was, and was shielding him. He shook his head again. He would not tell me anything the first day I went to him after he was arrested. And still, after two years in prison, he will not speak. Michael will never say anything."

The despair in Wentworth's voice met the advancing chill of the waning afternoon. The sun had gone. The gold had faded into grey. A frosty breath was stirring the dead leaves. The butterfly had closed his wings for the last time, and clung feebly, half reversed, to his snowdrop. A tiny trembling had laid hold upon him. He was tasting death.

Fay shivered involuntarily, and drew her fur cloak around her.

"I must go in," she said.

They walked slowly to the wooden, ivied gate which separated the woods from the gardens. A thin, white moon was already up, peering at them above the gathering sea mist.

They stood a moment together by the gate, each vaguely conscious of the consolation of the other's presence in the face of the great grief which had drawn them together.

"I will come again soon, if I may," he said diffidently, "unless seeing me reminds you of painful things." His voice had lowered itself involuntarily.

"I like to see you," said Fay in a whisper, and she slipped away from him like a shadow among the shadows.

The entire dejection of her voice and manner sheared from her words any possible reassurance which Wentworth might otherwise have found in them, which he suddenly felt anxious to find in them.

He pondered over them as he rode home.

How she had loved her husband! People had hinted that they had not been a happily assorted couple, but it was obvious that her grief at his loss was still overwhelming. And what courageous affection she had shown towards Michael, whom she had known from a boy; first in trying to shield him when he had taken refuge in her room, and afterwards in her sorrowing compassion for his fate. And what a steadfast belief she had shown from first to last in his innocence, against overwhelming odds!

Wentworth did not know till he met Fay that such women existed. Women he was aware were an enigma. Men could not fathom them. They were fickle, mysterious creatures, on whom no sane man could rely, whom the wisest owned they could not understand, capable alternately of devotion and treachery, acting from instincts that men did not share, moved by sudden, amazing impulses that men could not follow.

But could a woman like Fay, who towered head and shoulders above the ordinary run of women, removed to a height apart from their low level of pettiness and vanity, by her simplicity and nobility and capacity for devotion—*could such a woman love a second time?*

The thirst to be loved, to be the object of an exquisite tenderness, what man has not, consciously or unconsciously longed for that? What woman has not had her dream of giving that and more, full measure, running over?

To find favour in a woman's eyes a man need only do his stupid bungling best. But it is doubtful whether Wentworth had a best of any kind in him to do.

At twenty-five he would not have risked as much for love as even cautious men of robuster fibre will still ruefully but determinedly risk in the forties. And now at forty he would risk almost nothing.

Where Michael was concerned Wentworth's love had reached the strength where it could act, indefatigably, if need be. Michael had been so far the only creature who could move his brother's egotism beyond the refinements of bedridden sentiment.

It was as well for Fay that she did not realise, and absolutely essential for Wentworth that he did not realise either, that in spite of an undoubted natural attraction towards her he would have seen no more of her unless she had come within easy reach.

A common trouble had drawn them towards each other. A common interest, a common joy or sorrow, a house within easy distance—these are some of the match makers between the invalids of life, who are not strong enough to want anything very much, or to work for what they want. For them favourable circumstance is everything.

Wentworth could ride four and a half miles down a picturesque lane to see Fay. But he could not have taken a journey by rail.

A few years before Wentworth met Fay he had been tepidly interested in the youthful sister of one of his college friends and contemporaries, an Oxford Don at whose house he stayed every year. The sister kept house for her brother. It was the usual easy commonplace combination of circumstances that has towed lazy men into marriage since the institution was first formed. He saw her without any effort on his part. He arrived at a kind of knowledge of her. He found her to be what he liked. She was sympathetic, refined, shy, cultivated, unselfish, and of a wild rose prettiness. After a time he kept up, mainly on her account, a regular intercourse with the brother, who was becoming rather prosy, as was Wentworth himself. Presently the brother married, and the sister ceased to live with him.

Wentworth's visits to Oxford gradually ceased to give him pleasure. He found his friend's wife middle-class, self-absorbed, and artificial, the friend himself donnish, cut and dried, and liable to anecdotic seizures of increasing frequency. The intimacy dwindled and was now moribund. But it never entered his mind to enquire into the whereabouts of the sister, and to continue his acquaintance with her independently. If he had continued to meet her regularly he would almost certainly have married her. She on her side seemed well disposed towards him. As it was he never saw her again. He gradually ceased to think of her, except on summer evenings, as a charming possibility which Fate had sternly removed, as one lost to him for ever. He wrote a little poem about her, beginning, "Where are you now?"

(She was at Kensington all the time.) Wentworth never published his verses. He said there was no room for a new poet who did not advertise himself. There had been room for one of his college friends, but that had been a case of log rolling.

I do not know whether it was a fortunate or an unfortunate fate that had prevented the gay little lady of the pink cheeks from being at that moment installed at Barford as the wife of a poet who scorned publicity.

If Wentworth had been riding home to his wife on that February evening he would not have taken unconsciously another of the many steps which entailed so many more, by saying to himself, thinking of Fay:

"Could a woman like that love a second time?"

Then he hastened his speed as he remembered that his old friend the Bishop of Lostford had by this time arrived at Barford.

CHAPTER XI

If you feel no love, sit still; occupy yourself with things, with yourself, with anything you like, only not with men.

—TOLSTOY.

In Wentworth's youth he had been attracted towards many, besides the Bishop, among the bolder and less conventional of his contemporaries. Their fire, their energies, their enthusiasm, warmed his somewhat under-vitalized nature. He regarded himself as one of them, and his refinement and distinction drew the robuster spirits towards himself. But gradually, as time went on, these energies and enthusiasm took form, and, alas! took forms which he had not expected—he never expected anything—and from which his mind instinctively recoiled. He had supposed that energy was energy. He had not realised that it was life in embryo, that might develop, not always on lines of beauty, into a new policy, or a great discovery, or a passion, or a vocation. He hated transformations, new births, all change. His friends at first rallied him unmercifully, then lost patience, and finally fell from him, one by one. Some openly left him, the more good-natured among them forgot him, and if by chance they found themselves in his society, hurried back with affectionate cordiality to reminiscences of school and college life, long-passed milestones before the parting of the ways.

The Bishop when he plunged into his work also for a time lost sight of Wentworth, but when he was appointed to the See of Lostford, within five miles of Barford, the two men resumed, at first with alacrity, something of the old intercourse.

Wentworth had an element of faithfulness in him which enabled him to take up a friendship after a long interval, but it was on one condition, namely that the friend had remained *planté là* where he had been left. If in the meanwhile the friend had moved, the friendship flagged.

It was soon apparent that the Bishop had not by any means remained *planté là*, and the friendship quickly drooped. It would long since have died a natural death if it had not been kept alive by the Bishop himself, a man of robust affections and strong compassions, without a moment to spend on small resentments. After Michael's imprisonment he had redoubled his efforts to keep in touch with Wentworth, and the great grief of the latter, silently and nobly endured, had been a bond between the two men which even a miserable incident which must have severed most friendships had served to loosen, not to break.

The Bishop had in truth arrived at Barford, and was now sitting apparently unoccupied by the library fire. To be unoccupied even for an instant except during recuperative sleep was so unusual with the Bishop, so unprecedented, that his daughter would have been terrified could she have seen him at that moment. He had only parted from her and her husband at mid-day, yet it was a sudden thought suggested by his visit to them which was now holding him motionless by the fire, his lean person bulging with unanswered letters.

The Bishop was a small ugly man of fifty, unconventional to the core, the younger son of a duke, and a clergyman by personal conviction. He had been born in a hurry, and had remained in a hurry ever since. He had neither great administrative capacities, nor profound scholarship, but what powers he had were eked out by a stupendous energy. His Archbishop said that he believed that the Bishop's chaplains died like flies, and that he merely threw their dead bodies into the Loss, which flowed beneath his palace windows, without even a burial service. His chaplains and secretaries certainly worked themselves to the bone for him. They could have told tales against him, but they never did. For it was a strain to serve the Bishop, to get his robes thrown over him at the right—I mean the last—second, to thrust him ruthlessly into his carriage just in time to catch the tail ends of departing trains—he generally travelled with the guard. His admirable life had been spent in a ceaseless whirl. He had never had time to marry. He had hurried to the altar when he was an eager curate with a pretty young bride who was a stranger to him, whom his mother had chosen for him. During the years that followed what little he saw of her at odd moments he liked. After ten years of what he believed to be married life she died, leaving one child; tactful to the last, pretty to the last, having made no claim from first to last, kissing his hand, and thanking him for his love, and for the beautiful years they had spent together.

His friends said that he bore her loss with heroism, but in reality he missed her but little. Her death occurred just after he had become an ardent suffragan. His daughter grew up in a few minutes, and quickly took her mother's place. She was her mother over again in character and appearance. His wife had lived in his house for ten years, his daughter for twenty. By dint of time he learned to know her as he had never known her mother. At twenty she married his chaplain.

The chaplain was a tall, stooping, fleckless, flawless, mannerless, joyless personage, middle-aged at twenty-eight, with a voice like a gong, with a metallic mind constructed of thought-tight compartments, devoted body and soul to the Church, an able and indefatigable worker, smelted from the choice ore of that great middle class from which, as we know, all good things come. That he was a future ornament, or at any rate an iron girder of the Church was sufficiently obvious.

The Bishop saw his worth, and ruefully endured him until the chaplain, in the most suitable language, desired to become his son-in-law, and that at the most inconceivably awkward moment, namely, just when the Bishop had presented him with a living. The marriage had to be. The daughter wished it with an intensity that amazed her father. And gradually the Bishop discovered that he detested his paragon of a son-in-law. But why? It was not jealousy. He really was a paragon, not a sham. To the Bishop it seemed, and with truth, that any other woman would have done as well as his daughter, that her husband neither understood her nor wished to understand her, that he accepted ruthlessly without knowing that he accepted it, her selfless devotion, that he used her as a cushion to make his rare moments of leisure more restful, that her love was not even a source of happiness to him, only a solace. And she, extraordinary to behold, was radiantly content.

"*Just like her mother over again*," the Bishop had wrathfully said to himself as he drove away from his daughter's door. And at that moment a slide was drawn back from his mind, and he saw that the marriage was a replica of his own, except in so far that his son-in-law, greatly assisted by circumstances, had actually taken a little trouble to arrange his marriage for himself, while the Bishop's—what there was of it—had been done for him by his mother.

Till this morning he had believed his marriage to have been an ideally happy one, that he had felt all that man can feel; and he had been inclined to treat as womanish the desperate desolation of men who had after all only suffered the same bereavement as he had himself, and which he had quickly overcome. He saw now that he had missed happiness exactly as his son-in-law was missing it. The same thing had befallen them both. Love could do there no mighty works because of their unbelief. When he remembered his wife's face he realised that her joy had been something beyond his ken. He had not shared it. He had not known love, even when it had drawn very nigh unto him.

As he waited motionless for Wentworth to come in, his strong, intrepid mind worked. The Bishop at fifty went to school to a new thought. It was that power of going to school at fifty to a new thought which had made his Archbishop, who loved him, give him the See of Lostford, to the amazement of the demurer clergy who were scandalised by his unconventionality, and his fearful baldness of speech. They could only account for the appointment by the fact that he was the son of a duke. It was that power which made the Bishop seem a much younger man than Wentworth, who was in reality ten years his junior. The Bishop was still a learner. He still moved with vigour mentally. Wentworth, on the contrary, had arrived—not at any place in particular, but at the spot where he intended to remain. His ideas, and some of them had been rather good ones at twenty-five, had suffered from their sedentary existence. They had become rather stout. He called them progressive because in the course of years he had perceived in them a slight glacier-like movement. To others they appeared fixed.

Wentworth's attitude towards life, of which he was so fond of speaking, was perhaps rather like that of a shrimper who, in ankle-deep water, watches the heavily freighted whale boats come towering in. He does not quite know why he, of all men, with his special equipment for the purpose, and his expert handling of the net, does not also catch whales. That they seldom swim in two-inch water does not occur to him. At last he does not think there are any whales. He has exploded that fallacy. For, in a moment of adventurous enthusiasm, counting not the cost, did he not once wade recklessly up to his very shoulders in deep water: *and there were no whales*,—only pinching crabs. Crabs were the one real danger, the largest denizens of the boundless main, whatever his former playmates the whalers might affirm.

When the shrimper and the whaler had dined together, and the Bishop had heard with affectionate sympathy the little there was to hear respecting Michael, and the conversation tended towards more general topics, the radical antagonism between the two friends' minds threatened every moment to make itself felt.

The Bishop tried politics somewhat tentatively, on which they had sympathised in college days, but it seemed they had widely diverged since. Wentworth, though he frequently asserted that no one enjoyed more than he "the clashing of opposite opinions," seemed nevertheless only able to welcome with cordiality a mild disagreement, just sufficiently defined to prove stimulating to the expression of his own views. A wide divergence from them he met with a chilly silence. He did so now. The Bishop looked at his neat ankle, and changed the subject.

"Have you seen or heard anything of Everard Constable since he came into his kingdom, such a very unexpected kingdom, too?"

"No. I fancy he is still abroad. But I can't say that for some time past I have found Constable's aims in life very sympathetic. His unceasing struggle after literary fame appears to me somewhat undignified."

"Oh! come. Give the devil his due. Constable can write."

"Of course, of course. That is just what I am saying. But he and I differ too widely in our outlook on life to remain really intimate. He cares for the big things, ambition, popularity, a prominent position, luxury. He will enjoy being a personage, and having wealth at his command. For my part, I am afraid I care infinitely more for the small things of life, love, friendship, sympathy."

"The *small* things! Good Lord!" said the Bishop, and his jaw dropped. He also dropped the subject.

"I ran up against Grenfell last week," he continued immediately. "Do you see *him* now? You and he used to be inseparable at Cambridge."

Wentworth became frigid.

Grenfell had accused him at their last meeting of being an old maid, an accusation which had wounded Wentworth to the quick, and which he had never forgotten or forgiven. He had not in the least realised that Grenfell was not alluding to the fact that he happened to be unmarried.

"I can't say I care to see him now," he said. "He has become entirely engrossed in his career. A simple life like mine, the life of thought, no longer interests him. He is naturally drawn to people who are playing big parts."

"What nonsense! He is just the same as ever. A little vehement and fiery, but not as much as he was. They say he will be the next Chancellor of the Exchequer to a certainty."

"I daresay he will. He has the art of keeping himself before the public eye. Being myself so constituted—it is not any virtue in me, only a constitutional defect—that I cannot elbow for a place, it is difficult for me to understand how another, especially a man like Grenfell, can bring himself to do so. I had always thought he was miles above that kind of thing."

"So he is. So he is. A blind man can see Grenfell's unworldliness. It sticks a yard out of him. My dear Wentworth, if energetic elbows were, as you imply, the key to success, how do you account for the fact that hundreds of painful persons have triumphantly passed that preliminary examination who never achieve anything beyond a diploma in the art of pushing?"

Wentworth did not answer.

He firmly believed that in order to attain the things he had not attained, had never striven for, of which he invariably spoke disparagingly, but which he secretly and impotently desired, the co-operation of certain ignoble qualities was essential, sordid allies whom he would have disdained to use.

"I don't blame Grenfell," he said at last. "He had his way to make. I know how blinding the glamour of ambition is, how insidious and insistent the claims of the world may become. I don't pretend to be superior to certain temptations if they came in my way. But I happen to have kept out of their way. That is all."

"You have certainly kept out of the way of—nearly everything."

"For my part, I daresay I am hopelessly out of date, but I value beauty and peace and simplicity higher than a noisy success. But a noisy success is the one thing that counts nowadays."

"Does it?"

"And Grenfell has taken the right steps to gain it. If a man craves for popularity, if he really thinks the bubble worth striving for, he must lay himself out for it. If he wants a place he must jostle for it. If he wants power he must discard scruples. If he wants social success it can be got—we see it every day—by pandering to the susceptibilities and seeking the favour of influential persons. Everything has its price. I don't say that everyone obtains these things who is ready to bid for them. But some do. Grenfell is among those who have. I don't blame him. I am not sure that I don't rather envy him."

The Bishop could respect a conviction.

"Are you not forgetting Grenfell's character?" he said gently, as one speaks to a sick man. "Think of him, his nobility, his integrity, his enthusiasm, his transparent unworldliness which so often in the old days put us all to shame!"

"That is just what makes it all so painful to me," said Wentworth, and there was no possibility of doubting his sincerity. "That contact with the world can taint even beautiful natures like his. He was my ideal at one time. I almost worshipped him at Cambridge."

"I love him still," said the Bishop. "A cat may look at a king, so I suppose a poor crawler of a bishop may look at a man like Grenfell. Don't you think, Wentworth, that sometimes a man who succeeds may have worked as nobly as a man who fails—you always speak so feelingly of failure, it is one of the many things I like about you. Don't you think that perhaps sometimes success may be—I don't say it always is—as high-minded as failure, that a hard-won victory may be as honourable as defeat, that achievement may *sometimes* be the result not of chance or interest, but of unremitting toil? Don't you think you may be unconsciously cutting yourself adrift from Grenfell's friendship by attributing his success to unworthy means which a man like him could never have stooped to?"

"It is he who has cut himself adrift from me," said Wentworth icily. "I have not changed."

"That is just it. A slight change, shall we say expension on your part, might have enabled you to"—the Bishop chose his words as carefully as a doctor counts drops into a medicine glass—"to keep pace with him?"

"I do not regard friendship as a race or a combat of wits," said Wentworth. "Friendship is to my mind something sacred. I hope I can remain Grenfell's friend without believing him to be absolutely faultless. If he is so unreasonable as to expect that of me, which I should not for a moment expect of him, why then——" Wentworth shrugged his shoulders.

One of the few friends who had not drifted from him looked at him with somewhat pained affection.

Why does a life dwelt apart from others tend to destroy first generosity and then tenderness in man and woman? Why does one so often find a certain hardness and inhumanity encrusting those who have withdrawn themselves behind the shutters of their own convenience, or is it, after all, their own impotence?

"Has he always been hard and cold by nature?" said the Bishop to himself, "and is the real man showing himself in middle age, or is his meagre life starving him?"

He tried again.

"You nearly lost my friendship a year ago by attributing a sordid motive to me, Wentworth."

Wentworth understood instantly.

"That is all past and forgotten," he said quickly. "I never think of it. Have I ever allowed it to make the slightest difference?"

"No," said the Bishop, looking hard at him, "and for that matter neither have I. We have never talked the matter out. Let us do so now. I don't suppose you have forgotten the odium I incurred over the living of Rambury. It had been held for generations by old men. It had become a kind of clerical almshouse. When it fell vacant there was of course yet another elderly cleric——"

"My uncle," said Wentworth, "a most excellent man."

"Just so, but in failing health. Rightly or wrongly I was convinced that it was my duty to give the place a chance by putting there a younger man, of energy and capacity for hard work. I gave it to my future son-in-law as you know."

Wentworth nodded. "Everyone said at the time he was an excellent man," he said with evident desire to be fair.

"I daresay, but that is not the point. The point is that I had no idea that iron traction engine wanted to marry my daughter or anybody's daughter. The tactless beast got up steam and proposed for her the day after I had offered him the living. He had never given so much as a preliminary screech on the subject, never blown a horn to show what his horrid intentions were—I only hope that if I had known I should still have had the moral courage to appoint him. The Archbishop assures me I should—but I doubt it. I was loudly accused of nepotism, of course. Your uncle, who died soon afterwards, forgave me in the worst of taste on his deathbed. I had no means of justifying myself. The Archbishop and Grenfell and a few other old friends believed. *Why were you not among those old friends, Wentworth?*"

"I *was* among them," said Wentworth, meeting the Bishop's sombre eyes. "You never answered it, so I suppose you never received it, but at the time I wrote you a long letter assuring you that I for one had not joined in the cry against you, even though my uncle did. I frankly owned that, while I regarded the appointment as an ill-considered one, I took for granted that Mr. Rawlings was suited for the place. I said that I knew you far too well to suppose even for a moment that you would have given the post to a man, even if he were your son-in-law, unless he had been competent to fill it. You never answered the letter, so I suppose it failed to reach you."

"I received it," said the Bishop slowly. "I felt it to be an illuminating document, but it did not seem to call for an answer. It was in itself a response to a tacit appeal."

There was a pause, and then he continued cheerfully. "Rawlings has proved himself dreadfully competent as you prophesied, and Lucy is very happy in her new home. I came on from there this morning. My son-in-law, with the admirable promptitude and economy of time which endeared him to me as my chaplain, had arranged that every moment of my visit should be utilised; that I should christen their first child, dedicate a thank-offering in the shape of a lectern, consecrate the new portion of the churchyard, open a reading-room, and say a few cordial words at a drawing-room meeting before I left at mid-day. I told him if he went on like this he would certainly come to grief and be made a bishop some day. But he only remarked that he was not solicitous of high preferment. I think you would like Rawlings if you knew him better. You and he have a certain amount in common. I must own that I am glad that it is Lucy who has to put up with him and not I. I should think even God Almighty must find him rather difficult to live with at times. And now, Wentworth, if I am to be up and away at cock-crow, I must go to bed."

But the Bishop did not go to bed at once when Wentworth had escorted him to his room.

"It was no use," he said to himself. "It was worth trying, but it was no use. He never saw that he had misjudged me. He met my eye. He has a straight, clean eye. He is sincere as far as he goes, but how far *does* he go? He has never made that first step towards sincerity of doubting his own sincerity. He mistakes his moods for convictions. He has never suspected his own motives, or turned them inside out. He suspects those of others instead. He is like a crab. He moves sideways by nature, and he thinks that everyone else who moves otherwise is not straightforward, and that he must make allowances for them. According to his lights he has behaved generously by me. Has he! Damn him! God forgive me. Well, I must stick to him, for I believe I am almost the only friend he has left in the world."

CHAPTER XII

Shall soul not somehow pay for soul?—D. G. ROSSETTI.

Fay did not sleep that night.

For a long time past, she seemed to have been gradually, inevitably approaching, dragging reluctant feet towards something horrible, unendurable. She could not look this veiled horror in the face. She never attempted to define it to herself. Her one object was to get away from it.

It had not sprung into life full grown. It had gradually taken form after Michael's imprisonment. At first it had been only an uneasy ghost that could be laid, a spectre across her path that could be avoided; but since she had come home it had slowly attained gigantic and terrifying proportions. It loomed before her now as a vague but insistent menace, from which she could no longer turn away.

A great change was coming over Fay, but she tacitly resisted it. She did not understand it, nor realise that the menace came from within her gates, was of the nature of an insurrection in the citadel of self. We do not always recognise the voice of the rebel soul when first it begins to speak hoarsely, unintelligibly, urgently from the dark cell to which we have relegated it.

Some of us are so constituted that we can look back at our past and see it as a gradation of steps, a sort of sequence, and can thus gain a kind of inkling of the nature of the next step against which we are even now striking our feet.

But poor Fay saw her life only as shattered, meaningless fragments, confused, mutilated masses without coherence. The masses and the gaps between them were of the same substance in her eyes. She wandered into her past as a child might wander among the rubbish heaps of its old home in ruins. She was vaguely conscious that there had been a design once in those unsightly mounds, that she had once lived in them. On that remnant of crazy wall clung a strip of wall-paper which she recognised as the paper in her own nursery; here a vestige of a staircase that had led to her mother's room. And as a child will gather up a little frockful of sticks and fallen remnants, and then drop them when they prove heavy, so Fay picked up out of her past tiny disjointed odds and ends of ideas and disquieting recollections, only to cast them aside again as burdensome and useless.

The point to which she wandered back most frequently—to stare blankly at it without comprehension—was her husband's appeal to her on his deathbed. To-night she had gone back to it again as to a tottering wall. She had worn a little pathway over heaps of miserable conjectures and twisted memories towards that particular place.

She saw again the duke's dying face, and the tender fixity of his eyes. She could almost hear his difficult waning voice saying:

"The sun shines. He does not see them, the spring and the sunshine. Since a year he does not see them. Francesca, how much longer will you keep your Cousin Michael in prison?"

Since a year he does not see them.

It was two years now.

The shock to Fay at the moment those words were spoken had been that her husband had known all the time. That revelation blotted out all other thoughts for the time being. It even blotted out all considerations of her own conduct towards Michael, which it might conceivably have rendered acute. It made her mind incapable of receiving the impression that the duke had perhaps hoped his deliberate last words might make on it; that surely she would not, after his death, still keep Michael in his cell. Throughout the early weeks of her widowhood Fay remained as one stunned. Even Magdalen, who hurried out to her, supposed at first that she was stunned by grief.

"Then Andrea knew all the time." That was the constant refrain of her bewildered, half-paralysed mind.

Gradually in the quiet monotonous life at Priesthope the question made itself felt. "*How did he know?*"

That question was never answered by Fay, deeply though she pondered over it. It remained a mystery to her all of her life. She recalled little scraps of his conversation, tiny incidents which might have shown her that he knew. But she had noticed nothing at the time. Her cheek burned when she recalled his tranquil, sarcastic voice.

"Not on the high road. You are in the right. How dusty, how dirty, is the high road! But I have known, not once, nor twice, women to murder men very quietly. Oh! so gently and cleanly—to let them die."

When first she remembered those words of her dead husband, a horrible revulsion of feeling against him seized her. She had been vaguely miserable and remorseful at his death until those words, so tranquilly spoken in a primrose dawn, came back to her.

Then she was suddenly glad he was dead, gone for ever. She almost hated him once more. It was dreadful to live with people whom she did not understand, who knew things they kept secret, whose minds and thoughts and motives were incomprehensible to her, who believed horrible untrue things of her. It had been a fixed idea with Fay during her husband's lifetime that he believed horrible untrue things about her. But what they were she would have found it difficult to say.

Fay's was not a suspicious nature in its normal state, but most persons of feeble judgment become suspicious when life becomes difficult. They cannot judge, and consequently cannot trust. Fay had never learnt even so much of her husband as that she might have trusted him entirely. Now that he was gone without betraying her, the knowledge that he had known her secret and had guarded it faithfully did not make her feel, with a flood of humble contrition, how deeply she had misjudged him, how loyal he had been from first to last; it only aroused in her a sense of fear and anger. How secretive Andrea had been, how underhand! Perhaps part of the doom of a petty, self-centred nature is that it does not know when it has been generously and humanely dealt with.

When Fay had somewhat recovered from the shock of her husband's dying speech she had turned with all her might to Magdalen, had cast herself upon her, clung to her in a sort of desperation. Magdalen at any rate believed in her.

For many months after she came to Priesthope, her mind remained in a kind of stupor, and it seemed at first as if she were regaining a sort of calm, caught as it were from Magdalen's presence.

But gradually miserable brooding memories returned, and it seemed at last as if something in Magdalen's gentle serenity irritated instead of soothing Fay as heretofore. Was Magdalen a sort of unconscious ally of that fainting soul within Fay's fortress? Were chance words of Magdalen's beginning to make the rebel stir in his cell? At any rate something stirred. Something was making trouble. Fay began to shrink from Magdalen, involuntarily at first, then purposely for long moody intervals. Then she would be sarcastic and bitter with her, jibe at the housekeeping, and criticise the household arrangements. A day later she would be humbly and hysterically affectionate once more, asking to be forgiven for her waywardness. She could not live without the comfort of Magdalen's tenderness. And at times she could not live with it. Magdalen preserved an unmoved front. She ignored her sister's petulance and spasmodic fault-finding. She knew they were symptoms of some secret ill, but what that ill was she did not know. She kept the way open for Fay's sudden remorseful return to affectionate relations, and waited.

Those who, like Magdalen, do not put any value on themselves, are slow to take offence. It was not that she did not perceive a slight, or a rebuff, or a sneer at her expense, but she never, so to speak, picked up the offence flung at her. She let it lie, by the same instinct that led her to step aside in a narrow path rather than that her skirt should touch a dead mole. No one could know Magdalen long without seeing that she lived by a kind of spiritual instinct, as real to her as the natural instincts of animals.

Fay became more and more haggard and irritable as the months at Priesthope drew into a year. A new element of misery was added to her life by the sight of Wentworth, and his visits were becoming frequent. His mere presence made acute once more that other memory, partially blurred, persistently pushed aside—the memory of Michael in prison. The figure of the duke had temporarily displaced that other figure in its cell.

But now the remembrance of Michael, continually stirred up by poor Wentworth, with his set, bereaved face, was never suffered to sleep. With every week of her life it seemed to Fay some new pain came.

Magdalen could not comfort her. Magdalen, who was so fond of Michael.

If Magdalen knew!

Magdalen must never, never know. She could not live without Magdalen. Magdalen was not like Andrea in that. She at any rate was concealing nothing, could know nothing. Now that Andrea was dead, only one living person beside herself *knew*—Michael. Fay was unconsciously growing to hate the thought of that one other person, to turn with horror from the remembrance of Michael: his sufferings, his patient life in death filled her with nausea, disgust. Her vehement selfish passion for him had been smothered by the hideous débris which had been cast upon it.

She had never loved him, as the duke well knew, and now the shivering remembrance of him, constantly renewed by Wentworth, had become like a poignard in a wound that would not heal. Wentworth had to-day yet again unconsciously turned the dagger in the wound, and her whole being sickened and shuddered. Oh! if she could only tear out that sharp-bladed remembrance and cast it from her, then in time the aching wound in her life might heal, and she might become happy and well and at peace once more;—at peace like Magdalen. An envious anger flared up in her mind against Magdalen's calm and happy face.

Oh, if poor Michael could only die! He wanted to die. If only he could die and release her. *Release her from what?*

From her duty to speak and set him free? Those were the words which she never permitted the rebel voice within to say. Still, they were there, silenced for the time, but always waiting to be said. Their gagged whisper reached her in spite of herself.

Oh! if only Michael were dead and out of his suffering, then she would never be tortured by them any more. Then, too, her husband's words would lose their poisoned point, and she could thrust them forth from her mind for ever.

"Francesca, how much longer will you keep your cousin Michael in prison?"

Oh! Cruel, cruel Andrea, vindictive to the very gates of death.

Down the empty, whispering gallery of ghostly fears in which her life crouched, Michael's voice spoke to her also. She could hear his grave, low tones. "Think of me as in fairy-land."

That tender, compassionate message had a barbed point which pierced deeper even than the duke's words.

Her lover and her husband seemed to have conspired together to revenge themselves upon her.

Fay leaned her pretty head against the window-sill and sobbed convulsively.

Poor little soul in prison, weeping behind the bars of her cell, that only her own hands could open!

Were not Fay and Michael both prisoners, fast bound: she in misery, he only in iron.

The door opened gently and Magdalen came in in a long white wrapper, with a candle in her hand.

She put down the candle and came towards Fay. She did not speak. Her face quivered a little. She bent over the huddled figure in the window seat, and with a great tenderness drew it into her arms. For a moment Fay yielded to the comfort of the close encircling arms, and leaned her head against Magdalen's breast.

Then she wrenched herself free, and pushed her sister violently from her.

"Why do you come creeping in like that?" she said fiercely. "You only come to spy upon me."

Magdalen did not speak. She had withdrawn a pace, and stood looking at her sister, her face as white as her night-gown.

Fay turned her tear-drenched face to the window and looked fixedly out. There was a faint movement in the room. When she looked round Magdalen was gone.

Fay, worn with two years of partially eluded suffering, restless with pain, often sick at heart, was at last nearing the last ditch:—but she had not reached it yet.

Many more useless tears, many more nights of anguish, many more days of sullen despair still lay between her and that last refuge.

CHAPTER XIII

Il n'y a point de passé vide ou pauvre, il n'y a point d'événements misérables, il n'y a que des événements misérablement accueillis.

—MAETERLINCK.

Magdalen went back to her own room, and set down her candle on the dressing-table with a hand that trembled a little.

"I ought not to have gone," she said half aloud, "and yet—I knew she was awake and in trouble. And she nearly spoke to me to-day. I thought—perhaps at last—the time had come like it did with Mother. But I was wrong. I ought not to have gone."

The large room which had been her mother's, the elder Fay's, seemed to-night crowded with ghostly memories: awakened by the thought of the younger Fay sobbing in the room at the end of the passage.

In this room, in that bed, the elder Fay had died eighteen years ago.

How like the mother the child had become who had been named after her.

Magdalen saw again in memory the poor pretty apathetic mother who had taken so long to die; a grey-haired Fay, timid as the present Fay, unwise, inconsequent, blind as Fay, feebly unselfish, as alas! Fay was not.

There is in human nature a forlorn impulse, to which Mrs. Bellairs had yielded, to speak at last when the great silence draws near, of the things that have long cankered the heart, to lay upon others part of the unbearable burden of life just when death is about to remove move it. Mrs. Bellairs had always groped feebly in heavy manacles through life, in a sort of twilight, but her approaching freedom seemed towards the last to throw a light, faint and intermittent but still a light, on much that had lain confused and inexplicable in her mind. Many whispered confidences were poured into Magdalen's ears during those last weeks, faltered disjointed revelations, which cut deep into the sensitive stricken heart of the young girl, cutting possibly also new channels for all her after life to flow through.

Did the mother realise the needless anguish she inflicted on the spirit of the grave, silent girl of seventeen. Perhaps she was too near the great change to judge any longer—not that she had ever judged—what was wise or unwise, what was large or small. Trivial poisoned incidents and the deep wounds of life, petty unreasonable annoyances and acute memories were all jumbled together. She had never sorted them, and now she had ceased to know which was which. The feeble departing spirit wandered aimlessly among them.

"You must stand up to your father, Magdalen, when I'm gone. I never could. I was too much in love with him at first, and later on when I tried he had got the habit of my yielding to him, and it made a continual wretchedness if I opposed him. He always thought I did not love him if I did not consent to everything he wished, or if I did not think him right whatever he did. I did try to stand up about the children, but at last I gave up that too. I was not fit to have children, if I sacrificed their wellbeing to his caprice and his whim, but that was what I did. I have been a poor mother, and an unfaithful friend, and an unjust mistress. Women like me have no business to marry....

"You don't remember Annie, do you? She was second housemaid, the best servant I ever had. She was engaged to William, the footman with the curly hair. He is butler now at Barford. She cared for him dreadfully, poor soul. But your father could not bear her because she had a squint, and he never gave me any peace till I parted with her. I did part with her—and I got her a good place—but—I spoilt her marriage. It did not take much spoiling perhaps, for after she was gone he soon began to walk with the kitchen maid, but—she had been kind to me. So good once when I was ill, and my maid was ill. She did everything for me. I have often cried about that at night since."

"Mother always used to tell me and I never believed it, but it is true—men are children and it is no good thinking them different. They never grow up. I don't know if there are any grown up men anywhere. I suppose there must be—but I have never met one. I don't know any Prime Ministers or Archbishops, but I expect they are just the same as your father in home life."

"I daresay your father will be sorry when I'm gone. People like your father are always very fond of someone who is dead, who has no longer any claim upon them: a mother or a sister, whom they did not take much trouble about when they were alive.

"Of course I am going to die first, but I sometimes used to think if your father died before me and if he were allowed to come back after death—such things do happen—I had a friend who saw a ghost once—whether he would be as vexed then at any little change as he is now. You know, Magdalen, it has always been a cross to me that the writing-table in my sitting-room is away from the light. My eyes were never strong. I moved it near the window when I first came here, but your father was annoyed and had it put back where it is now, because his mother always had it there. But I really could not see to write there. And I have often thought if he came back after he was dead whether he would mind if he found I had moved it nearer the window."

"The Bishop of Elvaston married us. I daresay you don't remember him, my dear. He died a few years later. He had a wart on his chin and he once shook hands with baby's feet. But he was good. He told me I must sacrifice all to love. But what has been the use of all my sacrifices, first of myself and then of others? Your father has not been the happier or the better for it, but the worse. I have let him do so many cruel little things for which others have suffered. It was not exactly that he did not see what he was doing. He would not see. Some people are like that. They won't look, and they become dreadfully angry if they are asked to look. I gave it up at last. Oh, my poor husband! I knew I had failed everybody else, but at any rate not him. But I see now,"—the weak voice broke—"I see now that I have failed him, too. We ought never to have married. Love is not any guide to happiness. Remember that, Magdalen. We were both weak. He was weak and domineering. I was weak and yielding. I don't know which is the worst."

As the shadows deepened all the tacit unforgiveness of a weak, down-trodden nature which has been vanquished by life whispered from the brink of the grave.

"I have never been loved. I have given everything, and I have had nothing back. Nothing. Nothing. Don't marry, Magdalen. Men are all like that. Lots of women say the same. They take everything and they give nothing. It is our own fault. We rear them to it from their cradles. From their schooldays we teach them that everything is to give way to them, beginning with the sisters. With men it is Take, Take, Take, until we have nothing left to give. I went bankrupt years ago. There is nothing left in me. I *have* nothing and I *am* nothing. I'm not dying now. I have been dead for years."

"You say I am going to be at peace, Magdalen, but how do you know? I daresay I'm not. I daresay I am going to hell, but if I do I don't care. I don't care where I go so long as it is somewhere where there aren't any more husbands, and housekeeping, and home, weary, weary home, and complaints about food. I don't want ever to see anything again that I have known here. I am so tired of everything. I am tired to death."

Poor mother and poor daughter.

Who shall say what Magdalen's thoughts were as she supported her mother's feeble steps down to the grave. Perhaps she learned at seventeen what most of us only learn late, so late, when life is half over.

Bitterness, humiliation, the passionate despair of the heart which has given all and has received nothing,—these belong not to the armed band of Love's pilgrims, though they dog his caravan across the desert.

These are only the vultures and jackal prowlers in Love's wake, ready to pounce on the faint hearted pilgrim who through weakness falls into the rear, where fang and talon lie in wait to swoop down and rend him.

If we adventure to be one of Love's pilgrims we must needs be long suffering and meek, if we are to win safe with him across the desert, and see at last his holy city.

Tears welled up into Magdalen's eyes as one piteous scene after another came back to her, enacted in this very room.

Poor little mother, who had seemed to Magdalen then so old and forlorn, who, when she died, had only been a year or two older than Magdalen herself was now.

And poor little wavering life sobbing in the room at the end of the passage over some mysterious trouble.

The elder Fay lived on in the younger Fay. Was she also to be vanquished by life, to become gradually embittered and resentful? There seemed to be nothing in her lot to make her so. What was it, what could it be that was casting a blight over Fay's life?

How to help her, how to release her from the self-imposed fetters in which her mother had lived and—died.

Just as some persons have the power of making something new out of refuse—paper out of rags—so Magdalen seemed to have the power of cherishing and transforming the weaker, meaner elements of the characters with which she came in contact. Certain qualities in those we are inclined to love daunt us. Insincerity, callousness, selfishness, treachery in its more refined aspects, these are apt to arouse at first incredulity and at last scorn in us. But they aroused neither in Magdalen. She saw them with clearness, and dealt tenderly with them.

What others discarded as worthless, she valued. To push aside the feeble and intermittent affection of a closed and self-centred nature, believing it is giving its best, what is that but to push aside a poor man's little offering. Many years ago Magdalen had accepted not without tears, one such offering from a very poor man indeed.

Loving-kindness, tenderness, have their warped, stunted shoots as well as their free-growing, stately blossoms. It is the same marvellous, fragrant life struggling to come forth through generous or barren soil. There are some thin, dwarfed, almost scentless flowers of love and friendship, of which we can discern the faint fragrance only when we are on our knees. But some of us have conscientious scruples about kneeling down except at shrines. Magdalen had not.

She knew that Fay cared but little for her in reality. But she also knew that she did care a little. Fay had turned to her many times, and had repulsed and forgotten her not a few times.

Magdalen had a good memory.

"When she really wants me she will turn to me again," she said tranquilly to herself.

CHAPTER XIV

Toute passion a son chemin de croix.

And Michael?

What of him during these two endless years?

What did he think about during his first year in prison: what was the first waking in his cell like, the second, the third, the gradual discovery of what it means to be in prison? Was there a bird outside his window to wound him? The oncome of summer, the first thrill of autumn, how did he bear them?

His was not a mind that had ever dwelt for long upon itself. The egoist's torturing gift of introspection and self-analysis was not his. He had never pricked himself with that poisoned arrow. So far he had not thought it of great importance what befell him. Did he think so now? Did he brood over his adverse fate? Did he rebel against it, or did he accept it? Did angels of despair and anguish wrestle with him through the hot nights until the dawn? Did his famishing youth rise up against him? Or did that most blessed of all temperaments, the impersonal one, minister to him in his great need?

Perhaps at first he was supported by the thought that he was suffering voluntarily for Fay's sake. Perhaps during the first year he kept hold of the remembrance of her love for him. Perhaps in time he forgot what he had read in the depths of her terror-stricken eyes as he had emerged from behind the screen. There had been no thought of him at that moment in those violet eyes, no anxiety for him, no love.

Or perhaps he had *not* forgotten, and had realised that her love for him was very slenderly built. Perhaps it was the foreshadow of that realisation that had made him know in his first weeks in prison, before the trial, that she would not speak.

Michael had unconsciously readjusted several times already in pain his love for Fay. He did it again during that first year in prison. He saw that she was not capable of love as he understood it. He saw that she was not capable of a great sacrifice for his sake. The sacrifice which would have exonerated him had been altogether too great. Yes, he saw that. It had been cruel of him to think even for a moment that she might make it. What woman would! His opinions respecting the whole sex had to be gently lowered to meet the occasion. Nevertheless she *did* love him in her own flower-like way. She would certainly have made a *small* sacrifice for his sake. His love was tenderly moved and re-niched into a smaller demand on hers, one that she could have met without too much distress. His bruised mind comforted itself with the conviction that if a slight sacrifice on her part could have saved him she would indubitably have made it.

After a year in prison the news tardily reached Michael through his friend, the doctor, that the duke was dead.

The news, so long expected, gave him a pang when it did at last arrive. He had liked the duke. For a moment they had been very near to each other.

But now, *now*, Fay would release him. It would still be painful to her to do so, but in a much lesser degree than heretofore. She would have to endure certain obvious, though groundless, inferences from which her delicacy would shrink. But she was free to marry him now, and that made all the difference as to the explanation she would have to give. A little courage was all that was needed, just enough to make a small sacrifice for him. She would certainly have that amount. The other had been too much to expect. *But this*——

Michael leaned his forehead against the stone wall of his cell, and sobbed for joy.

Oh! God was good. God was merciful. He knew how much he could bear. He knew that he was but dust. He had not tried him beyond his strength.

Michael was suffused with momentary shame at the joy that the death of his friend had brought him.

Nevertheless, like a mountain spring that will not be denied, joy ever rose and rose afresh within him.

Fay and he could marry now. The thought of her, the hungered craving for her was no longer a sin.

It was Sunday evening. The myriad bells of Venice were borne in a floating gossamer tangle of sound across the water.

Joy, overwhelming, suffocating joy inundated him.

He stumbled to his feet, and clung convulsively to the bars of his narrow window.

How often he had heard the bells, but never with this voice!

He looked out across the wide water with its floating islands, each with its little campanile. His eyes followed the sails of the fishing boats from Chioggia, floating like scarlet and orange butterflies in the pearl haze of the lagoon.

How often he had watched them in pain. How often he had turned his eyes from them lest that mad rage for freedom which entered at times into the man in the next cell, when the boats passed, should enter also into him, and break him upon its wheel.

He looked at the boats now with tears in his eyes. They gleamed at him like a promise straight from God. How freely they moved. Free as air; free as the sea-mew with its harsh cry wheeling close at hand under a luminous sky.

He also should be free soon, should float away past the gleaming islands, over a sea of pearl in a boat with an orange sail.

For Fay would come to him. The one woman in the world of counterfeits would come to him, and set him free. She would take him in her arms at last, and lay her cool healing touch upon his aching life. And he would lean his forehead against her breast, and his long apprenticeship to love would be over. It seemed to Michael that she was here already, her soft cheek against his.

He pressed his face to the stone wall, and whispered as to her:

"Fay, have I served you?"

He almost heard her tremulous whisper, "Yes."

"Do you still love me?"

"Yes."

"We may love each other now."

Again Fay's voice very low. "Yes."

It had to be like that. This moment was only a faint foreshadowing of that unendurable joy, which inevitably had to come.

A great trembling laid hold on Michael. He could not stand. He fell on his knees, but he could not kneel. He stretched himself face downwards on his pallet. But it was not low enough. He flung himself on the floor of his cell, but it was not low enough. A grave would hardly have been low enough. The resisting stone floor had to do instead.

And through the waves of awe and rapture that swept over him came faintly down to him, as from some dim world left behind, the bells of Venice, and the thin cry of the sea-mew rejoicing with him.

Can we call a life sad which has had in it one such blessed hour?

Luminous day followed luminous day, and the nights also were full of light. His work was nothing to him. The increasing heat was nothing to him. His chains were nothing to him.

But at last when the weeks drew into a month, two months, a chill doubt took up its abode with him. It was resolutely cast out. But it returned. It was fought against with desperation. It was scorned as want of faith. Michael's strength waned with each conflict. But it always returned. At last it became to him like a mysterious figure, always present with him.

"Fay," he whispered over and over again through the endless burning nights of summer. "Dear one, come soon."

There was neither speech nor language, only the lying bells in the dawn.

The shadow deepened.

A frightful suspense laid its cold, creeping hold on Michael.

What could have happened?

Was she ill?

Was she dead?

He waited, and waited, and waited. Time stood still.

Let no one say that he has found life difficult till he has known what it is to wait; till he has waited through the endless days that turn into weeks more slowly than an acorn turns into a sapling; through the unmoving weeks that turn into months more slowly than a sapling turns into a forest tree,—for a word which does not come.

Late in the autumn, six months and five days after the death of the duke—Michael marked each day with a scratch on the wall—he received a letter from Wentworth. He was allowed to receive two letters a year.

He dreaded to open it. He should hear she was dead. He had known all the time that she was dead. That flowerlike face was dust.

With half blind eyes, that made the words flicker and run into each other, he sought through Wentworth's long letter for her name. Bess, the retriever, had had puppies. The Bishop of Lostford's daughter had married his chaplain—a dull marriage, and the Bishop had not been able to resist appointing his son-in-law to a large living. The partridges had done well. He had got more the second time over than last year. But he did not care to shoot without Michael.

He found her name at last on the third sheet, just a casual sentence.

"Your cousin, the Duchess of Colle Alto, has come to live at Priesthope for good. She has been there nearly six months. I see her occasionally. At first she appeared quite stunned by grief, but she is becoming rather more cheerful as time passes on."

The letter fell out of Michael's hand.

"*Rather more cheerful as time passes on.*"

Someone close at hand laughed, a loud, fierce laugh.

Michael looked up startled. He was alone. He never knew that it was he who had laughed.

"*Rather more cheerful as time passes on.*"

He looked back and saw the months of waiting that lay behind him,—during which the time had passed on. He saw them pieced together into a kind of map; an endless desert of stones and thorns, and in the midst a little figure in the far distance, coming toiling towards him, under a blinding sun.

That figure was himself. And this was what he had reached at last. He had touched the goal.

She had left Italy for good. She had gone back to her own people; not lately, but long ago, months ago. When he had first heard of the duke's death, even while he was counting daily, hourly, on her coming as the sick man counts on the dawn; even then she was arranging to leave Italy for good. Even then, when he was expecting her day by day, she must have made up her mind not to speak. She would not face anything for his sake. She had decided to leave him to his fate.

She who looked so gentle, was hard; she who wept at a bird's grief over its rifled nest, was callous of suffering. She, who had seemed to love him—he felt still her hands holding his hands against her breast—had never loved him. She did not know what love was.

She was inhuman, a monster. He saw it at last.

There is in love a spiritual repulsion to which physical repulsion at its worst is but a pale shadow. Those who give love to one who cannot love may not escape the stroke of that poisoned fang. Sooner or later that shudder has to come.

Only while we are young do we believe that the reverse of love is hate. We learn later, and that lesson we never forget, for love alone can teach it, that the reverse of love is egotism. The egoist cannot love. Can we endure that knowledge and go on loving? Can we be faithful, tender, selfless to one who exacts all and gives nothing, who forgets us and grieves us, even as day by day we forget and grieve our unforsaking and faithful God?

Can we endure for love of man what God endures for love of us?

The duke's words came back to Michael.

"Why do you deceive yourself, my friend? There is only one person for whom she has a permanent and deep affection—for her very charming self."

He had thought of her as his wife for six months and four days.

Michael beat his manacled hands against the wall till they bled. He broke his teeth against his chains.

If Fay had come in then he would have killed her, done her to death with the chains he had worn so patiently for her sake.

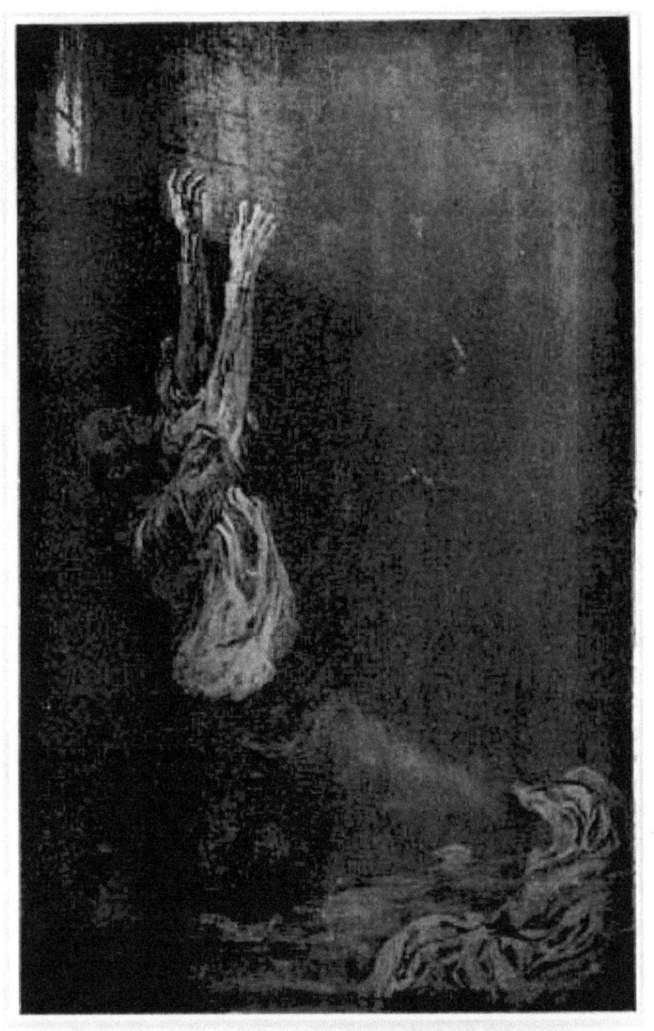

"IF FAY HAD COME IN THEN HE WOULD HAVE KILLED HER, DONE HER TO DEATH WITH THE CHAINS HE HAD WORN SO PATIENTLY FOR HER SAKE"

And that night the convict in the next cell, who had at times such wild outbursts of impotent rage when the boats went by, heard as he lay awake a low sound of strangled anguish, that ever stifled itself into silence, and ever broke forth anew, from dark to dawn.

CHAPTER XV

Qui sait ce qui peut advenir de la fragilité des femmes? Qui sait jusq'où peut aller l'inconstance de ce sable mouvant?

—ALFRED DE MUSSET.

The Italian winter was closing in. The nights were bitter cold.

Had Michael reached at last the death of love? Was its strait gate too narrow for him?

After that one night he held his peace, even with himself, even with the walls of his cell. He did not sleep nor eat. He had no time to sleep or eat. He was absorbed in one idea.

Michael was not a thinker. He was a man of action, whose action, sharp, rapier-like, and instantaneous, was unsheathed only by instinctive feeling, by chivalry, honour, indignation, compassion, never by reflection, judgment, experience. He could not really think. What he learned had to reach him some other way. His mind only bungled up against ideas, hustled them, so to speak, till they turned savage.

He sat idly in his cell when his work was done. There was a kind of pressure on him, as if the walls were closing in on him. Sometimes he got up, and pushed them back with his hands.

The sun had shifted his setting as the winter drew in, and for a few minutes every afternoon laid a thong of red light upon his wall. He looked at it sternly while it burned. It looked back sternly at him.

He had no wish to be free now, no wish for anything.

The doctor came to see him, and looked closely at him, and spoke kindly to him. He was interested in the young Englishman, and, like several of the warders, was convinced of his innocence.

Michael took no notice of him, barely answered his questions. He was impatient of any interruption.

He was absorbed in one thought.

He had loved Fay for a long time. How long was it? Five years? Ten years? Owing to his peculiar fate love had usurped in Michael's life too large a place, the place which it holds in a woman's life, but which is unnatural in a man's. He did not know it, but he had travelled a long way on the road towards an entire oblivion of Fay when he came to Rome. But the one great precaution against her he had not taken. He had not replaced her, and "Only that which is replaced is destroyed." He had grown accustomed to loving her.

In these days he went over, slowly, minutely, every step of his long acquaintanceship with her, from the first day, when he was nineteen and she was seventeen, to the last evening six years later, when he had kissed the cold hand that could have saved him, and did not.

Old people, wise old learned people, smoke-dried Dons and genial bishops sitting in their dignified studies, had spoken with guarded frankness to him in his youth on the temptations of life. They had told him that love, save when it was sanctified by marriage, was only a physical passion, a temporary madness, a fever which all men who were men underwent, but to which a man of principle did not succumb, and which if vigorously suppressed soon passed away.

Why had it not been so with him? He had never had to contend with the coarse forms of temptation of which his elders had spoken, as if they were an integral part of his youth.

Why, then, had he loved this pretty, false, selfish woman so long? Why had he allowed himself to be drawn back into her toils after he had known she was false? Why was he more weak, more credulous, more infatuated than other men?

The duke had actually been her husband, had actually possessed that wonderful creature, and yet he, under the glamour of her personal presence, which it made Michael gasp to think of, he, the duke, had not been deceived.

Why had he, Michael, been deceived?

He remembered the exhortations of his tepid-minded, painlessly married tutor at Oxford, who read the vilest French novels as a duty, and took a walk with his wife on fine afternoons; and whose cryptic warnings on the empire of the passions would have made a baboon blush.

Michael laughed suddenly as he recalled the mild old-maidish face. What was the old prig talking about? What did he know, dried up and shrivelled like a bit of seaweed between the leaves of a folio.

Everyone had told him wrong.

Why had they decried this awful power, why had they so confused it with sensual indulgence that he had had to disentangle it for himself? Why had they not warned him, on the contrary, that the love of woman was a living death, a pitfall from which there was no escape, from the depths of which you might stare at the sky till you starved to death, as he was doing now.

With all their warnings they had not warned him, these grave men, these instructors of youth, who had never known any world except their little world of books, who ranged women into two camps, one in which they held a docile Tennysonian place, as chaste adorners of the sacred home, mothers of children, man's property, insipid angel housekeepers of his demure middle age; the other where they were depicted as cheap, vulgar temptresses, on a level with the wine cup and the gambling table.

Why had he allowed himself to be duped and hoodwinked by his elders and by his own shyness, into chastity? They had entreated him to believe it was the only happy life. *It was not.* To be faithful to his future wife. Ha! Ha! That was the beginning of the trap, the white sand neatly raked over the hidden gin.

If he had only lived like other men! If he had only listened to the worst among them, if he had only torn the veil early from every limb of that draped female figure, that iron maiden, if he had only seen it in its horror of nudity, with its sharp nails for eyes, and its jagged knives where the bosom should be, he should not be pressed to death in its embrace now.

He had been deceived, betrayed, fooled. That was why he was shut up. He had believed in a woman, had believed that the cobra's bite was only a wasp's sting. Good Lord, what an imbecile! He was insane of course, raving mad. And he had been here eighteen months and only saw the joke now.

Michael laughed again, shouted with laughter.

The sun was setting again. It was always setting now. It set in the mornings as well. The red thong of light was on the wall again. Blood red! He rocked to and fro shaking with laughter.

The doctor and a warder came in. It was just like them. They were always coming in when they were not wanted.

He pointed at the bar of light, stumbled to it, and tried to tear it from the wall. It had been there long enough. Too long. And as he tore at it with hands dyed crimson, something that was pressing upon him lightened suddenly, and the blood gushed forth from his mouth, flooding the sun-stained wall.

"I have put out that damned sunset at last," he said to himself as he fell.

CHAPTER XVI

So we must keep apart,
You there, I here,
With just the door ajar
That oceans are,
And prayer,
And that pale sustenance
Despair!

—EMILY DICKENSON.

It was a little after Christmas when Michael first began to take notice of his surroundings once more. There was no love or tenderness that Wentworth could have shown him which the grave young Italian doctor did not lavish on him.

Little by little the mist in which Michael lay shifted and cleared, and closed in on him again. But the times when it cleared became nearer together. He felt that the great lethargy in which he lay would shift when the mist shifted. Dimly, as if through innumerable veils, he was aware that something indefinable but terrible crouched behind it. Days passed. Blank days and blank nights. He had forgotten everything.

He had been lying awake a long time, years and years. The doctor had been in to see him just before sunrise, had raised him, and made him drink, and laid him back upon his pillow. And now he felt full of rest. How clear everything was becoming. He raised his hand to his head. He had not taken the trouble to do that before. He looked long at his wasted hands laid on the coarse cotton sheeting. What were these marks on the wrists? They seemed like an answer to a riddle of which he had forgotten the question. If he only knew what those marks were he should know numbers of other things as well. He raised his long right hand, and held it close to his eyes.

These marks were bruises. A line of bruises went round the wrist. And here over the bone was a scar. It was healed now, but it had been a deep sore once.

When?

If only he could remember!

The mist in his mind cleared a little.

Those bruises were made by chains.

A deadly faintness came over him.

Michael knew at last that he was in prison. The past filtered back into his feeble mind drop by drop. He knew why he was there. He knew what he had done to bring him there; he realised that he had been ill a long time, many weeks. But there was still something sinister, mysterious, crouching in the back of his mind.

The doctor sought to distract him, to rouse him. He was a botanist, and he shewed Michael his collection of grasses. Michael did not want to have the fatigue of looking at them, but he feigned an interest to please the doctor. He gazed languidly at a spray, now dry and old. The doctor explained to him that it was the sea lavender, which, in the early autumn, had flushed the shallows of the lagoon with a delicate grey lilac.

"I remember," said Michael, whitening.

It rushed back upon him, that time of waiting, marked by the flowering and the fading of the sea lavender. The colour was seared upon his brain.

"A hundred years it is lilac," he said, "and a hundred thousand years it is a purple brown."

The doctor, bending lovingly over a specimen of a rare water plant, looked up to see Michael's quivering face. He withdrew the book gently and took it away.

Michael trembled exceedingly. He was on the verge of some abyss which he should see clearly in another moment. The sea lavender grew on the very edge of it. It yawned suddenly at his feet. The abyss was Fay's last desertion. He looked down into it. It was quite dark.

A few days later the doctor brought another book. It was butterflies this time. He saw that an increasing pressure was upon Michael's mind, and he feared for his brain. He was too weak to read. He might perhaps like to look at pictures.

The doctor opened the book at an attractive illustration of an immense butterfly, with wings of iridescent blue and green. He could not stay, but he left the cherished volume open on Michael's knee.

Michael turned his maimed mind slowly from the abyss into which it had been looking ever since he had seen that sprig of sea lavender.

Yes. He knew that particular butterfly. He had seen them by thousands once in a field in Corfu, long ago on an Easter holiday, when he had been abroad with Wentworth. They had all glinted together in the sunshine, wheeling together, sinking together, rising together like an army of fairies.

How heavy the book was on his knee.

He had not the energy to turn another page. Yes, he must. The doctor would be disappointed if he found the book open at the same place when he came back. One leaf. Come! He owed it to his friend. Just one leaf.

Were there English butterflies here as well?

Yes. Here was a sheet of them.

He knew that little yellow one with red tips to its wings. It was common enough in the south of England.

He looked idly at it.

And somewhere out of the past, far, far back from behind the crystal screen of childhood, came a memory clear as a raindrop.

He remembered as a tiny child lying in the sun watching a butterfly like that; watching it walk up and down on a twig of whortleberry, opening and shutting its new-born wings. It was the first time he had noticed how beautiful a butterfly's wings were. His baby hand went out towards it. The baby creature did not fly, was not ready to fly. He grasped it, and laughed as he felt it flutter, tickling his hot little palms, closed over it. It gave him a new sense of power. Then he slowly pulled off its wings, one by one, because they were so pretty.

He remembered it as if it were yesterday, and the sudden disgust and almost fear with which he suddenly tossed away the little mutilated ugly thing with struggling legs.

The cruelty of it filled him even now with shamed pain.

"It was not I who did it," he said to himself "I did not understand."

And a bandage was removed from his eyes, and he looked down, as we look into still water, and he saw that Fay did not understand either. She had put out her hand to take him. She had pulled his wings off him. She had cast him aside. Perhaps she even felt horror of him now. But nevertheless she had not done it on purpose, any more than he had done it on purpose to that other poor creature of God. *She did not understand.*

Her fair, sweet face, which he had shuddered at as at a leper's, came back to him, smiling at him with a soft reproach. Ah! It was a child's face. That was the secret of it all. That was one of the reasons why he had so worshipped it, that dear face. She had not meant to hurt him with her pretty hand.

Later on, some day, not in this world perhaps, but some far-off day she would come to herself, and, looking back, she would feel as he felt now at the recollection of his infant cruelty, only a thousand times more deeply. He hoped to God he might be near her when that time of grief came, to comfort her, to assure her that the pain she had inflicted had been nothing, nothing, that it did not hurt.

An overwhelming, healing compassion, such as he had never known in all the years of his great tenderness for Fay, welled up within his arid heart.

Michael's racked soul was steeped in a great peace and light!

Time and time again his love for Fay had been wounded nearly to the death, and had been flung back bleeding upon himself. He had always enfolded it, and withdrawn it, and cherished it anew in a safer place.

A love that has been thus withdrawn and protected does not die. It shrinks home into the heart, that is all. Like a frightened child against its mother, it presses close and closer against the Divine Love that dwells within us, which gave it birth. At last the mother smiles, and takes her foolish weeping child, born from her body, which has had strength from her to wander away from her—back into her arms.

CHAPTER XVII

And no more turn aside and brood
Upon Love's bitter mystery.

—W. B. YEATS.

It seems is if in the early childhood of all of us some tiny cell in the embryo brain remains dormant after the intelligence and other faculties have begun to quicken and waken. While that cell sleeps the child is callous to suffering, even ingenious in inflicting it. The little cell in the brain wakes and the cruelty disappears. And the same cell that was slow to quicken in the child is often the first to fall asleep in the old. The ruthless cruelty of old age is not more of a crime than the ruthless cruelty of young children. Childhood does not yet understand. Old age ceases to understand.

But some there are among us who have passed beyond childhood, beyond youth, into middle age, in whose brain that little cell still sleeps and gives no sign of waking, though all the other faculties are at their zenith; imagination, intellect, lofty sentiment, religious fervour. Where they go pain follows. They leave a little trail of pain behind them, to mark their path through life. They appear to have come into the world to be ministered to, not to minister. If love could reach them, call loudly to them from without, it seems as if the dormant cell might wake. But if they meet love, even on an Easter morning, and when they are looking for him, they mistake him for the gardener. They can only be loved and served. They cannot love—as yet. They exact love and miss it. They feel their urgent need of its warmth in their stiffening, frigid lives. Sometimes they gain it, lay their cold hand on it, analyse it, foresee that it may become an incubus, and decide that there is nothing to be got out of it after all.

They seem inhuman because they are not human—as yet. They seem variable, treacherous, because a child's moral sense guiding a man's body and brain must so seem. They are not sane—as yet.

And all the while the little cell in the brain sleeps, and their truth and beauty and tenderness may not come forth—as yet.

We who love them know that, and that our strained faithfulness to them now may seem almost want of faith, our pained tenderness now shew like half-heartedness on the day when that little cell in the brain wakes.

Michael knew this without knowing that he knew it. His mind arrived unconsciously at mental conclusions by physical means. But in the days that followed, while his mind remained weak and wandering, he was supported by the illusion—was it an illusion—that it was Fay really who was in prison, not himself, and that he was allowed to take her place in her cell because she would suffer too much, poor little thing, unless he helped her through.

He became tranquil, happy, serene. He felt no regret when he was well enough to resume the convict-life, and the chains were put on him once more. Did he half know that Fay's fetters were heavier than his, that they were eating into her soul, as his had never eaten into his flesh?

When he sent her a message the following spring that he was happy, it was because it was the truth. Desire had rent him and let him go—at last. Vague, inconsequent and restful thoughts were Michael's.

His body remained feeble and emaciated. But he was not conscious of its exhaustion. His mind was at peace with itself.

CHAPTER XVIII

What she craved, and really felt herself entitled to, was a situation in which the noblest attitude should also be the easiest.

—EDITH WHARTON.

On a stormy night, towards the end of March, Magdalen was lying awake listening to the wind. Her tranquil mind travelled to a great distance away from that active, monotonous, daily life which seemed to absorb her, which had monopolised her energies but never her thoughts for so many years past.

Suddenly she started slightly and sat up. A storm was coming. A tearing wind drowned all other sounds, but nevertheless she seemed to listen intently.

Then she slowly got out of bed, lit her candle, stole down the passage to Fay's door, and listened again. No sound within. At least none that could be distinguished through the trampling of the wind over the groaning old house.

She opened the door and went in. A little figure was crouching over the dim fire, swaying itself to and fro. It was Fay.

Magdalen put down her candle, and went softly to her, holding out her arms.

Fay raised a wild, wan face out of her hands and said harshly:

"Aren't you afraid I shall push you away again like I did last time?"

Then with a cry she threw herself into the outstretched arms.

Magdalen held the little creature closely to her, trembling almost as much as Fay.

Outside the storm broke, and beat in wild tears against the pane. Within, another storm had broken in a passion of tears.

Fay gasped a few words between the paroxysms of sobbing.

"I was coming to you, Magdalen,—I was trying to come—and I couldn't—I had pushed you away when you came before—and I thought perhaps you would push *me* away—no—no—I didn't, but I said to myself you would. I hardened myself against you. But I was just coming, all the same because—

because,"—Fay's voice went thinner and thinner into a strangled whimper, "because I can't bear it alone any more."

"Tell me about it."

But Fay tore herself out of her sister's arms and threw herself face downwards on the bed.

"I can't," she gasped. "I must and I can't. I must and I can't."

Magdalen remained standing in the middle of the room. She knew that the breaking moment had come and she waited.

She waited a long time.

The storm without spent itself before the storm within had spent itself.

At last Fay sat up.

Then Magdalen moved quietly to the dying fire. She put on some coal, she blew the dim embers to a glow.

Fay watched her.

Magdalen did not look at her. She sat down by the fire, keeping her eyes fixed upon it.

"I have done something very wicked," said Fay in a hollow voice from the bed. "If I tell you all about it will you promise, will you swear to me that you will never tell anybody?"

"I promise," said Magdalen after a moment.

"Swear it."

"I swear."

Fay made several false starts and then said:

"I was very unhappy with Andrea."

Magdalen became perceptibly paler and then very red.

"He never cared for me," continued Fay, slipping off the bed, and kneeling down before the fire. "It's a dreadful thing to marry a man who does not really care. I sometimes think men can't care. They are too selfish. They don't know what love is. I was very young. I did not know anything about life. He was kind, but he never understood me."

Magdalen's eyes filled with tears. In the room at the end of the passage she had listened to her mother's faint voice in nights of wakeful weakness speaking of her unhappy marriage. Did all women who failed to love deep enough say the same things? And as Magdalen had listened in silence then so she listened in silence now.

"He did not trust me. And then I had no children, and he was dreadfully disappointed. And he kept things to himself. There was no real confidence between us, as there ought to be between husband and wife, those whom God has joined together. Andrea never seemed to remember that. And gradually his conduct had its natural effect. I grew not to care for him, and—he brought it on himself—I'm not excusing myself, Magdalen—I see now that I was to blame too—I ended by caring for someone else—someone who *did* love me, who always had since we were boy and girl together."

"Not Michael!"

"Yes. Michael. And when he came out to Rome it began all over again. It never would have done if Andrea had been a good husband. I did my best. I tried to stave it off, but I was too miserable and lonely and I cared at last. And he was madly in love with me. He worshipped me."

Fay paused. She was looking earnestly into her recollections. She was so far withholding nothing. As she knelt before the fire making her confession Magdalen saw that according to her lights she was speaking the whole truth and nothing but the truth.

"Of course he found it out at last and—and we agreed to part. We decided that he must leave Rome. He wished to see me once to say good-bye. Was it *very* wrong of me to let him come once,—just once?"

"It was perhaps natural. And after Michael had said good-bye why did not he leave Rome?"

"He was arrested the same night," faltered Fay. "I said good-bye to him in the garden, and then the garden was surrounded because they were looking for the murderer of the Marchese, and Michael could not get out. And he was afraid of being seen for fear of compromising me. So he hid behind the screen in my room. And then—you know the rest—the police came in and searched my rooms, and Michael came out and confessed to the murder, and said I had let him hide in my room. It was the only thing to do to save my reputation, and he did it."

"And what did you say?"

"Nothing. What could I say? Besides, I was too faint to speak."

"And later on when you were not too faint?"

"I never said anything later on either." Fay's voice had become almost inaudible. "I hoped the real murderer would confess."

"But when he did not confess?"

"I have always clung to the hope. I have prayed day and night that he might still confess. Sinners do repent sometimes, Magdalen."

There was a terrible silence, during which several fixtures in Magdalen's mind had to be painfully and swiftly moved, and carefully safeguarded into new positions. Magdalen became very white in the process.

At last she said, "Did Andrea *know* that Michael was innocent of the murder?"

"I never thought so at the time, but just before he died he said something cruel to me which shewed he knew Michael's innocence for certain, had known it from the first."

"Then if he knew Michael had not murdered the Marchese, how do you suppose he accounted for his being hidden in your rooms at midnight, after he had ostensibly left the house?"

Fay stared at her sister aghast.

"I never thought of that," she said.

"What *can* Andrea have thought of that?"

"Andrea was very secretive," faltered Fay. "You never could tell what he was thinking. And I was the last person he ever told things to. Roman Catholics are like that. The priest knows everything instead of the wife."

There was another silence.

Magdalen's question vaguely alarmed Fay. Natures such as hers if given time will unconsciously whittle away all the sinister little incidents that traverse and render untenable the position in which they have taken refuge. They do not purposely ignore these conflicting memories, but they don't know what has weight and what has not, and they refuse to weigh them because they cannot weigh anything. Their minds, quickly confused at the best of times, instinctively select and retain all they remember that upholds their own view of the situation and—discard the rest.

Fay could not answer Magdalen's trenchant question. She could only restate her own view of her husband's character.

Magdalen did not make large demands on the truthfulness of others if they had very little of it. She did not repeat her question. She waited a moment, and then said:

"You seem to think that Andrea never guessed the attachment between yourself and Michael. But he must have done so. And if he had not guessed it till Michael was found in your rooms, at any rate he knew it *then*—for certain. *For certain*, Fay. Remember that is settled. There was no other possible explanation of Michael's presence there, if you bar the murder explanation, which is barred as far as Andrea is concerned. Now from first to last Andrea retained his respect for Michael and his belief in your innocence in circumstances which would have ruined you in the eyes of most husbands. You say Andrea did not understand you or do you justice. On the contrary, it seems to me he acted towards you with great nobility and delicacy."

Fay was vaguely troubled. Her deep, long-fostered dislike of her husband must not be shaken in this way. She could not endure to have any fixtures in her mind displaced. So much depended on keeping the whole tightly wedged fabric in position.

"You don't know what cruel words he said to me on his deathbed," she said. "I don't call it nobility and delicacy never to give me the least hint till the day he died that he knew why Michael was in prison."

"Perhaps he hoped—hoped against hope—that——" Magdalen did not finish her sentence. She fixed her eyes on Fay's. A great love shone in them, and a great longing. Then, with a kind of withdrawal into herself, she went on. "Andrea was loyal to you to the last. He went away without a word to anyone except, it seems, to you. I always liked him, but I see now that I never did him justice. I did not know with his Italian hereditary distrust of woman's honour that he could have risen to such a height as that. Think of it, Fay. What grovelling and sordid suspicions he might have had of you, must inevitably have had of you and Michael if he had not followed a very noble instinct, that of entire trust in you both in the face of overwhelming proof to the contrary. Dear Fay, the proof was overwhelming."

Fay was silent.

"Just as we all believed in Michael's innocence of the murder, so Andrea believed in your innocence of a crime even greater, never faltered in his belief, and went to his grave without a word of doubt. Oh! Fay, Fay, do you suppose there are many men like that?"

And Magdalen, who so seldom wept, suddenly burst into tears. Perhaps the thought forced itself through her mind, "If only once long ago I had met with one little shred of such tender faith!"

"Andrea was better than I thought," Fay faltered. The admission made her uneasy. She wished he had not been better, that her previous view of him had not been disturbed.

Magdalen's tears passed quickly. She glanced again at Fay through a veil of them, looking earnestly for something she did not find.

"And Michael," she went on gently. "Dear, dear Michael. He gave himself for you, spent in one moment, not counting the cost, his life, his future, his good name—for your sake. And he goes on day by day, month by month, year in year out, enduring a living death without a word—for your sake. How long has Michael been in prison?"

"Two years." Fay's voice was almost inaudible.

"Two years! Is it only two? To him it must seem like a hundred. But if his strength remains he will go on for thirteen more. Oh! Fay, was any man since the world began so loyal to any woman as your husband and your lover have been to you? You said just now that men were selfish and could not love. I have heard many women say the same. But *you*! How can *you* say such a thing! To have met one man who was ready to love and serve them is not the lot of many women. Very few of us ever find anything more than a craving to be loved in the stubborn material of men's hearts. And we are thankful enough when we find that. But to have stood between two such men who must have crushed you between them if either of them had had one dishonouring thought of you. A momentary selfishness, a momentary jealousy in either of them, and—where would *you* have been?"

"No one knows how good Michael is better than I do," said Fay, "but what you don't seem to realise is how awful these years have been for *me*. He has suffered, but sometimes I think I have suffered more than he has. No, I don't *think* it, I *know* it. He can't have suffered as much as I have."

Magdalen put out her hand, and touched Fay's rough head with a tenderness that seemed new even to Fay, to whom she had been always tender.

"You have suffered more than Michael," she said. "I have endured certain things in my life, but I could never have endured as you have done the loss of my peace of mind. How have you lived through these two years? What days and nights upon the rack it must have meant!"

Oh! the relief of those words. Fay leaned her head against her sister's knee, and poured forth the endless story of her agony. She had someone to confide in at last, and the person she loved best, at least whom she loved a little. She who had never borne a mosquito bite in silence, but had always shewn it to the first person she met, after rubbing it to a more prominent red, with a plaintive appeal for sympathy, was now able to tell her sister everything.

The recital took hours. A few minutes had been enough on the subject of the duke and Michael, but when Fay came to dilate on her own sufferings, when the autobiographical flood-gates were opened, it seemed as if the rush of confidences would never cease. Magdalen listened hour by hour. Is it given even to the wisest of us ever to speak a true word about ourselves? Do our whispered or published autobiographies ever deceive anyone except ourselves? We alone seem unable to read between the lines of our self-revelations. We alone seem unable to perceive that sinister ghost-like figure of ourselves which we have unconsciously conjured up from our pages for all to see; the cruelly faithful reflection of one whom we have never known. Those who love us and have kept so tenderly for years the secret of our egotism or our false humility or our meanness, how can they endure to hear us unconsciously proclaim to the world what only Love may safely know concerning us?

Magdalen heard, till her heart ached to hear them, all the endless bolstered-up reasons why Fay was not responsible for Michael's fate. She heard all about the real murderer not confessing. She heard much that Fay would have died rather than admit. Gradually she realised that it was misery that had driven Fay to a partial confession, not as yet repentance, not the desire to save Michael. Misery starves us out of our prisons sometimes, tortures us into opening the doors of our cells bolted from within, but as a rule we make a long weary business of leaving our cells when only misery urges us forth. I think that Magdalen's heart must have sunk many times, but whenever Fay looked up she met the same tender, benignant look bent down upon her.

"Oh! why didn't I tell you before?" she said at last. "I always wanted to, but I thought—at least I felt—I see I did you an injustice—I thought you might press me to—to——"

"*To confess*," said Magdalen, her low voice piercing to Fay's very soul.

"Y-yes, at least to say something to a policeman or someone, so that Michael might be let out. I was afraid if I told you you would never give me any peace till Michael was released."

"Have you *had* any peace since he was put into prison?"

Fay shook her head.

"Make your mind easy, Fay, I shall never urge you to"—Magdalen hesitated—"to go against your conscience."

"What would you have done in my place?" said Fay hastily.

"I should have had to speak."

"You are better than me, Magdalen, more religious. You always have been."

"I should have had to speak, not because I am better or worse than you, but simply because I could not have endured the misery of silence. It would have broken me in two. And if I had not had the courage to speak in Andrea's lifetime, I would have spoken directly he was dead, and have released Michael and married him. You have not told me why you did not do that."

"I never thought of it. I somehow regarded it as all finished. And I have never even *thought* of marrying Michael or anyone when I was left a widow. I was much too miserable. I had had enough of being married."

There was a difficult silence.

"I should never have a moment's peace if—if I *did* speak," said Fay at last.

"Yes, you would," said Magdalen with sudden intensity. "That is where peace lies."

Fay raised herself to her knees and looked into Magdalen's eyes. The dawn had come up long ago, and in its austere light Magdalen's face showed very sharp and white in a certain tender fixity and compassion. She had seen that look once before in her husband's dying eyes. Now that she was suddenly brought face to face with it again she understood it for the first time. Had not Andrea's last prayer been that she might be given peace!

CHAPTER XIX

> There is no wild wind in his soul,
> No strength of flood or fire; He knows no force beyond control,
> He feels no deep desire.
>
> He knows no altitudes above,
> No passions elevate; All is but mockery of love,
> And mimicry of hate.
>
> —EDGAR VINE HALL.

The morning after the storm Wentworth was sitting in the library at Barford, looking out across the garden to the down. Behind the down lay Priesthope, where Fay was.

He was thinking of her. This shewed a frightful lapse in his regulated existence. So far he had allowed the remembrance of Fay to invade him only in the evenings over his cigarette, or when he was pacing amid his purpling beeches.

Was she now actually beginning to invade his mornings, those mornings sacred to the history of Sussex? No! No! Dismiss the extravagant surmise. Wentworth was far more interested in his attitude towards a thing or person—in what he called his point of view—than in the thing viewed.

He was distinctly attracted by Fay, but he was more occupied with his feelings about her than with herself. It was these which were now engrossing him.

For some time past he had been working underground—digging out the foundations—and as a rule invisible as a mole within them—of a tedious courtship undertaken under the sustaining conviction that marriage is much more important to a woman than to a man. This point of view was not to be wondered at, for Wentworth, like many other eligible, suspiciously diffident men, had so far come into contact mainly with that large battalion of women who forage for themselves, and who take upon themselves with assiduity the work of acquaintanceship and courtship. He had never quite liked their attentions or been deceived by their "chance meetings." But his conclusions respecting the whole sex had been formed by the conduct of the female skirmishers who had thrown themselves across his path; and he, in common with many other secluded masculine violets, innocently supposed that he was irresistible to the other sex; and that when he met the *right* woman she would set to work like the others, only with a little more tact, and the marriage would be conveniently arrived at.

But Fay showed no signs of setting to work, no alacrity, no apparent grasp of the situation: I mean of the possible but by no means certain turn which affairs might one day take.

At first Wentworth was incredulous, but he remembered in time that one of the tactics of women is to retreat in order to lure on a further masculine advance. Then he became offended, stiff with injured dignity, almost anxious. But he communed with himself, analysed his feelings under various headings, and discovered that he was not discouraged. He was aware—at least, he told himself that he was aware—that extraordinary efforts must be made in love affairs. I don't know how he reconciled that startling theory with his other tenets, but he did. The chance suggestions of his momentary moods he regarded as convictions, and adopted them one day and disowned them the next with much *naïf* dignity, and offended astonishment, if the Bishop or some other old friend actually hinted at a discrepancy between diametrically opposed but earnestly expounded views. He imagined that he was now grappling with the difficulties inherent to love in their severest form. It was of estrangements like these that poets sang. He opened his Browning and found he was on the right road, passing the proper milestones at the correct moment. He was sustained in his idleness this morning by the comfortable realisation that he was falling desperately in love. He shook his head at himself and smiled. He was not ill pleased with himself. He would return to a perfectly regulated life later on. In the meanwhile he would give a free rein to these ecstatic moods, these wild emotions. When he had given a free rein to them they ambled round a little paddock, and brought him back to his own front door. It was delicious. He had thoughts of chronicling the expedition in verse.

I fear we cannot escape the conclusion that Wentworth was on the verge of being a prig. But he was held back as it were by the coat-tails from the abyss by a certain *naïveté* and uprightness of character. The Bishop once said of him that he was so impressed with the fact that dolls were stuffed with sawdust that it was impossible not to be fond of him.

Wentworth in spite of his sweeping emotions was still unconsciously meditating a possible retreat as regards Fay, was still glancing furtively over his shoulder. Strange how that involuntary, self-protective attitude on a man's part is never lost on a woman, however dense she may otherwise be, almost always ends by ruining him with her. Others besides Lot's wife have become petrified by looking back.

Fay, he reflected, must make it perfectly clear to him that if he did propose he would be accepted—she in short must commit herself—and then—after all a bachelor's life had great charm. But still—at any rate he might come back from Lostford this afternoon by way of Pilgrim Road. That would tie him to nothing. She often walked there. It would be an entirely chance meeting. Wentworth had frequently used this "short cut" of late which did not add more than two miles to the length of his return journey from Lostford.

It was still early in the afternoon when he rode slowly down Pilgrim Road feeling like a Cavalier. There was no hurry. The earth was breathing again after the storm. Everything was resting, and waking in the vivid March sunshine. As he rode at a foot's pace along the mossy track dappled with anemones, as he noted the thin powder of green on the boles of the beech trees, and the intense blue through the rosy haze of myriad twigs, the slight hunger of his heart increased upon him. There was a whisper in the air which stirred him vaguely in spite of himself.

At that instant he caught sight of a slight black figure sitting on a fallen tree near the track.

For one moment the Old Adam in him actually suggested that he should ride past, just taking off his hat. But he had ridden past in life, just taking off his hat, so often that the action lacked novelty. He almost did it yet again from sheer force of habit. Then he dismounted and walked up to Fay, bridle in hand.

"What good fortune to meet you," he said. "I so seldom come this way."

This may have been the truth in some higher, rarer sense than its obvious meaning, for Wentworth was a perfectly veracious person. Yet anyone who had seen him during the last few weeks constantly riding at a foot's pace down this particular glade, looking carefully to right and left, would hardly have felt that his remark dovetailed in with the actual facts. The moral is—morals cluster like bees round certain individuals—that we must not ponder too deeply the meanings of men like Wentworth.

"I often used to come here," said Fay, "but not of late. I came to get some palm."

She had in her bare hand a little bunch of palm, the soft woolly buds on them covered with yellow dust. She held them towards Wentworth, and he looked at them with grave attention.

The cob, a privileged person, of urbane and distinguished manners, suddenly elongated towards them a mobile upper lip, his sleek head slightly on one side, his kind, sly eyes half shut.

"Conrad," said Wentworth, "we never ask. We only take what is given us."

Fay laughed, and gave them both a twig.

Wentworth drew his through his buttonhole. Conrad twisted his in his strong yellow teeth, turned it over, and then spat it out. The action, though of doubtful taste in itself, was ennobled by his perfect rendering of it. He brought it, so to speak, forever within the sphere of exquisite manners.

Wentworth led him back to the path, tied him to a tree, and then came back and sat down at a little distance from Fay on the same trunk. He had somehow nothing to say, but of course he should think of something striking directly. One of Fay's charms was that she did not talk much.

A young couple close at hand were not hampered by any doubts as to a choice of subject.

From among the roots of a clump of alder rose a sweet little noise of mouse talk, intermittent, *affairé*, accompanied by sudden rustlings and dartings under dead leaves, momentary glimpses of a tiny brown bride and bridegroom. Ah! wedded bliss! Ah! youth and sunshine, and the joy of life in a new soft silken coat!

Fay and Wentworth watched and listened, smiling at each other from time to time.

"I am forced to the conclusion," said Wentworth at last, "that even in these early days Mrs. Mouse does not listen to all Mr. Mouse says."

"How could she, poor thing, when he never leaves off talking?"

"Well, neither does she. They both talk at once. I suppose they have not our morbid craving for a listener."

"Do you think—I mean really and truly—that they are talking about themselves?" said Fay, looking at Wentworth as if any announcement of his on the subject would be considered final.

"No doubt," he said indulgently, willing to humour her, and feeling more like a cavalier than ever.

Then he actually noticed how pale she was.

"You look tired," he said. "I am afraid the storm last night kept you awake."

"Yes," she said, and hung her head.

Wentworth, momentarily released from his point of view, looked at her more closely, and perceived that her lowered eyelids were heavy with recent tears. And as he looked, he realised, by some other means than those of reasoning and deduction, by some mysterious intuitive feeling new to him, that all these weeks when he had imagined she was drawing him on by feminine arts of simulated indifference she had in reality been thinking but little of him because she was in trouble. The elaborate edifices which he had raised in solitude to account for this and that in her words one day, in her attitude towards him another day, toppled over, and he saw before him a simple creature, who for some unknown and probably foolish reason, had cried all night.

He perceived suddenly, without possibility of doubt, that she had never considered him in the light of a lover, had never thought seriously about him at all, and that what he had taken to be an experienced woman of the world was in reality an ignorant child at heart.

He felt vaguely relieved. There were evidently no ambushes, no surprises, no pitfalls in this exquisite nature. There was really nothing to withdraw from. He suddenly experienced a strong desire to go forward, a more imperative desire than he had ever known about anything before. Even as he was conscious of it Fay raised her eyes to his and it passed away again, leaving a great tranquillity behind, together with a mounting sense of personal power.

If Fay had spoken to him he had not heard what she had said. But he did not mind having missed it. The meaning of the spring was reaching him through her presence like music through a reed. He had never understood it till now. Poor empty little reed! Poor entranced listener mistaking the reed for music!

Can it be that when God made His pretty world He had certain things exceeding sharp and sweet to say to us, which it is His will only to whisper to us through human reeds: the frail human reeds on which we sometimes deafly lean until they break and pierce our cruel hands?

The mystery of the spring was becoming clear and clearer. What Wentworth had believed hitherto to be a deceptive voice was nothing but a reiterated faithful prophecy, a tender warning to him so that he might be ready when the time came.

"The primroses will soon be out," he said as if it were a secret.

"Very soon," she said, though they were out already. Fay always assented to what was said.

"I must be going," she said, getting up. "I have walked too far. If I sit here any longer I shall never get home at all."

"Let me take you home on Conrad."

Fay hesitated.

"I am frightened of horses."

"But not of Conrad. He is only an armchair stuffed to look like a horse. And I will lead him."

Fay still hesitated.

He took an authoritative tone. He must insist on her riding home. She was tired already, and it was a long mile up hill to Priesthope.

Fay acquiesced. To-day of all days she was not in a condition for anything but a dazed acceptance of events as they came.

Wentworth lifted her gently onto the saddle, and put one small dangling foot into a stirrup shortened to meet it.

She was alarmed and clutched Conrad's mane, but gradually her timidity was reassured, and they set out slowly together, Wentworth walking beside her, with his hand on the rein.

The little bunch of palm was forgotten. It had done its part.

Wentworth talked and Fay listened, or seemed to listen. Her mind wandered if Conrad pricked his ears, but he did not prick them very often.

Wentworth felt that it was time Fay made more acquaintance with his mind, and he proceeded without haste, but without undue delay to indicate to her portions of his own attitude towards life, his point of view on various subjects. All the sentiments which must infallibly have lowered him in the eyes of a shrewder woman he spread before her with childish confidence. He gave her of his best. He expressed a hope that he did not abuse for his own selfish gratification his power of entering swiftly into intimacy with his fellow creatures. He alluded to his own freedom from ambition, his devotion—unlike other men—to the *small* things of life, love, friendship, etc.: we know the rest. Wentworth had been struck by that sentence when he first said it to the Bishop, and he repeated it now. Fay thought it very beautiful. She proved a more sympathetic listener than the Bishop.

I don't know whether like Mrs. Mouse she did not listen to all Mr. Mouse said. But at any rate she noticed for the first time how lightly Wentworth walked, how square his shoulders were, and the beauty of his brown thin hand upon the bridle; and through her mind a little streak of vanity came back to the surface, momentarily buried under the *débris* of last night's emotion. Wentworth was interested in her. He admired her. *He* did not know anything uncomfortable about her—*as Magdalen did.* He thought a great deal of her. It was nice to be with a person who thought highly of one. It had been a relief to meet him. How well he talked! What a wide-minded, generous man!

The gate into the gardens must have been hurrying towards them, it was reached so soon. Wentworth, after a momentary surprise at beholding it, stopped the cob, and helped Fay with extreme care to the ground. One of Fay's attractions was her appearance of great fragility. Men felt instinctively that with the least careless usage she might break in two. She must be protected, cheered, have everything made smooth for her. She was in reality much stronger than many of her taller, more robust-looking sisters, who, whether wives or spinsters, if they required assistance, had to look for it in quinine. An uneasy jealousy of Fay led Lady Blore frequently to point out that Fay was always well enough to do what she wanted. Aunt Mary's own Roman nose and stalwart figure warded off from her the sympathy to which her severe cramps undoubtedly entitled her.

"When shall I see you again?" said Wentworth, suddenly realising that the good hour was over.

Fay did not answer. She was confused. A very delicate colour flew to her cheek.

Wentworth, reddening under his tan, said: "Perhaps Pilgrim Road is a favourite walk of yours?"

"Yes. I often go there in the afternoon."

"I have to pass that way, too, most days," he said. "It is a short cut to Lostford."

He had forgotten that an hour before he had announced that he seldom used that particular path. It did not matter, for Fay had not noticed the contradiction any more than he did. Fay was easy to get on with because she never compared what anyone said one day with what they said the next. She never would feel the doubts, the perplexities that keener minds had had to fight against in dealing with him.

For the first time she looked at his receding figure with a sense of regret and loss.

Magdalen was in the house waiting to give her her tea, dear Magdalen who was so good, and so safe, such a comforter—*but who knew*. Fay shrank back instinctively as she neared the house, and then crept upstairs to her own room, and had tea there.

"FAY NOTICED FOR THE FIRST TIME HOW LIGHTLY WENTWORTH WALKED, HOW SQUARE HIS SHOULDERS WERE"

Wentworth rode home feeling younger that he had done for years. What is thirty-nine? No age for a thin man. (He was in reality nearly forty-one.) He was pleased with himself. How quaintly amusing he had been about the mouse. He regretted, not for the first time, that he did not write novels, for little incidents like that, which the conventional mind of the ordinary novelist was incapable of perceiving, would intertwine charmingly with a love scene. The small service he had rendered Fay linked itself to a wish to do something more for her—he did not know exactly what—but something larger than to-day. Any fool, any bucolic squireen, could have given her a lift home on a cob. He would like to do something which another person could *not* do, something which would cheer her, console her, and at the same time place him in a magnanimous light.

We all long for an opportunity to act with generosity and tenderness to the one we love. We need not trouble ourselves to seek for such an occasion, for though many things fail us in this life the opportunity so to act has never yet failed to arrive, and has never arrived alone, always hand in hand with some prosaic hideously difficult circumstance, which, if we are of an artistic temperament, may appear to us too ugly.

Wentworth had never wished to do anything for the gay little lady who, a few years ago, had crossed his path. The principal subject of his cogitations about her had been whether she would be able to adapt herself to him and his habits, to understand his many-sided wayward nature, and to add permanently to his happiness; or whether, on the contrary, she might not prove a bar to his love of solitude, a drag on his soaring spirit. So I think we may safely conclude that his feelings for her had not gone to breakneck length. But the germ in his mind of compassionate protection and instinctive desire to help Fay had in it the possibility of growth, of some expansion. And what other feeling in Wentworth's clean, well-regulated, sterilized mind had shown any power of growth?

The worst of growth is that a small acorn does not grow into a large acorn as logical persons expect. It ought to, but it does not. It grows instead into something quite unrecognisable from its small beginnings, something for which, perhaps, beyond a certain stage, there is no room,—not even a manger.

Those who love must discard much. Wentworth had not yet felt the need of discarding anything, and he had not the smallest intention of doing so. He intended instead to make a small ornamental addition, a sort of portico, to his life. His mind had got itself made up this afternoon, and he contemplated the proposed addition with some complacency as already made.

There is, I believe, a method of planting an acorn in a bottle, productive of the happiest results—for those who love small results. You only give the acorn a little water every day,—no soil of course. The poor thing will push up a thin twig of stem through the bottle neck, and in time will unfold a few real oak leaves. Men like Wentworth would always prefer the acorn to remain an acorn, but if it shews signs of growth, some of them are wise enough, take alarm early enough, to squeeze it quickly down a bottle neck before it has expanded too much to resist the passage.

Had Fate in store for Wentworth a kinder, sterner destiny than that, or would she allow him to stultify himself, to mutilate to his own convenience a great possibility?

CHAPTER XX

Look through a keyhole, and your eye will be sore.

During the weeks which followed Fay's confession Magdalen became aware that she watched her, and aware also that she avoided her, was never alone with her if she could help it.

At this time Fay began to do many small kindnesses, and to talk much of the importance of work for others, of the duty of taking an interest in our fellow creatures. This was a new departure. She had not so far evinced the faintest interest in the dull routine of home duties which are of the nature of kindnesses, and had often reproached Magdalen for spending herself in them. To play halma with zest all the evening with a parent who must always win, to read the papers to him by the hour, not while he listened, but while he slept—Fay scorned these humble efforts of Magdalen's. She shewed no disposition to emulate them; but she did shew a feverish tendency towards isolated acts of benevolence outside the home life, which precluded any claim upon her by arousing a hope of their continuance, which tied her to nothing. Fay began to send boxes of primroses to hospitals, to knit stockings for orphans, to fatigue herself with enormous walks over the downs with illustrated papers for the Saundersfoot work-house.

It was inevitable at this juncture that she should feel some shocked surprise at the supineness of those around her. Her altruistic efforts were practically single-handed. She had hoped that when she inaugurated them, Magdalen at any rate would have followed suit, would have worked cheerfully under her direction. But Magdalen, whose serene cheerfulness had flagged of late, fell painfully below her sister's expectation. Fay came to the conclusion that it was more lack of imagination than callousness on her sister's part which held her back.

Many careworn souls besides Fay have discovered that the irritable exhaustion, the continual ache of egotism can be temporarily relieved by taking an inexpensive interest in others. The remedy is cheap and efficacious, and it is a patent. Like Elliman applied to a rheumatic shoulder it really does do good—I mean to the owner of the shoulder. And you can stop rubbing the moment you are relieved. Perhaps these external remedies are indispensable to the comfort of those who dwell by choice, like Fay, in low-lying swampy districts, and have no thought of moving to higher ground.

Magdalen knew these signs, and sometimes her heart sank.

Was Fay unconsciously turning aside to busy herself over little things that were not required of her, in order to shut her eyes to the one thing needful—a great act of reparation?

If Fay was watching Magdalen, someone else was watching Fay. Bessie's round, hard, staring eyes were upon her, and if Bessie did anything she did it to some purpose.

One afternoon in the middle of April Bessie came into Magdalen's sitting room and sat down with an air of concentration.

"I have reason to be deeply ashamed of myself," she said. "I *am* ashamed of myself. If I tell you about it it is not in order that you may weakly condone and gloss over my conduct."

Magdalen reflected that Bessie had inherited her father's graceful way of approaching a difficulty by finding a preliminary fault in his listener.

Bessie shut her handsome mouth firmly for a moment, and then opened it with determination.

"I thought that whatever faults I had I was at any rate a lady, but I find I am not. I discovered something by the merest chance a short time ago, and since then, for the last fortnight I have been acting in a dishonourable and vulgar manner, in short, spying upon another person."

"That must have made you miserable."

"It has. I am miserable. But I deserve that. I did not come to talk about that. The point is this——"

"Bessie, I don't want to hear what you evidently ought not to know."

"Yes, you must, because someone else needs your advice."

"We won't trouble our minds about the someone else."

Bessie had, however, inherited another characteristic trait of her father's. She could ignore when she chose. She chose now.

"I may as well put you in possession of the facts," she continued. "A few weeks ago I was coming home by Pilgrim Road. I was not hurrying because I was struck, as I always am struck—I don't suppose I am peculiar in this—by the first appearance of spring. Pilgrim Road is a sheltered place. Spring always comes early there."

"It does."

"I will even add that I was recalling to myself verses of poetry connected with the time of year, when I saw a couple in front of me. They were walking very slowly with their backs towards me, taking earnestly together. They were Fay and Wentworth."

Magdalen made no movement, but her face, always pale, became suddenly ashen grey.

If Fay were seriously attracted by Wentworth would she ever confess, ever release Michael!

"There was no harm in their walking together," she said tremulously.

"There was one harm in it," retorted Bessie. "It made me so angry that I did not know how to live. They did not see me, and I struck up into the wood, and I had to stay an hour by myself holding on to a little tree, before I could trust myself to come home."

"It does not help matters to be angry, Bessie. I was angry once for two years. I said at the time like Jonah that I did well, but I see now that I might have done better."

"I don't particularly care what helps matters and what does not. I now come to my own disgraceful conduct. I have spied upon Fay steadily for the last fortnight. She is so silly she never even thinks she is watched. And she meets Wentworth in Pilgrim Road nearly every afternoon. I once waylaid her as if by accident, on her way home, and asked her where she had been, and she said she had been on her way to Arleigh wood, but had not got so far, as she was too tired. Too tired! She had been walking up and down with Wentworth for over an hour. I timed them. She never meant to go to Arleigh wood. And when they said Good-bye, he—he kissed her hand. Since Fay has come back to live here I have gradually formed the meanest opinion of her. She is not truthful. She is not sincere. She is absolutely selfish. I was inclined to be sorry for her at first, but I soon saw through her. She did not really care for Andrea. She only pretended. Everything she does is a kind of pretty pretence. She does not really care for Wentworth. She is only leading him on for her own amusement."

"I think it is much more likely that she is drifting towards marriage with him without being fully aware of what she is doing. But women like you and me are not in the same position towards men as Fay is. Consequently it is very difficult for us to judge her fairly."

"I don't know what you mean."

"You and I are not attractive to men. Fay is. You saw Wentworth kiss her hand. You naturally infer, but you are probably wrong, that Fay had been leading him on, as you call it."

"It will take a good deal to disabuse me of that at any rate. I believe my own eyes."

"I should not if I were you. If anyone kissed your hand or mine it would not only be an epoch in our lives, but also the sign manual of some ponderous attachment which you, my dear, would carefully weigh, and approximately value. But do you suppose for one moment that Fay attaches any importance to such an everyday occurrence!"

"I see what you are driving at, that Fay is not responsible for her actions. But she is. She must know when she does things or lets them be done, that will make others suffer."

"If you could look into Fay's heart, Bessie, you would find that Fay is suffering herself and attributing her pain to others. As long as we do that, as long as we hold the stick by the wrong end, we must inflict pain in some form or other. Fay is not happy. You cannot look at her without seeing it."

"I would not mind so much if it were not for Wentworth," said Bessie with dreadful courage. "I know it is partly jealousy, but it is not only jealousy. There are a few crumbs of unselfishness in it. I thought at first—I reasoned it out with myself and it appeared a logical conclusion—that father was the ostensible but not the real object of Wentworth's frequent visits. I took a great interest in his conversation; it is so lucid, so well informed, so illuminative. I do not read novels as a rule, but I dipped into a few, studying the love scenes, and the preliminary approaches to love scenes in order to aid my inexperience at this juncture. I am sorry to say I fell into the error that he might possibly reciprocate the growing interest I felt in him, in spite of the great disparity in age. It was a mistake. I have suffered for it."

The two roses of Bessie's cheeks bloomed on as unflinchingly as ever.

Magdalen's eyes were fixed on her own hands.

"You would not have suited each other if he had cared for you," she said after a moment, "for you would not have done him justice when you got to know him better, any more than you do Fay justice now that you *do* know her better. Wentworth is made of words, just as other men are made of flesh and blood. How would you have kept any respect for him when you had become tired of words? You are too straightforward, too sledge-hammer to understand a character like his."

"In that case Fay ought to suit him," said Bessie grimly. "No one, not even you, can call her straight-forward. But I begin to think, Magdalen, that you actually wish for the marriage."

"I had never thought of it as possible on her side until a few minutes ago, when what you said took me by surprise. Of course I had noticed the attraction on his side, but it appeared to me he was irresolute and timid, and it is better to ignore the faint emotions of half-hearted people. They come to no good. If you repel them they are mortally offended and withdraw, and if you welcome them they are terrified and withdraw."

"I don't think Wentworth intends withdrawing."

"No. These meetings look as if he had unconsciously drifted with the current till the rowing back would be somewhat arduous." There was a moment's silence, in which Magdalen recalled certain lofty sentiments which Wentworth had aired with suspicious frequency of late. She knew that when he talked of his consciousness of guidance by a Higher Power in the important decisions of his life he always meant following the line of least resistance. In this case the line of least resistance *might* tend towards marriage.

"It never struck me as possible till now," she said aloud, "that Fay would think seriously of him."

"I don't suppose she is. She is only keeping her hand in. Don't you remember how cruel she was to that poor Mr. Bell."

"I am convinced that she is not keeping her hand in."

"Then you actually favour the idea of a marriage." Bessie got up and stalked slowly to the door. "You will help it on?" she said over her shoulder.

"No." Magdalen's voice shook a little. "I will do nothing to help it, or to hinder it."

CHAPTER XXI

The dawn broke dim on Rose Mary's soul—
No hill-crown's heavenly aureole,
But a wild gleam on a shaken shoal.

—D. G. ROSSETTI.

If Fay's progress through life could have been drawn with a pencil it would have resembled the ups and downs, like the teeth of a saw, of a fever chart.

To Magdalen it appeared as if Fay could undergo the same feelings with the same impotent results of remorse or depression a hundred times. They seemed to find her the same and leave her the same. But nevertheless she did move, imperceptibly, unconsciously—no, not quite unconsciously. The sense—common to all weak natures—not of being guided, but of being pushed was upon her.

Once again she tried to extricate herself from the pressure of some mysterious current. There seemed no refuge left in Magdalen. There seemed very few comfortable people left in the world, to whom a miserable woman might turn. Only Wentworth. *He did not know.*

Perhaps Fay would never have turned to him if she had not first confided in and then shrunk from Magdalen. For the second time in her life she longed feverishly to get away from home, the home to which only a year ago she had been so glad to hurry back, when she had been so restlessly anxious to get away from Italy. Wentworth was beginning to look like a means of escape. The duke had at one time worn that aspect. Later on Michael had looked extremely like it for a moment. Now Wentworth was assuming that aspect in a more solid manner than either of his predecessors. She was slipping into love with him, half unconsciously, half with *malice prepense.* She told herself continually that she did not want to marry him or anyone, that she hated the very idea of marriage.

But her manner to Wentworth seemed hardly to be the outward reflection of these inward communings. And why did she conceal from Magdalen her now constant meetings with him?

Wentworth had by this time tested and found correct all his intimate knowledge of Woman, that knowledge which at first had not seemed to work out quite smoothly.

Nothing could be more flattering, more essentially womanly than Fay's demeanour to him had become since he had set her mind at rest as to his intentions on that idyllic afternoon after the storm. (How he had set her mind at rest on that occasion he knew best.) It seemed this exquisite nature only needed the sunshine of his unspoken assurance to respond with delighted tenderness to his refined, his cultured advances. He was already beginning to write imaginary letters to his friends, on the theme of his engagement: semi-humourous academic effusions as to how he, who had so long remained immune, had succumbed at last to feminine charm; how he, the determined celibate—Wentworth always called himself a celibate—had been taken captive after all. To judge by the letters which Wentworth conned over in his after-dinner mind, and especially one to Grenfell, the conclusion was irresistible to the meanest intellect that he had long waged a frightful struggle with the opposite sex to have remained a bachelor—a celibate, I mean—so long.

We have all different ways of enjoying ourselves. In the composition of these imaginary letters Wentworth tasted joy.

In these days Fay's boxes of primroses jostled each other in the postman's cart, on their way to cheer patients on their beds of pain in London hospitals.

Fay read the hurried, grateful notes of busy matrons, over and over again. They were a kind of anodyne.

On a blowing afternoon in the middle of April she made her way across the down with her basket to a distant hazel coppice to which she had not been as yet.

A fever of unrest possessed her. She had thought when she confessed to Magdalen that her misery had reached its lowest depths. But it had not been so. Her wretchedness, momentarily relieved, had since gone a step deeper, that was all. She had endeavoured to allay her thirst with a cup of salt water, which had only increased it to the point of agony.

As she walked a bare tree stretched out its naked arms to waylay her. It was the very tree under which Michael and she had kissed each other, six spring-tides ago. She recognised it suddenly, and turned her eyes away, as if a corpse were hanging in chains from one of its branches. Her averted eyes fell upon a seagull wheeling against the blue, the incarnation of freedom and the joy of life. She turned away her eyes again and hurried on, looking neither to right nor left.

A light wind went with her, drawing her like a "kind constraining hand."

She stumbled across the bare shoulder of the down to the wood below.

Magdalen came by the same way soon afterwards, but not to gather primroses. Magdalen usually so serene was becoming daily more troubled. The thought of Michael in prison ground her to the earth. Fay's obvious wayward misery, which yet seemed to bring her no nearer to repentance, preyed upon her. She was crushed beneath her own promise of secrecy. Every day as it passed seemed to cast yet another stone on the heap under which she lay.

Could she dare to keep that promise? How much longer could she dare to keep it? And yet if she broke it, what would breaking it avail? Certainly not Michael's release. No creature would believe her unsupported word. She had not even been in Italy at the time. She would only appear to be mad. The utmost she might achieve would be to cast a malignant shadow over her sister. Even if Fay herself confessed the difficulties of obtaining Michael's release after this lapse of time would be very great. Unless the confession came from her they would be insuperable.

As Magdalen walked her strong heart quailed within her. Long ago in her passionate youth she had met anguish and had vanquished it alone. But how to bear the burden of another's sin without sharing the sin? How to help Fay and Michael? Fay had indeed cast her burden upon her. She knew not how to endure it, she who had endured so much.

She reached the wood, and entered one of the many aimless paths that wandered through it. The uneven ground sloped downwards to the south, and through the manifold branches of the undergrowth of budding hazels the sea lay deeply blue, far away. The primroses were everywhere among the trees. A winding side path beckoned to her. She walked a few steps along it, and came suddenly upon a clearing in the coppice.

She stood still, dazed.

The primroses had taken it for their own, had laid tender hold upon that little space, cleared and forgotten in the heart of the wood.

Young shoots of hazel and ash pricked up here and there from ivy-grown stumps, moss gleamed where it could, through the flood of primroses. The wild green of the mercury, holding its strong shield to the sun, the violets, and the virgin white of the anemones were drowned in the uneven waves and billows and shallows of that sea of primroses. They who come in meekness year by year to roadside hedgerow and homely meadow had come in power. The meek had inherited the earth.

The light wind impotently came, and vainly went. Overhead a lark sang and sang in the blue. But none heeded them. The wind and the song were but a shadow and an echo. They that are the very core of spring hung forgotten on her garments' fringe. All the passion of the world was gathered into the still, upturned faces of the primroses, glowing with a pale light from within. All the love that ever had been, or could be, all rapture of aspiration and service and self-surrender were mirrored there.

Magdalen wept for Fay, as once in bygone years she had wept for Everard: as perhaps some woman of Palestine may have wept when Jesus of Nazareth passed by, speaking as never man spake, and her lover went with him a little way and then turned back.

"There is no sorrow," said the primroses. "There is neither sorrow nor sin. You are of one blood with us. You have come through into light, as we have done, and those others are coming, too. There is no sorrow, only a little pressure through the brown earth. There is no sin, only a little waking and stirring in the dark. Why then grieve, oh little faith! They are all waking and coming. For the Hand that made us made them. The Whisper that waked us, wakes them. The Sun that draws us, draws them. The Sun will have us come."

Fay had already passed by that way, had picked a few primroses, and had gone on. *Was she never to be at peace again?* Was she never to know what it is to lie down in peace at night, never to know what it is to be without fear. Her whole soul yearned for peace, as the sick man yearns for sleep. Andrea had prayed that she might find peace. Magdalen had told her where peace lay. But all that she had found was despair.

On her way homewards she came again upon the clearing and stopped short. The place seemed to have undergone some subtle change. A tall figure was standing motionless in it. The face was turned away, but Fay recognised it instantly. As she came close Magdalen turned. For a moment Fay saw that she did not recognise her, that she was withdrawn into a great peace and light.

Then recognition dawned in Magdalen's eyes and with it came a look of tenderness unspeakable.

"Fay," she said in a great compassion. "How much longer will you torture yourself and Michael? How much longer will you keep him in prison?"

Fay was transfixed.

Those were the same words that Andrea had said on his deathbed. Those words were alive, though he was dead. Never to any living creature, not even to Magdalen, had she repeated them. Yet Magdalen was saying them. She could not withstand them any longer. The very stones would shriek them out next.

She fell at Magdalen's feet with a cry.

"I will speak," she gasped in mortal terror. "I will speak." And she clung for very life to her sister's knees, and hid her face in her gown.

CHAPTER XXII

To-day unbind the captive,
So only are ye unbound.

—EMERSON.

The following afternoon saw Magdalen and Fay driving together to Lostford, to consult the Bishop as to what steps it would be advisable to take in the matter of Michael's release. Magdalen felt it would be well-nigh impossible to go direct to Wentworth, even if he had been at Barford. But he had been summoned to London the day before on urgent business. And with Fay even a day's delay might mean a change of mind. It was essential to act at once.

But to Magdalen's surprise Fay did not try to draw back. When the carriage came to the door she got into it. She assented to everything, was ready to do anything Magdalen told her. She was like one stunned. She had at last closed with the inevitable. She had found it too strong for her.

Did Fay realise how frightfully she had complicated her position by her own folly? She lay back in her corner of the brougham with her eyes shut, pallid, silent. Magdalen held her hand, and spoke encouragingly from time to time.

You had to be constantly holding Fay's hand, or kissing her, or taking her in your arms if you were to make her feel that you loved her. The one light austere touch, the long grave look, that between reserved and sympathetic natures goes deeper than any caress, were nothing to Fay.

It was a long drive to Lostford, and to-day it seemed interminable.

The lonely chalk road seemed to stretch forever across the down. Now and then a few heavily-matted, fatigued-looking sheep, hustled by able-bodied lambs, got in the way. The postman, horn on shoulder, passed them on his way to Priesthope with the papers.

Once a man on a horse cantered past across the grass at some distance. Magdalen recognised Wentworth on Conrad. She saw him turn into the bridle path that led to Priesthope. He had then just returned from London.

"He is on his way to see Fay," said Magdalen to herself, "and he is actually in a hurry. How interested he must be in the ardour of his own emotions at this moment. He will have a delightful ride, and he can analyse his feelings of disappointment at not seeing her, on his way home to tea."

Magdalen glanced at Fay, but she still lay back with closed eyes. She had not seen that passing figure.

Magdalen's mind followed Wentworth.

"Does she realise the complications that must almost certainly ensue with Wentworth directly her confession is made?

"Will her first step towards a truer life, her first action of reparation estrange him from her?"

The Bishop was pacing up and down in the library at Lostford, waiting for Magdalen and Fay, when the servant brought in the day's papers. He took them up instantly with the alertness of a man who can only make time for necessary things by seizing every spare moment.

"Oh! you two wicked women," he said as he opened the *Times*. "Why are you late? Why are you late?"

They were only five minutes late.

His swift eye travelled from column to column. Suddenly his attention was arrested. He became absorbed. Then he laid down the paper, and said below his breath "Thank God."

At that moment Magdalen and Fay were announced.

For a second it seemed as if the Bishop had forgotten them. Then he recollected and went forward to meet them. He knew that only a matter of supreme urgency could have made Magdalen word her telegram as she had worded it, and when he caught sight of Fay's face he realised that she was in jeopardy.

All other preoccupations fell from him instantly. He welcomed them gravely, almost in silence.

The sisters sat down close together on a sofa. Fay's trembling hand put up her long black veil, and then sought Magdalen's hand, which was ready for it.

There was a short silence. Magdalen looked earnestly at her sister.

Fay's face became suddenly convulsed.

"Fay is in great trouble," said Magdalen. "She has come to tell you about it. She has suffered very much."

"I can see that," said the Bishop.

"I wish to confess," said Fay in a smothered voice.

"That is a true instinct," said the Bishop. "God puts it into our hearts to confess when we are unhappy so that we may be comforted. When we come to see that we have done less well than we might have done—then we need comfort."

Fay looked from him to Magdalen with wide, hardly human eyes, like some tiny trapped animal between two executioners.

The Bishop's heart contracted.

Poor, poor little thing!

"Would you like to see me alone, my child?" he said, seeing a faint trembling like that of a butterfly beginning in her. "All you say to me will be under the seal of confession. It will never pass my lips."

It was Magdalen's turn to become pale.

"Shall I go?" she said, looking fixedly at her sister.

"Yes," said Fay, her eyes on the floor.

Magdalen went slowly to the door, feeling her way as if half blind.

"Come back," shrieked Fay suddenly. "Magdalen, come back. I shall never say it all, I shall keep back part unless you are there to hold me to it. Come back. Come back."

Magdalen returned and sat down. The Bishop watched them both in silence.

"I have confessed once, already," said Fay in a low hurried voice, "under the promise of silence. Magdalen promised not to say, and I told her everything, weeks ago. I thought I should feel better then, but it wasn't any good. It only made it worse."

"It is often like that," said the Bishop. "We try to do something right but not in the best way, and just the fact of trying shows us there is a better way—only harder, so hard we don't know how to bring ourselves to it. Isn't that what you feel?"

"Yes."

"But there is no rest, no peace till we come to it."

"No," whispered Fay. "Never any rest."

"That is God's Hand drawing you," said the Bishop, his mind seeming to embrace and support Fay's tottering soul. "There are things He wants done, which He needs us to do for Him, which perhaps only we can do for Him. At first we don't understand that, and we are so ignorant and foolish that we resist the pressure of His Hand. Then we suffer."

Fay shivered.

"That resistance is what some people call sin. It is unendurable, the only real anguish in the world. You see we are not meant to bear it. And it is no manner of use to resist Him, for God is stronger than we are, and He loves us too much ever to lose heart with us, ever to blame us, ever to leave us to ourselves. He sees we don't understand that He can't do without us, and that we can't do without Him. And at last, when we feel God's need of us, then it becomes possible"—the Bishop paused—"to say the difficult word, to do the difficult deed."

Did she understand? Who shall say! Sometimes it seems as if no actual word reaches us that Love would fain say to our unrest and misery. But our troubled hearts are nevertheless conscious by some other channel, some medium more subtle than thought and speech, that Love and Peace have drawn very near to us. It is only reflected dimly through dear human faces that some of us can catch a glimpse of "the light that lighteth every man that cometh into the world."

The small tortured face relaxed between the two calm ones. The sunny room was quite still. Fear shrank to a shadow.

Suddenly the fire drew itself together with a little encouraging sound.

Fay started slightly, looked at it, and began to speak rapidly in a low clear voice.

As Magdalen listened she prayed with intensity that Fay might really tell the Bishop the whole story, as she had told it to herself, that stormy night in March, half a life-time ago.

The little voice went on and on. It faltered, sank, and then struggled up again. One point after another was reached in safety, was passed. Nothing that Fay had already admitted was left out. Gradually, as Magdalen listened, a faint shame laid hold of her. Her whole life had for the time centred in one passionate overwhelming desire that Fay should make to the Bishop as full a confession as she had made to herself. Now she realised that Fay was saying even more than she had done on that occasion, was excusing herself less, was blaming others less.

Fay herself saw no discrepancy between her first and second account of the tragedy. But then she never did see discrepancies. Her mind had shifted a little towards the subject, that was all. This mysterious unconscious shifting of the mind had been hidden from Magdalen, who had felt with anguish that all she had said on that night of the storm had had no effect on Fay's mind. She had never seen till now a vestige of an effect. Fay had shrunk from her persistently afterwards, that was all.

Strong and ardent souls often wonder why an appeal which they know, if made to themselves, would clinch them forever into a regenerating repentance is entirely powerless with a different class of mind. But although an irresistible truth spoken in love will renovate our being, and will fail absolutely to reach the mind of another, nevertheless the weaker, vainer nature will sometimes pick out of the uncomfortable appeal, to which it turns its deaf ear, a few phrases less distressing to its *amour propre* than the rest. To these it will listen. Fay had retained in her mind Magdalen's vivid description of the love her husband and Michael had borne her. She had often dwelt upon the remembrance that she had been greatly loved. During the miserable weeks when she had virtually made up her mind not to speak, that remembrance had worked within her like leaven, unconsciously softening her towards her husband, drawing her towards compassion on Michael.

Now that she did speak again she did not reproach them. She who had blamed them both so bitterly a few short weeks ago blamed them no longer. Nor did she say anything about the culpable silence of the real murderer. That mysterious criminal, that scapegoat who had so far aroused her bitterest animosity had ceased to darken her mind.

Fay had passed unconsciously far beyond the limitations of Magdalen's anxious prayer on her behalf. The love of Andrea and Michael, tardily seen, only partially realised, had helped her at last.

The Bishop listened and listened, a little bent forward, his eyes on the floor, his chin in his hand. Once he made a slight movement when Fay reached Michael's arrest, but he quickly recovered himself.

The faint voice faltered itself out at last. The story was at an end. The Duke was dead and Michael was in prison.

"I have kept him there two years," said Fay, and was silent.

How she had raged against the cruelty of her husband's dying words. What passionate, vindictive tears she had shed at the remembrance of them. Now, unconsciously, she adopted them herself. She had ceased to resist them, and the sting had gone clean out of them.

"Two years," said the Bishop. "Two years. Fast bound in misery and iron. You in misery and he only in iron. You two poor children."

His strong face worked, and for a moment he shaded it with his hand.

Then he looked keenly at Fay.

"And you have come to me to ask me to advise you how to set Michael and yourself free?"

"Yes," whispered Fay.

"It was time to come."

There was a short silence.

"And you understand, my dear, dear child, that you can only rescue Michael by taking heavy blame upon yourself, blame first of all for having a clandestine meeting with him, and then blame for letting him sacrifice himself for your good name, and lastly blame for keeping an innocent man in prison so long."

Fay shook like a leaf.

The Bishop took her lifeless hands in his, and held them. He made her meet his eyes. Stern, tender, unflinching eyes they were, with a glint of tears in them.

"You are willing to bear the cross, and endure the shame?" he said.

Two large tears gathered in Fay's wide eyes, and rolled down her bloodless cheeks.

You could not look at her, and think that the poor thing was willing to endure anything, capable of enduring anything.

The Bishop looked at her, through her.

"Or would you rather go home and wait in misery a little longer, and keep him in his cell a little longer: another week—another month—another *year*! You know best how much longer you can wait."

Silence.

"And Michael can wait, too."

"Michael must come out," said Fay, with a sob. "He was always good to me."

"Thank God," said the Bishop, and he rose abruptly and went to the window.

Magdalen and Fay did not move. They leaned a little closer together. Fay's timid eyes sought her sister's like those of a child which has repeated its lesson, and looks to its teacher to see if it has done well.

Magdalen kissed her on the eyes.

"I have said everything, haven't I?"

"Everything."

"I wish I was dead."

Magdalen had no voice to answer with.

The Bishop came back, and sat down opposite them.

"Fay," he said, "as long as you live you will be thankful that you came to me to-day, that you were willing to make atonement by this great act of reparation. The comfort of that remembrance will sink deep into your troubled heart, and will heal its wounds. But the sacrifice is not to be exacted of you. I had to ask if you were willing to make it. But there is no longer any necessity for you to make it. Do you understand?"

The Bishop spoke slowly. The two women looked at him with dilated eyes.

"Is Michael dead?" said Magdalen.

"No. Michael is, I believe, well. The murderer of the Marchese di Maltagliala has confessed. It is in to-day's papers. The Marchese was murdered by his wife. It was quite sudden and unpremeditated, the work of an instant of terror. She has made a full confession on her deathbed. It exonerates Michael entirely. She implores his forgiveness for her long silence."

The Bishop's last words reached Fay from a great distance. The room with its many books, and the tall mullioned window with the bare elm branches across it, were all turning gently together in a spreading dimness. The only thing that remained fixed was Magdalen's shoulder, and even that shook a little. Fay leaned her face against it, and let all the rest go. The window with its tree quivered for a moment across the dark and then flickered out. The consciousness of tender hands and voices lingered a moment longer and then vanished too.

CHAPTER XXIII

All the heavy days are over.—W. B. YEATS.

It was very late when Magdalen and Fay reached home.

Bessie was on the lookout for them, and met them in the hall.

"Wentworth has been here," she said. "He arrived about an hour after you had started. As you were both out he asked to see me. He was greatly excited. He had come to tell us that Michael's innocence has suddenly been proved. He goes to Italy to-morrow. He said he would call here on his way to the station a little before eleven, to tell you both about it."

And punctually at a few minutes to eleven Wentworth appeared, and was ushered into the little white morning-room where Fay was waiting for him.

The room was full of sunshine. The soft air came gently in, bringing with it a breath of primroses.

Delight was in the room, tremulous, shining in Fay's eyes. Delight was in the whole atmosphere. An enormous boundless relief overflowed everything.

Wentworth was excited, softened, swept out of himself.

He held her soft hand in his. He tried to speak, but he could not. His eyes filled with tears. He was ashamed.

And when he looked up he saw Fay's eyes were wet, too. His heart went out to her. She was rejoicing with him. He pulled himself together, and told her what little he knew; not much more than the bare facts contained in the papers. It was now known by the Marchesa's confession that the murder took place inside the Colle Alto gardens. Everyone, including the police, had believed that the murder took place in the road, and that the assassin took advantage of the accident of the garden door being unlocked to drag the body into the garden, and hide it there. But the Marchesa stated that she stabbed her husband in the garden suddenly without premeditation, but with intent to kill him, because of his determination to marry their seventeen year old daughter to a friend of his, a *roué*, the old Duke of Castelfranco, who drank himself to death soon afterwards.

The Marchesa stated that she dragged the body behind a shrub, walked back through the garden to the house with the front of her gown covered with blood without being noticed, found no attendant in the cloak room, wrapped herself in a long cloak not belonging to her, told her servants that the Marchese would follow later, and drove home, partially burned her gown and the cloak as if by accident, and then awaited events. The first news she received of her husband's death next morning was accompanied by the amazing information that Michael had confessed to the murder.

The Marchesa in her tardy confession stated that she believed Michael, who had always shown her great sympathy, must have actually witnessed the crime, and out of a chivalrous impulse towards her, had immediately taken the guilt of it upon himself.

"That accounts for his extraordinary silence," said Wentworth, "not only to others, but to myself. He never would say a word pro or con, even when I told him it was no use trying to persuade me he was guilty. The mystery is cleared up at last. I shall reach Milan to-night, and I shall see him to-morrow. And I suppose we may be able to start home the following day. I say these things, but I don't believe them. I can't believe them. It all seems to me like some wonderful dream. And you are like a person in a dream, too, as if a fairy wand had passed over you?"

As he spoke Wentworth suddenly realised that this marvellous, radiant transformation which he beheld in Fay, which seemed to flow even to the edges of her lilac gown, was happiness, and that he had never seen her happy till this moment. She had always looked pathetic, mournful, listless. Now for the first time he saw her, as it were, released from some great oppression, and the change was almost that of identity. Her beauty had taken on a new magic.

There is no joy so rapturous, so perfect as the moment of relief from pain. There was, perhaps, no creature in the world on this particular April morning whose happiness approached Fay's. She raised her white eyelids and smiled at Wentworth.

His well-conducted heart nudged him suddenly like a vulgar, jocular friend.

"Is all your gladness for Michael?" he said boldly. "Have you none to spare for me?"

He was in for it.

"You must forgive me if I am too impetuous, too precipitate," he said, "but won't you make me doubly happy, Fay, before I go." He rose and came towards her. She looked down, half frightened, and he suddenly felt himself colossal, irresistible, a man not to be trifled with. "You have known for a long time that I love you," he said. "Won't you tell me that you love me a little, too?"

A delightful sense of liberty and newness of life were flowing in regenerating waves over Fay's spirit.

Wentworth seemed a part of this all-pervading joyousness and freedom. She made a little half unconscious movement towards him, and in a moment, that intrepid man, that dauntless athlete of the emotions had taken her in his arms.

CHAPTER XXIV

He who gives up the smallest part of a secret has the rest no longer in his power.

—JEAN PAUL.

The Marchesa's confession made a great and immediate sensation throughout Italy. Everyone who had known Michael, and a great many who had not, proclaimed with one consent that his innocence was no news to them. The possibility that he might be shielding someone had been discussed at the time of the trial, but had found no shred of confirmation.

And now the mystery was solved at last, and in the most romantic manner. Michael had come out with flying colours.

To many minds the romance was enhanced by the fact that the Marchesa was a gentle, middle-aged, grey-haired woman in no way attractive, whose whole interest in life centred in her daughter. Michael's transcendent act of chivalry towards the Marchesa, dramatically acknowledged by her at last upon her deathbed, appealed even to the most unimaginative natures. He became the hero of the hour. Telegrams of congratulation poured in from every quarter. Letters snowed in on him. Even before Wentworth could reach him enthusiastic strangers had tried to force their way into his cell. Determined young reporters came out in gondolas, and it was all the warders and the doctor could do to protect Michael from invasion.

He sat apparently stunned in his cell, the only person unmoved. Every servant and warder in that dreary establishment had come to offer him their congratulations. The other convicts had sent messages. The man in the next cell, slowly dying of gangrene, had crawled from his pallet to beat a tattoo on the wall. The doctor was beside himself with joy.

"You must keep calm," he kept saying in wild excitement. "Your brother will be here to-morrow morning. I implore you to be calm."

And he brought Michael his best pipe, and some of his most cherished tobacco, and a weird suit of black clothes, and urged him to spend the evening with him in his own sitting-room.

But Michael shook his head. He had no hatred of his striped blouse. He was accustomed to it. He said he would prefer to await his brother's arrival in his cell. He was accustomed to that, too. He felt as if he could not bear to have everything torn from him at once, as if he should be lost if all his landmarks were changed. He sat hour by hour, smoking, and every now and then reading Wentworth's telegram.

He tried to realise it. He said to himself over and over again: "I am free. I am going away. Wentworth is coming to take me home." But it was no good. His mind would not take hold.

He looked for the twentieth time at Wentworth's telegram. Wentworth was hurrying towards him at this moment, would be travelling all night, would reach him in the morning. Dear, dear Wenty, he would be happy again now.

Michael groaned.

"It's no kind of use. I *can't* believe it."

He tried to think of Fay. He should see *her* soon, touch her hand, hear her voice. Poor little darling! She had not the courage of a mouse. Perhaps she was a little glad at his release. Yes. No doubt she had been pleased to hear it. He hoped she would not feel shy of him at seeing him again. He hoped she would not thank him.

The door, no longer locked, was suddenly opened, and the head warder deferentially ushered in a visitor.

A tall, dark man in a tri-coloured sash came in, and the warder withdrew.

The man bowed and looked with fixity at Michael, who stared back at him, dazed and confused. Where had he seen that face before?

Ah! *He remembered!*

"I perceive that you have not forgotten me," said the Delegato. "It was I who arrested you. It was to me that you confessed to the murder of the Marchese di Maltagliala."

"I remember."

"I never was able to reach any certainty that you were really guilty," continued the Delegato. "I was not even convinced that you had had a quarrel with the Marchese."

"I had no quarrel with him."

"I knew that. That you might be shielding someone occurred forcibly to my mind. *But who?*"

Michael looked steadily at the official.

"And there was blood upon your hand and sleeve when you confessed."

"There was."

"It was not the Marchese's blood," said the Delegato, drawing a sallow finger across a blue chin. "It remained a mystery. I will own that it had not crossed my mind that that fragile and timid lady had killed her husband, and that as she at last confesses you were shielding her." The Delegato looked piercingly at Michael.

Michael was silent.

"You have always been silent. Is not the moment come to speak?"

Michael shook his head.

The Delegato bowed.

"I came to ask you to discuss the affair openly," he said, "to relieve my perplexity as a matter of courtesy. But you will not speak. Then I will speak instead. When first I read the Marchesa's confession it came into my mind that the Marchesa, who I believe was your friend, might for some reason, possibly the sentimental devotion of an older woman for a young man—such things have been—that she *might* have confessed on her deathbed to a crime which she had not committed in order to save you from—*this*"—he touched the wall of the cell. "I doubted that she really murdered her husband. *But she did.* I sought out the maid who had been with her when the Marchese died, and she, before the confession was published, informed me that she had not undressed the Marchesa on her return from the Colle Alto party. And that next morning part of the cloak which was not hers, and part of her gown were found to be burnt as stated in her confession. It was indeed necessary to burn them. The Marchesa murdered the Marchese."

There was a long silence.

"I cannot tell whether you witnessed the crime or not. At first I thought the blood on your hands and clothes might have come from helping her to drag the body into the garden. But it was not so. At the time I attached a great importance to the garden door being unlocked. Too great. It led me astray. The gardener, in spite of his oath that he had locked it, had probably left it unlocked. We now know from the Marchesa that the murder took place within the garden, and the locking and unlocking of the door was an accident which looked like a clue.... But, if you witnessed the murder, and wished to retire without raising an alarm, or denouncing that unhappy lady, I ask myself why did you not open the garden door from within—the key was in the lock, I saw it—and pass out on to the high road. Why did you, instead, try so hard to escape over the wall behind the ilexes that you tore your hands on the cut glass on the top? I found the place next day. There was blood on it. When you were struggling to escape over that wall you were not anxious to take the Marchesa's guilt upon yourself. When you were hiding behind the screen in the Duchess' apartment you were not—*at that moment*—very determined to shield the Marchesa from the consequences of her deed. All Italy is ringing with your quixotic, your chivalrous, your superb action. *Nevertheless*, if I had quitted the Duchess' apartment, if my natural and trained acuteness had not made one last effort respecting the screen, *I do not think you would have followed me into the garden to denounce yourself.*"

The Delegato paused.

Michael was quite unmoved. Everything reached him dimly as through a mist. He partly saw the difficulty in the official's mind, but it did not interest him. He was cleared. That was enough.

"In two years much is forgotten," said the Delegato, sententiously, "and it is, perhaps, I alone who recall the more minute details of the case, because I was present and my interest was overwhelming. I have not spoken of this to anyone but yourself. I shall not speak of it again. I have taken a journey to discuss it with you because I had hoped you would understand my professional interest in unravelling that which remains still obscure, a mystery, which is daily becoming to me a greater mystery than before the Marchesa's confession. You have it in your power to gratify my natural desire for elucidation by an explanation which can no longer injure you in any way. You are innocent. It is proved. But even now you will not speak. You prefer to preserve your attitude of silence to the end. Good! I will intrude on you no longer. I offer you my congratulations. I deplore your inevitable imprisonment. I withdraw."

The Delegato bowed yet again and went to the door.

"That of which you will not speak was known to your friend the Duke of Colle Alto," he said. "*The Duke knew.*"

"The Duke is dead," said Michael.

"I am aware of that," said the Delegato, frigidly. He bowed for the last time, and left the cell, gently closing the door.

CHAPTER XXV

Est-ce donc une monnaie que votre amour, pour qu'il puisse passer ainsi de main en main jusqu'à la mort? Non, ce n'est pas même une monnaie; car la plus mince pièce d'or vaut mieux que vous, et dans quelques mains qu'elle passe elle garde son effigée.

—A. DE MUSSET.

Wentworth came in the morning, tremulous, eager, holding Michael by the shoulders, as he used to do when Michael was a small boy, as he had never done since.

The brothers looked long at each other with locked hands, water in their eyes.

"Wenty," said Michael at last, with his grave smile.

And that was all.

They sat down together in silence on the little bed. Wentworth tried to speak once or twice, but it was no use.

"Fay cried with joy at the news," he said at last, looking with shy hungry love at his brother. "If you could have seen her radiant face. I never saw any creature so changed, so transfigured."

A faint flush rose to Michael's face.

"I know how she grieved over your imprisonment. She is the most tender-hearted woman in the world. I never knew anyone so sympathetic." Wentworth hesitated. Then he added tremulously. "My great grief has been her grief, too. She helped me to bear it."

"I did not know she had—minded so much," said Michael, almost inaudibly.

"You might have guessed it," said Wentworth, "knowing her to be what she is. She has always been so pale and sad, as if bowed down by trouble. But directly the news came that you were cleared—I went to see her at once—if you could only have seen her face, her tears of joy, her delight."

"Did she send a message, or a note? Just a line. Perhaps you have a letter with you."

"No, she did not write," said Wentworth, self conscious, but beaming. "There was not time. There was time for nothing. It was all such a rush. I only saw her on my way to the station. But I know she won't mind my telling you, Michael—you ought to know first of anyone—it all seems so wonderful. But I daresay—no, I see you have guessed it—I daresay I have said things in my letters that showed you it was coming—it was the grief about you that first drew us together. Fay and I are going to be married."

Michael put his hand to his head.

"Everything has come at once," said Wentworth. "I have you again. And I have her. I've nothing left to wish for."

Michael did not leave the prison in the gondola which had brought Wentworth, and which was waiting to take them both away. The excitement of his brother's arrival had proved too great, and he fell from one fainting fit into another. Wentworth was greatly alarmed, but the doctor was reassuring and cheerful. He said that Michael had borne the news with almost unnatural calmness, but that the shock must have been great, and a breakdown was to be expected. He laughed at Wentworth's anxiety even while he ministered to Michael, and assured him that no one in his experience had died of joy.

But later in the evening when Wentworth, somewhat pacified, had returned to Venice for the night, the doctor felt yet again for the twentieth time that the young Englishman baffled him.

It seemed to him that he was actually relieved when the kind, awkward, tender elder brother had reluctantly taken his departure, promising to come back early in the morning.

"Do not distress yourself, you will be quite well enough to leave to-morrow," the doctor said to him many times. "I expected this momentary collapse. It is nothing."

Michael's eyes dwelt on the kind face and then closed. There was that in them which the doctor could not fathom.

He took the food that was pressed on him, and then turned his face to the wall, and made as if he slept.

And the walls bent over him, and whispered to him, "Stay with us. We are not so cruel as the world outside."

And that night the dying convict in the next cell, nearly as close on freedom as Michael, heard all through the night a low sound of strangled anguish that ever stifled itself into silence, and ever broke forth anew, from dark to dawn.

The next morning Michael went feebly down the prison steps, calm and wan, leaning on Wentworth's careful arm, and smiling affectionately at him.

CHAPTER XXVI

Les caractères faibles ne montrent de la décision que quand il s'agit de faire un sottise.

—DANIEL DARC.

A week or two after the news of Michael's proved innocence had convulsed Hampshire, and before Michael and Wentworth had returned to Barford, Aunt Aggie might have been seen on a fine May afternoon walking slowly towards "The Towers." She had let her cottage at Saundersfoot for an unusually long period, and was marking time with the Blores. Whatever Aunt Mary's faults might be she was always ready to help her sister in this practical manner, when Aunt Aggie was anxious to add to the small, feebly frittered away income, on which her muddled, impecunious existence depended.

In spite of the most pertinent remarks to the contrary from her sister, Aunt Aggie believed herself to be an unsurpassed manager of restricted means. She constantly advised young married couples as to the judicious expenditure of money, and pressed on Magdalen the necessity of retrenching in exasperating directions, namely, where a minute economy entailed a colossal inconvenience.

In her imagination she saw herself continually consulted, depended on, strenuously implored to give her opinion on matters of the utmost delicacy, fervently blessed for her powerful spiritual assistance of souls in jeopardy, and always gracefully attributing the marvellous results of her intervention to a Higher Power of which she was but the unworthy channel.

These imaginary scenes were the unfailing solace of Aunt Aggie's somewhat colourless life, and the consciousness of them in the background gave her a certain meek and even patient self-importance, the basis of which was hidden from Lady Blore.

Aunt Aggie had also another perennial source of chastened happiness in recalling the romance of her youth, those halcyon days before the Archdeacon had been unsuccessfully harpooned and put to flight by Lady Blore.

Her clerical love affair perfumed her conversation, as a knife which has once associated with an onion inevitably reveals, even in estrangement, that bygone intimacy.

No one could breathe the word Margate without Aunt Aggie remarking that she had had a dear friend who had evinced a great partiality for Margate. Were the clergy mentioned in her presence with the scant respect with which the ministry and other secular bodies have to put up, Aunt Aggie vibrated with indignation. *She* had known men of the highest talents holding preferment in the Church.

But in her imagination her affair of the heart had passed beyond reminiscence. Far from being buried in the past it remained the chief factor in her life, colouring and shaping the whole of her future.

Aunt Aggie could at any moment dip into a kind of sequel to that early history. In the sequel the Archdeacon's wife was, of course, to die; but, owing to circumstances which Aunt Aggie had not yet thoroughly worked out, that unhappy lady was first to undergo tortures in some remote locality, nursed devotedly—poor thing—by Aunt Aggie. The result of her ministrations was never in doubt from the first. The Archdeacon's wife was, of course, to succumb, calling down blessings on the devoted stranger at her bedside, with the enigmatical smile which spoke of some sacred sorrow.

Aunt Aggie had shed many delicious tears over that deathbed scene, and the chastened grief of the saintly Archdeacon, quite overshadowed by his boundless gratitude to herself. At this crisis his overwhelming desolation wrung from him—with gross disloyalty to the newly dead—a few disjointed sentences which revealed only too clearly how unsuited to him his wife had been, how little she had understood him, how lonely his wedded life had been. She had evidently been one of those tall thin maypoles of women who have but little tenderness in them.

Aunt Aggie, after giving the children a sample of what a real mother could be, was to retire to her little home at Saundersfoot. Here the real joy of the situation was to begin.

After a decent interval the Archdeacon was to be constantly visiting Saundersfoot, was to be observed visiting Aunt Aggie at Saundersfoot, singling her out from among the numerous spinsters of that watering-place to make her the object of reverent attentions. Others younger and better looking than Aunt Aggie—especially Miss Barnett, the doctor's sister, who, it was whispered, wore an artificial cushion from Douglas's under her hair—were to set their caps or cushions at the dignified Archdeacon, seen pacing the sands. But it was all of no avail. He had eyes for no one but the gentle, retiring Miss Bellairs. Aunt Aggie was to become the object of burning jealousy and detraction on the part of the female—that is to say almost the whole—population of Saundersfoot. But she herself, while envious calumny raged round her, went on her way calm and grave as ever.

But the proposal long warded off could not be parried forever. The frenzied passion of the Archdeacon was at last not to be restrained. Aunt Aggie had in her mind a set of proposals, all good, out of which it became harder and harder as time went on to select one. But her answer was ever the same, a pained but firm refusal. She was happy in her lot. She was greatly needed where she was. She did not wish to marry. She was no longer young. This last reason was an enormous concession to realism on Aunt Aggie's part.

Then came the cream of the whole story. The Archdeacon was to pine secretly. His work was to be neglected. He was to be threatened with a nervous breakdown. He was to confide his sorrow to the paternal bosom of his Bishop. When Aunt Aggie was in her normal state it was the Bishop in whom the Archdeacon was to confide. But sometimes in the evenings after a glass of cowslip wine, her imagination took a bolder flight. The Archbishop himself was to be the confidant of the distracted cleric. This presented no real difficulty after the first moment, for the Archbishop was in the flower of his age—the Archdeacon's age—and might easily have been at school with him. Aunt Aggie had once seen Lambeth from a cab window as she passed over Westminster Bridge. Under that historic tower she heard the first subject of the King urge his brother prelate to take heart, promising assistance.

We will pass over Aunt Aggie's amazed reception of a cordial invitation to stay at Lambeth, her hesitating acceptance, her arrival, the magnificent banquet, crowded with ministers and bishops, the fact that the Archbishop himself singled her out as the object of courtly though somewhat anxious attentions. And then after dinner Aunt Aggie, in her plum-coloured satin, was to be unconsciously but skilfully withdrawn from the glittering throng by the Archbishop. And in his study he was to make a great, a fervent appeal to her. Aunt Aggie had bought a photograph of him in order to deaden the shock of this moment. But nevertheless whenever she reached this point she was always really frightened. Her hands really trembled. The Archbishop was to ask her with tempered indignation how much longer she intended to nullify the labours of his ablest colleague, how much longer her selfish predilection for celibacy was to wreck the life and paralyse the powers of a broken-hearted man. Her cruelty was placed before her in glowing colours. She was observed to waver, to falter. A tear was seen in spite of her marvellous self-control to course down her cheek. The eye of an Archbishop misses nothing. With an ejaculation of profound relief he beckons to a distant figure which appears in a doorway. The Archdeacon in his evening gaiters rushes in. Aunt Aggie gives way!

After this final feat of the imagination Aunt Aggie generally felt so worn out by emotion that food was absolutely necessary to her.

On this occasion she sat down quivering on a heap of stones by the roadside, and drew forth a biscuit which she had secreted at luncheon at the Vicarage an hour before. It must be owned that she was fond of food, though not in the same way that most of us are addicted to it. She liked eating buns out of paper bags at odd moments in the open air, and nibbling a sponge cake half forgotten and suddenly found in a drawer with her handkerchiefs. But in justice to her it ought to be added that she seemed only to care for the kind of provender which yielded the largest increment in the way of crumbs.

As she sat and nibbled an uneasy recollection stole across her mind.

This recollection was becoming more disconcerting day by day. And yet she had acted for the best. That fact did not insure to her immunity from blame on the part of that awful personage, her sister Mary. Good intentions had never yet received their due as extenuating circumstances in Lady Blore's sweeping judgments.

If a certain secret chivalrous action of Aunt Aggie's "turned out wrong," she knew well the intonation in which Lady Blore would ask her why she had been such a fool. Nevertheless she, Aunt Aggie, had only done with consummate tact what Mary herself had contemplated doing in her rough way, and had been persuaded not to do.

Some weeks ago Aunt Aggie had concocted in secret, recopied about twenty times, and had finally despatched a letter to Lord Lossiemouth anent Magdalen. It had been the boldest action of her life. At first, even after she had seen that she was the only person able to deal adequately with so delicate a matter, she had feared that she would not have the strength to perform her mission. But strength had apparently been lent to her for the occasion. The letter had actually been posted.

The moment it was irrevocably gone Aunt Aggie fell into a panic. Supposing it failed in its object, and that Algernon or Mary discovered what she had done. She could not even face such a possibility. But then, supposing on the other hand that her missive united two loving, estranged hearts, and that dear Magdalen owed her happiness—and a titled happiness—to her. Then Algernon and Mary would be forced to admit that she had shown a courage and devotion greater than theirs. "We only talked, you acted," they would both say, and she would thenceforth be recognised in her true light, as an incomparable counsellor, and a judicious, far-seeing friend.

But three weeks had elapsed since Aunt Aggie, stealing out alone, had dropped that momentous letter into the village post-box. Nothing had happened. She had not even received an answer. She was becoming frightened and anxious. *Was he secretly married?* She wished she had thought of that possibility before she posted the letter.

Many simple-minded men of disengaged affections, cheerfully pursuing their virtuous avocations, would be thunderstruck if they knew the dark suspicions harboured against them in spinster bosoms, that they are concealing some discreditable matrimonial secret, which alone can account for their—well—their *extraordinary* behaviour in not coming forward!

It has actually been said that real life is not always like a novel. This feebly false assertion was disproved forever in Aunt Aggie's mind by the sight of a dog-cart coming rapidly toward her from the direction of Lostford. She glanced indifferently at it as it approached, and then her pale eyes became glued to it. In the dog-cart sat Everard Constable, now Lord Lossiemouth. She had not seen him for fifteen years, but nevertheless she recognised him instantly. There was no doubt it was he: thickened and coarsened, but still he. He whirled past leaning back in his seat, looking neither to right nor left.

Aunt Aggie's heart gave a thump that nearly upset her equilibrium. The biscuit dropped onto the road, with a general upheaval of crumbs from all parts of her agitated person.

Lord Lossiemouth!

Going in the direction of Priesthope!

Her letter!

She nearly swooned with joy and pride.

Now Mary and Algernon, now everyone would believe in her.

She raised herself from the heap of stones and with trembling legs hurried towards "The Towers." She must tell Mary at once.

She found Lady Blore seated at her writing-table in the drawing-room, which was choked by the eastern and Japanese impedimenta, the draperies, the krises, the metal bowls, the ivory boxes, which an Indian career seems so inevitably to entail. Sir John had brought back crates of the kind of foreign *bric-à-brac* cheap imitations of which throng London shop windows. The little entrance hall was stuffy with skins. Horned skulls garnished the walls, pleading silently for decent burial. Even the rugs had once been bears.

Aunt Mary was bored with her drawing-room, which looked like a stall at a bazaar, but, to her credit be it said, that she had never made any change in it, except to remove a brass idol from the writing-table, at which she was at this moment sitting.

By one of those sudden instincts which make people like Aunt Aggie the despair of those with whom they live, she instantaneously conceived the idea (for no reason except that she was thinking of her own letter) that her sister was at that moment writing to Lord Lossiemouth.

She "had a feeling" that this was the case. The feeling became in a second a rooted conviction. The butler came in, arranged an uncomfortable Indian table, placed a brass tray with tea things on it before Lady Blore, and asked if there were any more letters for the post. Aunt Mary was in the act of giving him one when Aunt Aggie intervened.

"Don't," she said in wild agitation, clasping her hands. "Mary, I beg of you, I conjure you not to post that letter."

"Why not? I have resolved to give him another chance."

"Keep it back one post, I implore you. I have a reason."

Aunt Mary looked attentively at her sister, and took back the letter. It was not like her to give way. She seemed less overbearing than usual.

"Well? Why not employ him again?" she said wearily. "The Irish butter is the cheapest after all. Why do you make such a point of my leaving him."

Aunt Aggie was entirely nonplussed. A thousand similar experiences had never lessened the shock of the discrepancy between what she expected her sister to say, and what she actually said.

"I thought, I thought," she stammered, "I felt sure that, I see now I was wrong, but I had a conviction that that letter—you see I knew you were thinking of writing—was to, was in short to Lord Lossiemouth."

Aunt Mary's face became magenta colour.

"To Lord Lossiemouth! Why should you think I was writing to him?"

"Well, I could not help knowing—don't you remember how you discussed the subject with me and dear Magdalen some weeks ago?—that the subject of a judicious and dignified letter was in your mind."

"I was careful not to mention the subject to Magdalen in your presence. I see now that you must have listened outside the door."

Aunt Aggie experienced a second shock. How did Mary always spy out these things?

"I can't think," continued Lady Blore, "how you can lower yourself to eavesdrop in the way you do; and if you must do these underhand actions, why you don't conceal them better. When you read a private letter of mine the other day, because I inadvertently left it for a moment on my writing-table——"

"You always say you lock up your private letters, you do, indeed, Mary. *Be* fair. I could not *tell* it was private."

"You would have been wiser not to have alluded next day to its contents. If you had not done so I might not have known you had read it."

Aunt Aggie burst into tears.

"The truth is I am not secretive like you, Mary," she said between her sobs. "It is as natural to me to be open and trustful with those I love as it is for you to be the reverse. Whatever I do you think wrong. But perhaps some day—and that before long—you will be forced to admit——"

At this moment the drawing-room door opened and Colonel Bellairs came in. He often came to tea at "The Towers," though the meeting seldom passed off without a sharp brush with Lady Blore.

"Draw up that chair, Algernon," said that lady, with grim but instant cordiality. "The tea will be ready in a moment."

Colonel Bellairs looked more floridly handsome than usual. He was evidently in a state of supreme self-satisfaction.

"Fine day," he said, "for the time of year."

At this moment a small parchment face, and bent figure leaning on a stick, might have been seen peering in through the closed windows. Sir John looked dispassionately at the family group, and shook his head. Then he hobbled back to his chair under the cedar. Tea was evidently a meal to be dispensed with this afternoon.

"I have news for you," said Colonel Bellairs, expanding his chest.

Lady Blore held the tea-pot suspended.

"Everard Constable—Lossiemouth, I should say—is at this moment sitting in the drawing-room at Priesthope, alone with Magdalen."

Colonel Bellairs was not disappointed in the effect of his words on his audience.

Aunt Aggie trembled and looked proudly guilty. Lady Blore put down the tea-pot suddenly, and said, "Thank God!"

Aunt Aggie, her mouth open to speak, began to choke. She looked piteously from her brother to her sister, struggling in vain to articulate. It was too cruel that she should be bereft of speech at this supreme moment.

Lady Blore turned putty pale and magenta colour alternately. A great relief softened her hard face. There were actually tears in her eyes. Then she said majestically, but with a tremor in her metallic voice:

"I am not surprised."

"It is my doing," shrieked Aunt Aggie, in the strangled squeak in which we always explain that it is "only a crumb" gone wrong. And she relapsed into a fresh spasm.

Lady Blore sternly bade her be silent. Colonel Bellairs was slightly annoyed.

"It is no use, Mary, your saying you are not surprised, for you are," he said judicially, "and really," relapsing into complacency, "so am I in a way. It is fifteen years since I forbade Everard the house. I fear that I was unduly harsh. I dismissed him, so it was for me to recall him. Now that the cat is out of the bag I don't mind telling you that I wrote to him a few weeks ago."

"You—wrote—to—him!" said Aunt Mary in great agitation. "Algernon, you sent me word by Magdalen that you refused to meddle in the matter."

"I daresay I did. I may not have liked the tone you took about it, Mary. You are so devilish high-handed. In short, I don't mind telling you that I was annoyed by your interference in the matter. But after mature consideration—I turned the matter over in my mind—I was not the least influenced by your long-winded epistle—that in fact rather put me off than otherwise—still after a time I wrote a manly, straightforward letter to Everard, not blinking the facts, and I told him that if his feelings were unchanged—mark that—as I had reason to believe Magdalen's were—he was at liberty to come to Priesthope and resume cordial relations with us all. You observe that I only asked him to come if his feelings were unchanged. *He is there now.*"

It would be impossible to describe the varying emotions which devastated Lady Blore, as her brother made his announcement. Her hands trembled so much that she was obliged to give up any pretence of holding her cup. It chattered against its saucer.

"When did you write?" she asked at last.

"About three weeks ago."

Aunt Mary seemed to make a mental calculation.

"It is my doing. I wrote a month ago," gasped Aunt Aggie. "Algernon, you must not take the credit of it. I waited till you and Mary had decided not to write—you know, Mary, you told Magdalen you would not—and then—and then—I could not stand by and see that dear child's happiness slip away for want of one bold word, one brave friend to say for her what she could not say for herself,—I have seen so many lives wrecked for want of a sympathetic hand to draw two severed hearts together,—that I wrote. I wrote a month ago. A week before you did."

"I might have known you would do some folly," said Colonel Bellairs with contempt. "I am glad this did not come to my ears earlier, or I should have been very angry. It was most unsuitable, most undignified, that you and I should both write. But," it was evidently impossible for him to be seriously annoyed by anything on this particular afternoon, "all's well that ends well. We will say no more about it, Aggie. Don't cry. You can't help being a fool. But don't do anything of that kind, or of any kind again. I might not be so easy going next time."

Lady Blore drank down a large cup of tea. Her black silk bosom heaved. Contrary to all precedent she did not turn on her quaking sister.

"Where are Fay and Bessie?" she asked.

"Fay is spending the afternoon with the Carters, and Bessie is out somewhere, I don't know where. But I saw her start after luncheon."

"How fortunate! Then you knew he was coming?"

"Yes. I had a telegram from him this morning saying he was in the neighbourhood, and would come over this afternoon."

"Of course you warned Magdalen?"

"Not I. I knew better than that. She has a cold, so I knew she could not go out. So directly I had seen him drive up I came off here. I did not think I was particularly wanted at home. Two is company and three's none."

"Oh, Algernon, what tact! Most men would never have thought of that," said Aunt Aggie.

"Have another cup, Algernon," said Lady Blore graciously.

Colonel Bellairs stroked his moustache. He had another cause, a secret one, for self-complacency. At last, after many rebuffs from charming women, thirty years his junior, he was engaged to be married. Should he mention it? Was not this a most propitious moment? Yes? No. Perhaps better not. Another time! The lady had accepted him some weeks ago, but had expressed altruistic doubts as to whether she could play a mother's part to daughters as old as herself, whether in short, much as she craved for their society, *they* might not feel happier, more independent in a separate establishment, however modest. It was on a sudden impulse of what he called "providing for the girls," that Colonel Bellairs had written to Lord Lossiemouth.

The renewal of his engagement to Magdalen would pave the way to Colonel Bellairs's marriage. He had already decided that Bessie would live with Magdalen, who would take her out. Fay had her jointure. But he had a not unfounded fear that his second nuptials would be regarded with profound disapproval, even with execration, by his sisters.

Magdalen alone knew about it as yet. She had taken the news, which her father had feared would crush her to the earth, very tranquilly. She was a person of more frigid affections than he had supposed. He had already asked her to break the news to Fay and Bessie. Perhaps it would be better to let her break it to his sisters too. If he did it himself they might, at the first moment, say things they might afterwards regret. Yes, he would leave the announcement to Magdalen.

CHAPTER XXVII

Our chain on silence clanks. Time leers between, above his twiddling thumbs.

—GEORGE MEREDITH.

Lord Lossiemouth had come into his kingdom. He was rich, but not vulgarly so. He had a great position, and what his artistic nature valued even more, the possession of one of the most beautiful places in England. The Lossiemouth pictures and heirlooms, the historic house with its wonderful gardens—all these were his.

He had at first been quite dazed by the magnitude of his good fortune. When it came to him it found him somewhat sore and angry at a recent rebuff which had wounded his vanity not a little. But the excitement of his great change of fortune soon healed what little smart remained.

A few months before he succeeded, he had fallen in love, not for the first time by many times, with a woman who seemed to meet his requirements. She was gentle, submissive, pretty, easily led, refined, not an heiress, but by no means penniless.

To his surprise and indignation she had refused him, evidently not without a certain tepid regret. He discovered that the mother had other views for her daughter, and that the daughter, though she inclined towards him, was quite incapable or even desirous of opposing her mother. She was gentleness and pliability itself. These qualities, so admirable in domestic life, have a tendency of which he had not thought before to make their charming owner, if a hitch occurs, subside into becoming another man's wife. If only women could be adamant until they reach the altar, and like wax afterwards.

When everything bitter that could be said at the expense of women had been ably expressed, Lord Lossiemouth withdrew. A month later, when he was making an angry walking tour in Hungary, he learned from an English paper, already many days old, of the two deaths which effected his great change of fortune. He communicated with his lawyer, arranged to return by a certain date, and continued his tour for another month.

On his return he had gone at once to Lossiemouth, which he had visited occasionally as a poor and peppery and not greatly respected relation.

Business of all kinds instantly engulfed him. He was impatient, difficult, *distrait*, slightly pleased with himself at showing so little gratification at his magnificent inheritance.

On the third day he sorted out the letters which looked like personal ones, from among a heap of correspondence, the accumulation of many weeks.

Quantities of envelopes were torn open, and the contents thrown aside, begging letters, decently veiled congratulations from "old friends" who had not so far shown any particular desire to make their friendship a joy to him.

Presently he came upon a long, closely written letter of several sheets, in a slanting hand, which he was about to dismiss as another begging letter when his eye fell on the signature. Bellows? Bulteel? Buller? *Bellairs?*

Aunt Aggie's signature was quite illegible. It was an arranged squiggle painfully acquired in youth, which through life had resulted in all kinds of difficulties with tradespeople, and in continual annoyance and inconvenience to herself. Letters and parcels were frequently directed to her as A. Buller, Esq. She could only account for this mistake by the business-like nature of her style and handwriting. She often told her friends that, unless people knew her personally, her letters were generally believed to be a man's.

It had never struck Aunt Aggie that Lord Lossiemouth might possibly, in an interval of fifteen years, have forgotten who *A.* Bellows might be.

But the words "my beloved niece Magdalen" strongly underlined, and the postmark on the envelope, showed him who A. Bellairs was. He thought he remembered an old aunt who lived near Priesthope.

He read the long sentimental effusion and bit his lip.

Ah, me! Was that half-forgotten, dim-in-the-distance boyish love of his to be raked up again now!

He sighed impatiently. Why had Fate parted him and Magdalen? He still regretted her in a way, when he was depressed or harassed, or disgusted with the world in general; and he was often depressed and harassed and disgusted.

More letters. What business had people to give him the trouble of reading them? The floor was becoming strewn with his correspondence. The empty fireplace had become a target for crumpled balls of paper.

A short one in a large, scrambling, illiterate hand with a signature that might mean anything. That tall capital, shaped like a ham, was perhaps a B.

The letter was written on Priesthope notepaper. "*My daughter Magdalen.*"

This, then, was from Colonel Bellairs.

It was not such a very bad letter, but it was a deplorably unwise one. When had Colonel Bellairs ever indited a wise one! But he made his precarious position even less tenable by ignoring the fact that Lord Lossiemouth's fortunes had altered, by asserting that he had had it in his mind to write to this effect the previous Christmas but had not had time. When Colonel Bellairs concocted that sentence he had felt, not without pride, that it covered the ground of his fifteen years' silence, and also showed that Lord Lossiemouth's wealth had nothing to do with his recall. For the letter was a recall.

"Blundering old idiot," said Lord Lossiemouth, but he had become very red.

All kinds of memories were surging up in him; Magdalen's crystal love for him, her indefinable charm, her gaiety, her humility, her shyness, her exquisite beauty.

Life had never brought him anything so marvellous, so enchanting, as that first draught of April passion. And he had quenched his thirst at many other cups since then. His lips had been blistered and stained at poisoned brims. Why had that furious old turkey-cock parted him and Magdalen! His heart sank for a moment at the remembrance of his first love.

But what was the use! The Magdalen he had loved had ceased to exist. The wand-like figure with its apple-blossom face faded, faded, and in its place rose up the image of the thin, distinguished-looking grey-haired woman who had supplanted that marvel. He had met Magdalen accidentally once or twice in London of late years, and had felt dismayed anger at the change in her, an offended anger not wholly unlike that with which he surveyed himself at his tailors', and inspected at unbecoming angles, through painfully frank mirrors, a thick back and a stout neck and jaw which cruelly misrepresented his fastidious artistic personality.

He returned to his letters.

Three sheets in a firm, upright hand.

"I do not suppose you remember me," it began, "but I intend to recall myself to your memory, which I believe to be none of the best. I am the wife of Sir John Blore, and aunt to Magdalen Bellairs."

He flung the letter down. But this was intolerable, a persecution. And what fools they were *all* to write. Had Magdalen set them on?

He groaned with sudden self-disgust. What unworthy thought would come to him next? Of course she knew nothing of this.

He looked at the date of each letter carefully. Aunt Aggie's according to her wont had only the day of the week on it, just Tuesday, or it might be Thursday—but Colonel Bellairs's and Lady Blore's were fully dated, and about a fortnight apart. Colonel Bellairs had written last.

Lord Lossiemouth divined that each of the three believed him or herself to be the only one to tackle the subject.

How ghastly! What a cruelly good short story it would make for a magazine!

Then he read Lady Blore's letter. Apparently it was not pleasant reading. It seemed to prick somewhat sharply. He winced once or twice, and spoke angrily to it.

"My good woman, as if I did not *know* that! Men are always behaving heartlessly to women in their opinion. It is the normal male state. It is an established fact that we are all brutes. Why do you want me to marry your paragon if you have such a low opinion of me?"

Still he could not put the letter down.

"It is possible though improbable," wrote that dauntless woman, "that your vacillating and selfish character may have improved sufficiently in the course of years for you to have become aware that you have behaved disgracefully to a woman, who, if she had had any sense, ought never to have given you a second thought, who was and still is deeply attached to you; probably the only person on this earth who has the misfortune to care two pins about you."

Lord Lossiemouth tried to feel sarcastic. He tried to laugh. But it was no use. Lady Blore's arrow had penetrated a joint in his harness.

After all he need take no notice of any of these monstrous effusions.

He was disgusted with opening letters. Nevertheless he hurried on. Perhaps he should find others less intolerable.

A somewhat formal letter from his cousin the Bishop of Lostford, who had never been cordial to him since his engagement to Magdalen had been broken off. The Bishop pointed out certain grave abuses connected with house property at Lostford, at which the late Lord Lossiemouth had persistently connived, but which he hoped his successor might enquire into personally and redress.

Quantities of other letters were torn open and aimed in balls at the empty grate. But at last he came to a long one which he read breathlessly.

It was from the mother of the girl who had so recently refused him, an involved tortuous epistle, which implied that the daughter was seriously attached to him, and hinted that if he were to come forward again he would not be refused a second time. There was also a short, wavering, nondescript note with nothing in particular in it from the girl herself. The mother had evidently made her write.

A very venomous expression settled on Lord Lossiemouth's heavy face. He suddenly took up a Bradshaw and looked out the trains for Lostford.

CHAPTER XXVIII

Tard oublie qui bien aime.

On this momentous afternoon Magdalen was sitting alone in the morning-room at Priesthope somewhat oppressed by an oncoming cold. It had not yet reached the violent and weeping stage. That was for to-morrow. She, who was generally sympathetically dressed, was reluctantly enveloped in a wiry red crochet-work shawl which Bessie had made for her, and had laid resolutely upon her shoulders before she went out.

She tried to read, but her eyes ached, and after a time she laid down her book, and her mind went back, as it had a way of doing—to Fay.

Fay had told her as "a great secret" that she had accepted Wentworth. She was so transfigured by happiness, so radiant, so absolutely unlike her former listless, colourless, carping self that Magdalen could only suppose that two shocks of joy had come simultaneously, the discovery that she loved her prim suitor, and the overwhelming relief to her tortured conscience of Michael's release.

Wentworth and Michael were still at Venice. Michael, it seemed, had been prostrated by excitement, and had been too weak to travel immediately. But they would be at Barford in a few days' time.

When Magdalen saw Fay entirely absorbed in trying on a succession of new summer hats, sent for from London in preparation for Wentworth's return, she asked herself for the twentieth time whether Fay had entirely forgotten her previous attraction for Michael, or that there might be some awkwardness in meeting her faithful lover and servant again, especially as the future wife of his brother.

Two years had certainly elapsed since that sudden flare-up of disastrous passion, and in two years much can be forgotten. But after two years everything may still be remembered, as Magdalen knew well. And she feared that Michael was among those who remember.

Magdalen had that day told Fay of her father's intention of marrying again, but she took almost no notice of the announcement. To use one of Aunt Aggie's metaphors, the news "seemed to slide off her back like a duck."

She only said, "Really! How silly of him!"

As Magdalen thought of Fay the door opened and Bessie, who was supposed to have gone for a walk, came in.

She had a spray of crab-apple blossom in her hand. She held it towards Magdalen as if it were a bill demanding instant payment. These little amenities were a new departure on Bessie's part.

Magdalen's pleasure in the apple blossom seemed to her somewhat exaggerated, but she made allowances for her, as she had a cold.

"Are you going out again?" asked Magdalen.

"No."

"Then I should like to have a little talk with you. I have something to tell you."

Bessie sat down.

"I am prepared for the announcement you have to make. I have seen it coming. It is about Fay."

"No, it is about Father. He has asked me to tell you that he is engaged to be married."

"Father!"

"Yes, it is not given out yet."

"Father!"

"It is to a Miss Barnett. You may have seen her. The doctor's sister at Saundersfoot."

"I know her by sight, a tall, showy-looking woman of nearly forty, with amber hair and a powdered nose."

"Yes."

"Father has sunk very low," said Bessie, judicially. "He must have been refused by a lot of others, younger and better-looking, and ladies, to be reduced to taking her. And fancy anyone in their senses being willing to take Father, with his gout, and his tendency to drink, and his total disregard of hygiene. Well, she looks a vulgar pushing woman, but I am sorry for her. And I must own that I am disappointed that if there was to be an engagement in our family it should be Father. There is not likely to be more than one going for a home like ours. It is just like him to grab it."

Magdalen tried not to laugh.

"I've looked round," continued Bessie. "I don't say that at present I could entertain the thought of marriage myself. I can't just yet, but I mean to in the future. It's merely a question of time. Marriage is the higher life. Besides, if one remains unmarried people are apt to think it is because one can't help it. It would certainly be so in my case. And I have looked round. There is not a soul in the neighbourhood for any of us to marry that I can see except Wentworth, who is of course extremely elderly. Hampshire seems absolutely bare of young men. And if there are a few sons in some of the houses, they are never accessible. And the really superior ones like Lord Alresford's only son would never look at me. It would be waste of time to try. There is positively no opening in Hampshire unless I marry the curate."

"That reminds me that he is to call this afternoon about the boot-and-shoe club. I wish, my dear, in the intervals between your aspirations towards the higher life, you would go through the accounts with him. My head is so confused with this cold."

"I will. And where on earth are you going to live when Father marries again? Of course, I shall graduate at Cambridge. He won't oppose that now. Magdalen, why don't you marry, too?"

"I can't, dear Bessie. No one wants me."

"May I go on?"

"No. Please don't."

"I think I will all the same. Why not marry Lord Lossiemouth after all? Don't speak. I want to place the situation dispassionately before you. I have thought it carefully over. You are an extremely attractive woman, Magdalen. I don't know what it is about you, I fail to analyse it, but one becomes attached to you. You can make even a home pleasant. And if a man once cared for you it is improbable that he would cease to care just because you are no longer young. I take my stand on the basic fact that there certainly has been a mutual attachment. I then ask myself——"

At this moment the door opened and the footman announced "Lord Lossiemouth."

The shock to both women was for the moment overwhelming.

Magdalen recovered herself almost instantaneously and welcomed him with grave courtesy, but she was unable to articulate.

He had seen the amazement in the four eyes turned on him as he came in, and cursed Colonel Bellairs in his heart. Why had not the old idiot warned Magdalen of his coming?

He had felt doubtful of his reception. A simulated coldness on Magdalen's part was, perhaps, to be expected. But for her blank astonishment he was not prepared.

"This is Bessie," she said in a shaking voice.

Bessie! This tall, splendid young woman. Could this be the tiny child of three who used to sit on his knee, and blow his watch open.

"I cannot be expected to remember you," said Bessie, advancing a limp hand. She fixed a round dispassionate eye on his heavy, irritable face, and found him unpleasant looking.

He instantly thought her odious.

And they all three sat down simultaneously as if by a preconcerted signal.

"Are you staying in the neighbourhood?" asked Magdalen, as a paralysed silence became imminent. A faint hectic colour burnt in her cheeks.

Lord Lossiemouth pulled himself together, and came to her assistance. Together they held back the silence at arm's length.

Yes, he was staying in the neighbourhood—at Lostford in fact. House property near the river. Liable to floods.

Did he mention the word floods?

Yes. Floods at certain seasons of the year. Time to take measures now before the autumn, etc.

Magdalen was glad to hear of some measures being taken. Long needed.

Yes, culpable neglect.

A wall?

Yes, a wall. Certainly a wall.

Bessie rose, marched to the door, opened it, hit her body against it, and went out.

A certain degree of constraint went with her.

"I had your Father's leave to come," he said after a moment. "I should not have ventured to do so otherwise."

"I wish Father had warned me," she said.

They looked away from each other. Here in this room fifteen years ago they had parted. Both shivered at the remembrance.

Then they looked long at each other.

Magdalen became very pale. She saw as in a glass what was passing through his mind; and for a moment her heart cried out against those treacherous deserters, her beauty and her youth, that they should have fled and left her thus, defenceless and unarmed to endure his cruel eyes. But she remembered that he had left her before they did. They had not availed to stay him. They had only slipped away from her in his wake. And at the time she had hardly noticed their departure, as he was no longer there to miss them.

Lord Lossiemouth had come determined to propose to Magdalen, his determination screwed "to the sticking point" by a deliberately recalled remembrance of the change the years had wrought in her. He had told himself he was prepared for that. Nevertheless, now that he was actually face to face with her, in spite of his regard and respect for her, a horrid chasm seemed to yawn between them, which only one primitive emotion can span, an emotion which, like a disused bridge, had fallen into the gulf years ago.

And yet how marvellously strong, how immortal it had seemed once—in this same room with this same woman. It had seemed then as if it could not break, or fall, or fade.

It had broken, it had fallen, it had faded.

As he looked earnestly at her he became aware that though she had been momentarily distressed a great serenity was habitual to her. The eyes which now met his had regained their calm. It seemed as if her life had been steeped in tranquil sunshine, as if the free air of heaven had penetrated her whole delicate being, and had left its clear fragrance with her.

Oh! if only they had been married fifteen years ago! What happiness they might have given each other. How perfect to have owed it all to each other. How fond he would still be of her. How tender their mutual regard would still be. Then his present feeling for her would not be amiss. They ought to be sitting peacefully together at this moment, not in this intolerably embarrassing personal relation towards each other, but at ease with each other, talking over their boy at Eton, and the new pony for their little daughters. He did not want to *begin* being married to her now.

She knew what he felt.

"Magdalen," he said, "I am distressed that I have taken you by surprise. I had hoped that you were prepared to see me. But my coming is not, I trust, painful to you."

A pulse fluttered in her cheek.

"I am glad to see you," she said. "If I did not seem so the first moment it was only because I was taken aback."

"A great change has come over my fortunes," he continued, anxious to give her time, and yet aware that no conversation except on the object of his visit was really possible. "I am at last in a position to marry."

"When I heard the news I thought that you would probably marry soon."

"Our engagement was broken off solely for lack of means," he continued. Her eyes dropped. "Now that that obstacle is removed I have come to ask you, to beg you most earnestly to renew it."

"It is very good of you," she said almost inaudibly. "I appreciate your—kindness."

He saw that she was going to refuse him. But he was prepared for that contingency. It was a natural feminine method of readjusting the balance between them. He would certainly give her the opportunity. He owed it to her. Besides, the refusal would not be final. He knew from her relations that she still loved him.

"If your feeling towards me is unchanged will you marry me?"

The door opened, and the footman announced "Mr. Thomson."

The new curate came slowly into the room, his short-sighted eyes peering about him, a little faggot of papers girdled by an elastic band, clasped in his careful hand against his breast.

Magdalen started violently, and Lord Lossiemouth experienced a furious exasperation.

Magdalen mechanically introduced the two men to each other, and they all three sat down, with the same sudden automatic precision as when Bessie had been present.

"The days are beginning to lengthen already," said Mr. Thomson. "I have noticed it, especially the last few days, and the rooks are clamourous—very clamourous."

"It was to be expected," faltered Magdalen.

"The accounts are, I am glad to say, in perfect order. I am proud to add, though I fear a statement so unusual may lay me open to a charge of romancing, that we have a small balance in hand."

How he had looked forward to saying these words. With what a flash of surprised delight he had expected this astounding, this gratifying announcement would be received.

He paused a moment to let his words sink in—evidently Miss Bellairs had not heard.

"Three pounds five and nine," he said.

"It is wonderful," said Magdalen emphatically.

"Quite wonderful. I never heard of a boot-and-shoe club which was not in debt. Have you?" And she turned to Lord Lossiemouth.

But Lord Lossiemouth's temper was absent. He found the situation intolerable. He only answered, "Never."

"Bessie is waiting to hear all about it in the schoolroom," continued Magdalen. "I have asked her to go over the papers with you. She will be as surprised and delighted as I am. Shall we go and tell her?"

And without waiting for an answer she rose and led the way to the schoolroom, followed by Mr. Thomson. Bessie was sitting alone there, staring in front of her, paralysed by Lord Lossiemouth's arrival, and indignant at the possibility that Magdalen might marry that "horrid old thing," who was not the least like the charming photograph of him in her sister's album. However, she grasped the situation, and after an imploring glance from Magdalen, grappled with all her might with the boot-and-shoe club.

Magdalen hurriedly tore off the little red shawl and returned to the morning-room, and closed the door. It was a considerable effort to her to close it, and by doing so to invite a renewal of Lord Lossiemouth's offer. But it could not be left open.

"It was not poor Mr. Thomson's fault," she said, "but I wish I could have saved you this annoyance."

He struggled to recover his temper. Her quivering face shewed him that she was suffering from the miserable accident of the interruption even more than he was.

"I was asking you to marry me," he said with courage, but with visible irritation. "Will you?"

"I am afraid I cannot."

"I knew you would say that. I expected it. But I beg you to reconsider it, that is if—if your feeling for me is still unchanged."

"It is unchanged."

"Then why not marry me?"

"Because you do not care for me."

"I felt certain you would say that. But I *do* care for you. Should I be here if I did not? We are two middle-aged people, Magdalen. The old raptures and roses would be out of place, but I have always cared for you. Surely you know that. Have you forgotten the old days?"

"No."

"Neither have I. All we have to do is to forget the years between." As he spoke he felt that the thing could hardly have been better put.

"I have no wish to forget them."

He had made a great effort to control his temper, but he found her unreasonable. His anger got the upper hand.

"It is one of two things that makes you refuse me. Either you can't forgive me, and I daresay I don't deserve that you should, I am not posing as a faultless character—or you have ceased to love me. Which is it?"

"I have not ceased to love you," she replied. "Have I not just told you so? But you would find yourself miserable in the—lop-sided kind of marriage which you are contemplating. It is unwise to try to make bricks without straw."

"Then if your mind was so absolutely made up beforehand to refuse me, why was I sent for?" he stammered, white with anger. He struck the table with his hand. "What was the use of urging me to come back, if I was to meet with a frigid, elegantly expressed, deliberately planned rebuff directly I set foot in the house!"

"Why were you *sent for*?" she said aghast. "Surely you came of your own accord. *Sent for! Who* sent for you?"

She sat down feebly. A horrible suspicion turned her faint.

"*Who* sent for me?" he said venomously. "Why am I here?"

He tore some letters out of his pocket, and thrust them into her hands. Always sensitive to a slight, he was infuriated by the low cunning, the desire to humiliate him, with which he imagined he had been treated. Others could be humiliated as well as himself.

"Read them," he said savagely, and he walked away from her, and stood by the window with his back to her.

Magdalen read them slowly, the three letters, her father's, Aunt Mary's, Aunt Aggie's. Then she put them back into their envelopes and wiped the sweat from her forehead.

Humiliation, shame, despair, the anguish of wounded love, she saw them creep towards her. She saw them crouch like wild beasts ready to spring, their cruel eyes upon her. She had known their fangs once. Were they to rend her again?

She sat motionless and saw them pass, as behind bars, pass quite away. They could not reach her. They could not touch her.

She looked at the lover of her youth, standing as she had so often seen him stand at that window in years gone by, with his hands behind his back, looking out to the sea.

She went softly to him, and stood beside him.

"I am more grieved that I can say about these," she said, touching the letters. "I did not know the poor dears had written. It was good of you to come back at the call of these unhappy letters. Will you not burn them, Everard, and forget them? There is a fire waiting for them."

She put them into his hand. She had not spoken to him by his Christian name before. His anger sank suddenly. He took them in a shamed silence, and dropped them into the fire. Magdalen sat down by the hearth, and he sat down near her. Together they watched them burn.

"I ought to have burnt them yesterday," he said remorsefully.

"I am glad you did not. I am so thankful to see you again, and that these foolish letters brought you. I have often longed to have a talk with you.

"It seems unreasonable," continued Magdalen, her clear eyes meeting his, "but the fact of your asking me to marry you makes it possible for me to tell you what I have long wished to tell you. I have often thought of writing it. I did write it once, but I tore it up. It seems as if a woman *can't* say certain things to a man till he has said, 'Will you marry me?' Then it is easy, because then nothing she may say can rouse a suspicion in his mind that she wants to make him say it."

"I have proposed to you twice, Magdalen. Is not that enough?" His voice was very bitter. "I venture to prophesy that you will be safe from my pestering you with a third offer."

"I am sure of it. I never dreamed that you would ask me this second time. I never thought we should meet again except by chance, as we did a year ago. But I have had you in my mind, and I have often feared—often—that I was a painful remembrance to you; that when you thought of me it was with regret that you had perhaps—it is not so easy to say after all—that you had spoilt my life."

"I did reproach myself bitterly with having made love to you when you were so very young and inexperienced, and when I ought to have remembered that I was not in a position to marry. Your father did rub that in. As if I could help my poverty."

"Father is not a reasonable person. You were nearly as young as I was. Looking back now it seems as if we had both been almost children."

"It was a great misfortune for both of us," he said, colouring. He had not felt it great after the first.

"Not for me," she said. "That is what I have long wished to tell you. It has been my great good fortune. Not at first—but after a time. I should never have known love—of that I am sure—unless it had been for you. You were the only person who could waken it in me. The power to love is the great gift; to be permitted to know that marvel, to be allowed once in one's life to touch the infinite. Love opens all the doors. Some opened in pain, but they did open. I never knew, I never guessed until long after you had come into my life, and gone away again, how much I owed to you. Then I began to see, first in gleams, and then plainly. Your momentary attraction towards me was a tiny spark of the Divine love, a sort of little lantern leading me home through the dark."

He stared at her amazed. Her transparency transfixed him. What is superficial is also often deep in clear natures such as Magdalen's, like a water lily whose stem goes down a long way.

"Love releases us from ourselves, our hard proud selves, and makes everything possible to flow in to us, happiness, peace, joy, gratitude. I thank God for having let me know you, for having made me love you. I might have missed it. I see others miss it. I might have gone through life not knowing. I might have had to bear the burden of life, without the one thing that makes it easy. I see other people toiling and moiling, and getting hopeless and miserable and exhausted till my heart aches for them. After the first I have never toiled, never grieved, never despaired. I have been sustained always. For there are not two kinds of love, Everard, but only one. The love of you is the cup of water, and the love of God is the well it is taken from.... You had better go now before anyone else comes in, but I want you to remember when you think of me that I bless and thank you, and am grateful to you. I have been grateful for years."

She took his leaden hand in both of hers, and held it for a moment to her lips.

Lord Lossiemouth's face was pinched and aged. His hand fell out of hers.

Then his face became suddenly convulsed, frightful to behold, like that of a man being squeezed to death.

"I never loved you," he said in a fierce, suffocated voice. "I was a little in love with you, that was all, and that was not much. I soon got over it."

"I know," she said.

"I felt pain for a time. You were very beautiful, and you were the first. I was the same as you then. But I found other beautiful women. I took what I could get out of life, and out of women. I rubbed out my pain that way. It was not your father who parted us, it was myself. I would not own it, I was always bitter against him, but it was my fault. I did not mean to work, and tie myself to an office stool: I had the chance, but I wanted to travel and see the world. It was not lack of means that parted us. I said a few minutes ago that it had been the only obstacle to our marriage, and your eyes dropped. You have known better all the time, but you wouldn't say. All these years I have put it down to that. But it was *not*. We were parted by lack of love."

"I know," she said again.

"On my side."

"It was not your fault. We can't love to order, or by our own will. It is a gift."

"Some of us can't love at all," he said fiercely. "That is about it. We have not got any room for it if—if it *is* given us. It could not get a foothold. It was crowded out. I was often glad afterwards that I did not tie myself to you. *Glad!* Do you hear, Magdalen? It left me free to—it did give me pain when I thought of you. I knew what I had done to you. I used to tell myself that you gave me up very easily, that you did not really want me. But I knew in my heart that you did. But it only made me bitter, and I put the thought away. That time, it is ten years ago; good God! it is all so long ago, when you nearly died of scarlet fever in London, I heard of it by chance when you were at your worst, I was shocked, but I did not really care, for I had long ceased to want you. I used to visit a certain woman every day in that street, and I once asked her who the straw was down for, and she said it was for a 'Miss Magdalen Bellairs.' I was in love with her at the moment, if you can call it love. I have dragged myself through all kinds of sordid passions since—we parted."

Tears of rage stood in his eyes. He looked at her through them. It seemed as if no wounding word under heaven would be left to say by the time he had finished.

"And I did not come back in order to make amends," he went on. "You know me very little if you think that. I came back solely out of pique. It was not those absurd letters which brought me, or held me back. It was another woman. I wanted to pay her out."

"I thought perhaps it was something like that," said Magdalen.

"It was a virtuous attachment this time. I am nearly forty. I am getting grey and stout. Young women have a difficulty in perceiving my existence. It was high time to settle, and to live on some attractive woman's money. There are thousands of women who must marry someone. So why not me? I found the attractive woman. I walked into love with her," he stammered with anger. "I regarded it as a constitutional. But the attractive woman, though she liked me a little, weighed the pros and cons exactly as I had done, and decided not to take her constitutional in my impecunious company. She refused me when I was poor, and *now*—now that I am rich—she is willing."

The harsh voice ceased suddenly. Magdalen looked for a moment at the savage, self-tortured face, and her heart bled.

"That is how I have treated you," he said, choking with passion. "Now you know the truth of me—for the first time. That is the kind of man I am, hard and vindictive and selfish to the core: the man whom you have idealised, whom you have put on a pedestal all these years."

"I have known always the kind of man you were," she said steadily. "I never idealised you, as you call it. I loved you knowing the worst of you. Otherwise my love could not have endured through. A foolish idealism would have perished long ago."

"And then I come down here, on a sudden despicable impulse, intending to use you as a weapon to strike her with, not that she is worth striking, poor feeble pretty toy. And I encouraged myself in a thin streak of patronising sentiment for you. I wrote a little cursed sonnet in the train how old affection outlasts youthful passion, like violets blooming in autumn. How loathsome! How incredibly base! And then, when my temper is aroused by your opposition, I am dastardly enough, heartless enough to try to humiliate you by shewing you those letters, to try to revenge myself on you. On you, Magdalen! On you! On you!"

She did not speak nor move. Her face was awed, as the face of one who watches beside the pangs of death or—birth.

Outside in the amber sunset a thrush piped.

"Magdalen," he said almost inarticulately, "you have never repulsed me. Don't repulse me now, for I am very miserable. Don't pour your love into the sand any more. Give it me instead. I am dying of thirst. Give me to drink. You can live without me, but I can't live without you. I have tried—I have tried everything. I am not thinking of you, only of myself. I am only asking for myself, only impelled towards you by my own needs. Does not that prove to you that I am at last speaking the truth? Does not that force you to believe me when I tell you that I want you more than anything in the world. I have wanted you all my life without knowing it. I don't want to make amends to you for the past. I want you yourself, for myself, as my wife. I swear to God if you won't marry me I will marry no one. You are the only woman I can speak to, the only one who does not fail, who holds on through thick and thin, the only one who has ever really wanted me. I daresay I shan't make you happy. I daresay I shall break your heart. God help me, I daresay I shall put my convenience before your happiness, my selfish whims before your health. I have always put myself first. But risk it. Risk it, Magdalen. Take me back. Love me. For God's sake marry me."

Each looked into the other's bared soul.

Something in his desperate face which she had always sought for, which had always been missing from it—she found.

"I will," she said.

They made no movement towards each other. They had reached a spiritual nearness, a passion of surrender each to each, which touch of hand or lip could only at that moment have served to lessen.

"You are not taking me out of pity? You are sure you can still love me a little?"

"More than in the early days," she said. "For you have not only come to me, Everard. You have come to yourself."

CHAPTER XXIX

Me, too, with mastering charm
From husks of dead days freeing, The sun draws up to be warm
And to bloom in this sweet hour. The stem of all my being Waited to bear this flower.

—LAURENCE BINYON.

It would be hardly possible to describe the unholy, the unmeasured rejoicing to which Magdalen's engagement gave rise in her family. It is, perhaps, enough to say that the twenty years of her cheerful, selfless devotion to the domestic hearth had never won from her father and her two aunts anything like the admiring approval which her engagement at once elicited. The neighbourhood was interested. Lord Lossiemouth was a brilliant match for anyone (if you left out the man himself). The announcement read impressively in the *Morning Post.* The neighbours remembered that there had been a youthful attachment, an early engagement broken off owing to lack of means. And now it seemed the moment he was rich he had come flying back to cast his faithful heart once more at her feet. It was a real romance. Magdalen was considered an extraordinarily fortunate woman by the whole countryside, but Lord Lossiemouth was placed on a pedestal. What touching constancy. What beautiful fidelity. What a contrast to "most men." "Not one man in a hundred would have acted in that chivalrous manner," was the feminine verdict of Hampshire.

A wave of cheap sentiment overflowed the Bellairs family, in which Colonel Bellairs floated complacently like a piece of loose seaweed, and in which even Aunt Mary underwent a dignified undulation.

Bessie alone was unmoved.

"You said, 'Yes' too soon," she remarked to Magdalen in private. "I should never have thought you would be so lacking in true dignity. He goes away for fifteen years and I should not wonder a bit if he had thought of someone else in the interim for all you know to the contrary—men are like that—and then he just lounges in and says 'Marry me,' and you agree in a second. You might at any rate have made him wait for his answer till after tea. In my opinion you have made yourself cheap by such precipitate action. He thinks he has only got to ask, and he can have."

Magdalen did not answer.

"I don't understand you," continued the pained monitor. "I have always had a certain respect for you, Magdalen, and when he came back I supposed you would give in to him in time if he pressed you without intermission, and was constant for a considerable period—say a couple of years; but I never thought it possible you would collapse like this. I fear you have not taken his character sufficiently into consideration. If I were in your place I should be afraid that Everard would not allow my nature free scope, or take an interest in my mental development, and that the sacrifices which make domestic life tolerable might have to be all on my side. He is absolutely unworthy of you, and his nose is quite thick. I daresay you have not remarked it, but I did at once. And in my opinion he ought for his own good to have been made to *realise* it. Even Aunt Mary, though she says she entirely approves of the marriage, admits that you have shown too much eagerness."

Fortunately for Magdalen the interest of the neighbours, and even of her own family, was speedily diverted to another channel by the return of Wentworth and Michael to Barford. The enthusiastic welcome which Michael received from all classes, and from distant families who had never evinced much cordiality to his elder brother, astonished Wentworth, touched him to the quick.

"I had no idea we had so many friends," he said repeatedly.

Michael smiled vaguely and took everything for granted. Wentworth was so anxious to shield him from fatigue and excitement that at first he was only too thankful that Michael took everything so quietly. But after a few days he became uneasy at his brother's inertness of mind and body. A great doctor, however, explained Michael's state very much as the Italian doctor had done. He was in an exhausted condition. What was essential to him was rest. He must not be made to see anyone or do anything he did not like.

"Your brother will regain his health entirely," the great man had said, "if he is left in peace, and nothing happens to overexcite him. He is worn to a shadow by that accursed prison. Many men in his condition can't rest. Then they die. He can. He has the temperament that acquiesces. He will cure himself if he is left alone. Let him lie in the sun, and give nature a chance."

In spite of his anxiety Wentworth saw that Michael's bodily strength was slowly returning. Every afternoon he left him half asleep in the sun, and rode over to see Fay. Since she had accepted him it had become a necessity to him to see her every day.

Wentworth had long been bent to the dust under the pain of Michael's imprisonment. Fay had been bent with anguish to the dust by the weight of her own silence which had kept him there.

And now in the twinkling of an eye they both stood erect, freed. Life was transfigured for both at the same instant.

This marvellous moment found them both just when they were deciding mildly to love each other. It took them and flung them together in a common overwhelming joy. It almost seemed as if the shock might make a man of Wentworth.

Did he half know (he was certainly always tacitly guarding himself against the assumption of such an idea in the minds of others) that he had so far been left out, not only from the whirl of life—he had deliberately withdrawn from that—but from the weft of life itself. The great loom had not swept him in. It had not appeared to need him. Some of us seem to hang on the fringe of life, of thought, of love, of everything. We are not for good or ill interwoven into the stuff, part of the pattern.

Wentworth felt young for the first time in his life, happy for the first time in his life, really energetic for the first time. A certain languid fatigue which had been with him from boyhood, which had always lain mournfully on its back waving its legs in the air like a reversed beetle, had now been jolted right side upper-most, and was using those legs, not as proofs of the emptiness of the world, but as a means of locomotion.

He had at first been enormously raised in his own self-esteem by his engagement to a young and beautiful woman. He was permanently relieved from the necessity of accounting to his friends for the fact that he was still unmarried, reminding them that it was his own fault. Perhaps at the bottom of his heart a fear lurked, implanted by the brutal Grenfell, that he was going to be an old maid. That fear was now dispelled. It was mercifully hidden from Wentworth that Grenfell and the Bishop and most of his so-called friends would still so regard him even if he were married.

But gradually and insensibly the many petty reasons for satisfaction which his engagement to Fay had given him, and even the delight in being loved, were overshadowed by a greater presence.

At first they had never been silent together. Wentworth liked to hear his own voice, and prosed stolidly on for hours with exquisite enjoyment and an eye to Fay's education at the same time, about his plans, his aspirations, his past life (not that he had had one), the hollowness of society (not that he knew anything about it), a man's need of solitude, and the solace of a woman's devotion, its softening effect on a life devoted hitherto, perhaps, too entirely to intellectual pursuits.

Fay did not listen to him very closely. She felt that his mind soared beyond her ken. But she was greatly impressed, and repeated little bits of what he had said to Magdalen afterwards. And she looked at him with rapt adoration.

"Wentworth says that consideration in little things is what makes the happiness of married life," she would announce pontifically.

"How true!"

"And he says social life ought to be simplified."

"Indeed! Does he happen to mention how it is to be done?"

"He says it ought to be regulated, and that everyone ought to be at liberty to lead their own life, and not to be expected to attend cricket matches and garden parties, if you are so constituted that you don't find pleasure in them. I used to think I liked garden parties, Magdalen, but I see I don't now. I care more for the big things of life now. Does Everard ever talk to you like that when you and he are alone?"

"Never. Never."

"And Andrea never did, either. Wentworth is simply wonderful. You should hear him speak about fame being shallow, and how the quiet mind looking at things truly is everything, and peace not being to be found in the market place, but in a walk by a stream, and how in his eyes a woman's love outweighs the idle glitter of a social success. Oh! Magdalen, I'm beginning to feel I'm not worthy of Wentworth. I've always liked being admired, so different from him. I did not know there were men so high-minded as he. He makes me feel very petty beside him. And he is so humble. He says I must not idealise him, that he does not *wish* it, for though he may not be worse or better than I think he is only too conscious of his many deficiencies. But I can't help it. Who could?"

And Fay let fall a tear.

"We needs must love the highest when we see it."

But the highest some of us can see is the nearest molehill.

What Michael and the Duke had failed to do for Fay Wentworth was accomplishing.

"You are made for each other," said Magdalen, with conviction. "Every day shows me that you and Wentworth bring out the best in each other. Perhaps, gradually, you will keep nothing back from each other, tell each other everything."

"He tells me everything now," said Fay. "He trusts me entirely."

"And you?" said Magdalen. "Do you tell him everything?"

Wentworth, too, had reached the conviction that he and Fay were made for each other. He might have starved out the deeper love, the truth and tenderness of a sincerer nature, if it had been drawn towards him. He had often imagined himself as being the recipient of the lavished devotion of a woman beautiful, humble, exquisite and noble, whose truth was truth itself, and had vaguely wondered why she had not come into his life. But perhaps if he had met such a woman, and if she had loved him as he pined to be loved, he would have become suspicious of her, and would have left her after many vacillations. He did not instinctively recognise humility and nobility when he met them, because they bore but slight resemblance to the stiff lay figures which represented those qualities in his mind. To meet them in reality would have been to him bewilderment, disappointment, disillusion.

Fay was not only what he seemed to want, what he had feebly longed for. She was more than this. Her nature was the complement of his. A lack of shrewdness, of mental grasp, a certain silliness were absolutely essential to the maintenance of a lifelong devotion to him. Wentworth had found the right woman to give him what he wanted. Fay had found the right man.

Love, which had been knocking urgently at their doors for so many futile years, heard at last a movement as of someone stirring within, and a hand upon the disused latch.

CHAPTER XXX

O Yanna, Adrianna,
They buried me away In the blue fathoms of the deep,
Beyond the outer bay.

But in the Yule, O Yanna,
Up from the round dim sea And reeling dungeons of the fog
I am come back to thee!

—BLISS CARMAN.

Wentworth stood at the open window of the library watching Michael.

Michael was lying on a deck chair on the terrace playing with a puppy. His face was losing a certain grey drawn look which it had worn since he had left prison. He looked more like himself since his hair had time to grow. Wentworth felt that he ought to be reassured about him, but a vague anxiety harassed him.

Suddenly, without a moment's warning, the puppy fell asleep. Michael made a movement to reach it, but it was just beyond his grasp.

In an instant Wentworth was beside him, lifting the sleeping mass of sleek fat on to Michael's knee. Michael's long hands made a little crib for it.

"He will sleep now for a bit," he said contentedly.

"Do *you* sleep better?" said Wentworth. He had not forgotten those first nights at Venice when Michael's feeble step had dragged itself to and fro in the next room half the night.

"I sleep like a top. I'm asleep half the time."

"You are much better the last few days."

"Oh! I'm all right."

"All Hampshire has been to call. I knew you would be bored, so I did not let them disturb you."

"Thanks."

"Is there anyone you would like to see?"

"No one that I know of."

"No one at *all*?"

Michael made a mental effort which did not escape Wentworth.

"I should like very much to see—presently—if it could be done——"

"Yes," said Wentworth eagerly. "Of *course* it can be done, my dear boy. You would like to see?"

"Doctor Filippi," said Michael, looking deprecatingly at Wentworth. "He was so good to me. And I am accustomed to seeing him. I miss him all the time. I wonder whether you would let him come and stay here for his holiday. He generally takes it in June. And—let me see—it's May now, isn't it?"

Wentworth's heart swelled with jealousy and disappointment. The jealousy was of the doctor, the disappointment was about Fay. The larger of the two emotions was jealousy.

"You have sent Doctor Filippi a very handsome present," he said coldly. "I chose it for you, a silver salver. I went up to London on purpose at your wish a week ago."

"Y-yes."

"And I don't think he would care to come here. No doubt he has his own friends. You must remember a man like that is poor. It would be putting him to expense."

Michael looked down at the sleeping puppy. He did not answer.

Wentworth was beginning to fear that his brother had an ungrateful, callous nature. Was Michael so self-absorbed—egotism revolted Wentworth—that he would *never* ask to see Wentworth's future wife, the woman who had shown such unceasing, such tender interest in Michael himself.

"I hoped there was someone else, someone very dear to me, and a devoted friend of yours, whom you might like to see again."

Wentworth spoke with deliberation.

"I could send him a cheque. He need not be at any expense," said Michael in a low voice. His exhausted mind, slower to move than ever, had not left the subject of Doctor Filippi. His brother's last remark had not penetrated to it.

Wentworth became scarlet. He made an impatient movement. Then part of the sense of his brother's last words tardily reached Michael's blurred faculties.

"An old friend of mine," he said, vaguely flurried. "What old friend?"

"Fay," said Wentworth, biting his lip. "Have you forgotten Fay *entirely*? How she tried to save you, how she grieved for you? Her great goodness to you? And what she is to *me*!"

"No," said Michael. "No. I don't forget. Her goodness to me. How she tried to save me. Just so. Just so. I don't forget."

"Won't you see her? She and Magdalen are driving over here this morning. You need not see Magdalen unless you like."

"I should like. She is going to be married, too, isn't she? I feel as if I had heard someone say so."

"Yes, to Lossiemouth. You remember him as Everard Constable, a touchy, ill-conditioned, cantankerous brute if ever there was one, who does not care a straw for anyone but himself. I can't think what she sees in him. But an Earl's an Earl. I always forget that. I have lived so much apart from the world and its sordid motives and love of wealth and rank that it is always a shock and a surprise when I come in contact with its way of looking at things. I never liked Magdalen. I always considered her superficial. But I never thought her mercenary—till now. But Fay——"

"I will see her, too," said Michael. "Yes, of course. I somehow thought of Fay as—as—but my mind gets so confused—as at a great distance, quite removed all this time. Hundreds and hundreds of miles away in England. Left Italy for good."

"My dear boy, she is living at Priesthope, four miles off. I've told you so over and over again. I go and see her every day."

"Yes, at Priesthope, of course. Four miles. I know the way. You can go by Wind Farm, or Pilgrim Road. You did tell me. More cheerful as time passes on."

Wentworth looked with perplexity at Michael's thin profile. The doctor had most solemnly assured him that his mind was only muffled and deadened by his physical weakness. But it sometimes seemed to Wentworth as if his brother's brain were softening.

He felt a sudden return of the blind despairing rage which was wont to grip him after his visits to Michael in prison. This inert, cold-blooded shadow; was this all that was left of his brother?

A great tenderness welled up in his heart, the old, old protective tenderness of many years. He put his strong brown hand on his brother's emaciated, once beautiful hand, now disfigured by coarse labour, and scarred and discoloured at the wrist.

"Get well, Michael," he said huskily.

Michael's hand trembled a little, seemed to shrink involuntarily.

Then a servant appeared suddenly, coming towards them across the grass, and Wentworth took back his hand instantly.

"The Duchess of Colle Alto and Miss Bellairs are in the library."

"Are you quite sure that you *really* wish to see them—that it will not tire you?" said Wentworth.

"Quite sure."

"I will bring them out."

"No. Send one at a time. Fay first."

Michael lay back and closed his eyes.

On this May morning as Fay and Magdalen drove together to Barford, Magdalen looked at her sister's radiant face, not with astonishment, she had got over that, but with something more like fear.

The happiness of some natures terrifies those who love them by its appearance of brittleness. To Magdalen Fay's present joy seemed like a bit of Venetian glass on the extreme edge of a cabinet at a child's elbow.

It is difficult for those who have imagination to understand the *insouciance* which looks so like heartlessness of the unimaginative. The inevitable meeting with Michael seemed to cast no shadow on Fay's spirits; Wentworth's ignorance of certain sinister facts did not seem to disturb her growing love for him.

Their way lay through a pine wood under the shoulder of the down. The whortleberry with its tiny foliage made a miniature forest of pale golden green at the feet of the dark serried trunks of the pines.

Small yellow butterflies hovered amid the topmost branches of this underfoot forest.

Fay leaned out of the pony carriage and picked from the high bank a spray of whortleberry with a butterfly poised on it.

"I thought for one minute I might find a tiny, tiny butterfly nest with eggs in it," she said. "I do wish butterflies had nests like birds, Magdalen, don't you? But this is a new butterfly, not ready to fly. I shall hurt it unless I'm careful."

She made her sister stop the pony, and knelt down amid the shimmering whortleberry, and tenderly placed the sprig with the butterfly still clinging to it in a little pool of sunshine. But as she did it the butterfly walked from its twig on to her white hand and rested on it, opening and shutting its wings.

It was a pretty sight to watch Fay coax it to a leaf. But Magdalen's heart ached for her sister as she knelt in the sunshine. Words rose to her lips for the twentieth time, but she choked them down again. What use, what use to warn those who cannot be warned, to appeal to deaf ears, to point out to holden eyes the things that belong to their peace?

The vision is the claim, but it must be our own eyes that see it. We may not look at our spiritual life through another man's eyes.

As Magdalen waited her eyes wandered to the blue haze between the tree trunks which was the sea, and marked a white band like a ribbon between the blue and the fields. That was a piece of land newly reclaimed from the sea. When a tract of land is thus captured, the first year that it is laid open to the ministry of sun and air and rain it bears an overflowing crop of white clover. The clover seed has lain dormant, perhaps a thousand years under the wash of the wave. The first spring tide after the sea is withdrawn it wakes and rushes up. It was so now in that little walled-in tract by the shore, where she had walked but yesterday. Surely it was to be so in Fay's heart, now that the bitter tides of remorse and selfishness were ceasing to submerge it, now that at last joy and tenderness were reaching it. Surely, love itself, the seeds of which lie dormant in every heart, love like a marvellous tide of white clover, was finding its chance at last, and would presently inundate her heart.

Then, unharassed, undelayed by vain words and futile appeals from without—all would go well.

At the last moment when the meeting with Michael was really imminent Fay's *insouciance* began, as Magdalen feared it might, to show signs of collapse. It deserted her entirely as they drove up to Barford.

"Come out with me," she whispered in sudden panic, plucking at her sister's gown, when Wentworth asked her to go and speak to Michael for a few minutes in the garden. But Magdalen had drawn back gravely and resolutely, and had engaged Wentworth's attention, and Fay had been obliged to go alone across the lawn, in the direction of the deck chair.

Her step, lagging and irresolute, was hardly audible on the grass, but Michael heard it, recognised it. We never forget the footfall, however light, that has trodden on our heart.

The footfall stopped and he opened his eyes.

Fay was standing before him.

And so they met again at last, those two who had been lovers once. She looked long at the man she had broken. He was worn down to the last verge of exhaustion, barely more than a shadow in the suave sunshine. She would hardly have recognised him if it had not been for the tranquil steady eyes, and the grave smile. They were all that was left of him, of the Michael she had known. The rest was unfamiliar, repellant. And his hands! His hands were dreadful. Oh! if only she had known he was going to look like that she would never have come. Never, never! Fay experienced the same unspeakable horror and repugnance as if, walking in long, daisy-starred grass, she had suddenly stumbled against and nearly fallen over a dead body.

The colour ebbed out of her face and lips. She stood before him without a word, shrinking, transfixed.

He looked long at her, the woman for whom he had been content to suffer, that he might keep suffering from her. Fay's self torture, her protracted anguish, her coward misery, these were written as it were anew in her pallid face. They had been partially effaced during the heedless happiness of the last few weeks, but the sudden shock of Michael's presence drew in again afresh with a cruel pencil the haggard lines of remorse and despair.

He had not been able to shield her from pain after all.

"Oh, Fay!" he said below his breath. "How you have suffered."

"No one knows what it has been," she said hoarsely, sinking into a chair, trembling too much to stand. "I could not live through it again. I couldn't bear it, and I had to bear it."

"You will never have to bear it again," he said with compassion. "It is over and done with. You are going to be happy now."

"You have suffered too," she said, reddening.

"Not like you. It has been worst for you. I never guessed that you had felt my imprisonment so much as I see now by your face you have."

"Not have felt it! Not have suffered from it!" said Fay, amazed. "Michael, how could I help grieving day and night over it?"

The question almost rose to his lips, "Why then did you not release me?" But the words were not spoken. There is one pain which we need not bear, but which some of us never rest till we have drawn it upon ourselves, that of extorting from the one we love vain excuses, unconscious lies, feeble, inadequate explanations that explain nothing. Let be. The excuses, the lies, these shadows of the mind will vanish the moment Love lights his lamp.

Till then their ghost-like presence, their semblance of reality but show that the chamber of the Beloved is dark.

Michael was silent. Though his body and mind were half dead, his spirit was alive and clear, moving swiftly where the spent mind could not follow.

"How could I help breaking my heart over the thought of you in prison?" said Fay again, wounded to the quick.

She stared at him, indignant tears smarting in her eyes. Another long look passed between them, on her side bewildered, pained, aghast at being so misunderstood, on his penetrating, melancholy, full of compassionate insight, that look which seems to herald the parting between two unequal natures, but which is in reality a perception that they have never met.

"I knew you would rejoice when I was set free," he said tranquilly, smiling at her. "Ah! Here are Magdalen and Wentworth. How radiant she looks!"

When Magdalen and Fay had departed, and Wentworth had seen them to the carriage, he came back and sat down by Michael.

"Not over-tired?" he said, smiling self-consciously, and poking holes in the turf with his stick.

"Not in the least."

"She was looking a little pale to-day." It was obvious that he wished to talk about Fay.

"She is more beautiful than ever," said Michael, willing to give his brother a leg-up.

"Isn't she!" said the affianced lover expansively. "But it isn't her beauty I love most, it is her *character*. She is so feminine, so receptive, so appreciative of the deeper side of life, so absolutely devoted. Her heart has been awakened for the first time, Michael. She has, I feel sure, never been loved before as I loved her."

"I imagine not."

"I can't believe she ever cared for the Duke. I saw him once, and he gave me the impression of a very cold-blooded individual."

"I don't think he was cold-blooded."

"Evidently not the kind of man capable of drawing the best out of a woman like Fay."

"Perhaps not."

The man who felt himself capable of this feat prodded a daisy and then went on:

"You used to see a good deal of them in Rome before—while you were *attaché* there. Did you gather that it was a happy marriage, a true union?"

"Not very happy."

"I daresay he was selfish and inconsiderate. That is generally the crux in married life. Fay has had an overshadowed life so far, but I shall find my chief happiness in changing all that. It will be my object to guard her from the slightest touch of pain in future. The masculine impulse to shield and protect is very strongly developed in me."

"It is sometimes difficult to guard people," said Michael half to himself.

"I hope some day," Wentworth went on shyly, colouring under his tan, "your turn may come, that you may meet the right woman, and feel as I do now. It will be a revelation to you. I am afraid it may seem exaggerated in a person like myself, who am essentially a man's man. (This was a favourite illusion of Wentworth's.) But some day you will understand, and you will find as I have done that love is not just slothfully accepting a woman's slavish devotion."

"Indeed!"

"No, Michael, believe me, it is something far greater. It is living not only for self, but as for her sake. To take trouble to win the smile of one we love, to gladly forego one's momentary pleasures, one's convenience, in order to serve her. That is the best reward of life."

Michael's eyes filled with tears. He felt a hundred years older than Wentworth at that moment. A tender pained compassion welled up within him. And with it came a new protective comprehension of the man beside him who had cherished him from his childhood onwards.

He put out his hand and gripped Wentworth's.

"God bless you, Wenty," he said.

And for a moment they who were so far apart seemed very near together.

CHAPTER XXXI

She sees no tears, Or any tone
Of thy deep groan
She hears: Nor does she mind Or think on't now
That ever thou
Wast kind.

—HERRICK.

It quickly became plain to Magdalen that Fay's peace of mind had been shaken by her interview with Michael. She had vouchsafed no word concerning it on her way home. But in the days that followed she appeared ill at ease, and a vague and increasing unrest seemed to possess her. Magdalen doubted whether she had as yet asked herself what it was that was disturbing her tranquillity. But it was at any rate obvious that she shrank from seeing Michael again, and that she was at times dejected in Wentworth's presence.

Wentworth perceived the change in her, and attributed it to a most natural and pardonable jealousy of Michael to which, while he made the fullest allowance for it, he had no inclination to yield.

Michael had for a moment seemed to take more interest in life after Fay's visit, and although he had quickly relapsed into apathy Wentworth told himself that he was anxious to foster this nascent interest by another meeting between him and Fay. At the same time he desired to rehearse the part of central figure poised between two great devotions which was to be his agreeable *rôle* in the future. For Michael would of course live with them after his marriage with Fay. And if there were any ebullitions of jealousy between Fay and Michael—Wentworth dwelt with complacency on the possibility—he felt competent to deal with them with tact and magnanimity, reassuring each in turn as to their equal share in his affections.

Michael at any rate showed no disinclination to meet Fay again, and even evinced something verging on a desire to see Magdalen. And presently Wentworth arranged to drive him over to luncheon at Priesthope. Throughout life he had always liked to settle, even in the most trivial matters, what Michael should do, with whom he should associate. The situation was not new, nor was there any novelty in Michael's pliability.

But when the day came Wentworth arrived without his brother, and evidently out of temper. Magdalen asked if Michael were less well, and was curtly assured that he was steadily improving. The luncheon dragged through somehow as under a cloud. Colonel Bellairs was fortunately absent on a visit to Miss Barnett at Saundersfoot. His absence was the only silver lining to the cloud. Fay hardly spoke. Magdalen was thankful that her prickly Lord Lossiemouth had departed the day before.

After luncheon, when they were sitting on the terrace over their coffee, Bessie left them, and Magdalen was about to do the same, when Wentworth said suddenly:

"I left Michael with the Bishop of Lostford. That is why he is not here now. The Bishop is inducting the new Rector of Wrigley this afternoon, and he sent a wire this morning—he is always doing things at the last moment—he never considers others—to say that he would call at Barford on his way to see Michael. Michael is his godson, and he has always been fond of him. I left them together."

Magdalen and Fay sipped their coffee in silence.

"Michael had been as inert and apathetic as usual," continued Wentworth sullenly, "until the Bishop appeared. The Bishop took him off into the garden, though I said I did not like his going out so soon after dressing—he was only just up—and it was perfectly plain they did not want me. I believe that was why they went out. I was of no account. The Bishop has always been like that, your friend one day, and oblivious of you the next. But he and Michael seemed to have a great deal to say to each other. I watched them from the library walking up and down. Michael can walk quite well when he wants to. Then when the victoria came round—I thought he would find that less fatiguing than the dogcart—I went to tell him that it was time to start, but he only stared vaguely at me, and the Bishop took his arm and said that you must excuse him for this once, as he did not mean to let him go at that moment. So I came away without him."

"There will be many more opportunities of seeing us, and one must clutch what few chances one can of seeing the Bishop," said Magdalen.

"When I went to warn Michael that the carriage was there," continued Wentworth, "he did not see me till I was quite near—there was a bush between—and I could not help hearing him say, 'That was half an hour before I was arrested.'"

There was an uneasy silence.

"It seems," said Wentworth with exceeding bitterness, "that I have not Michael's confidence. The Bishop has it, but I, his only brother. Oh, no. He can talk to the Bishop about his imprisonment, but to me—not a word, not a single word. At first when we were together at Venice I asked him quietly about it once or twice. I asked him why he had never said a word to *me* about it at the time, why he had not confided to me at any rate that he was shielding the Marchesa, but I soon saw that the subject distressed him. He always became confused, and he never would reply. Once, since we were back at Barford, when he seemed clearer, I asked him most earnestly to tell me one thing, whether he actually witnessed the murder of the Marchese by his wife, as she supposed, and what had first put it into his head to take the blame on himself. But it seemed that any allusion to the subject exhausted and worried him. I said to him at last: 'Do you still hate talking of it as much as ever?' And he said 'yes.' I could understand that, and from that day to this I never alluded to it again. But though he won't say a word to me, it seems he can to others."

The miserable jealousy in Wentworth's face touched Magdalen.

"He knew you had strained every nerve to save him," said Wentworth, turning to Fay. "Has he ever shown his gratitude for what you tried to do for him?"

"N-no," stammered Fay.

"His imprisonment has changed his nature, that is what it is. He went in alive, and he has come out dead. He has ceased to care for anything or anyone. He has been killed by inches. He was so affectionate as a boy. I was father and mother to him. He used to trot after me like a little dog. And if anyone had his whole confidence I had. I was everything to him. My one fear of marrying has always been that he might feel pained at seeing another person first with me." (Wentworth had never had this altruistic misgiving, but he stated it with conviction.) "But now he is not the same. I suppose he still has some affection for me. He shows it sometimes by a kind of effort. He seemed to wake up a bit after you came over, Fay. I think he had a sort of glimpse from things I said to him of what love can be, and just for a moment he was more like his old self, and appeared to enter into my feelings. But he soon sank back again. As often as not he seems to shrink from any real conversation. We sometimes sit whole evenings together without speaking. He does not really want me any more, or anyone. He talked at first a little about the Italian doctor, but he never mentions him now. And as for my marriage, as for being distressed by my caring for someone else," resentfully, "he is absolutely indifferent. You would think that Fay and I, the two people of all others who have done most for him, who have grieved most over him, who have shown him most affection, were nothing to him."

There was a ghastly silence.

"I don't blame him," said Wentworth with something nearer passion than he had ever experienced before, in which even his petty jealousy was momentarily extinguished. "At least, I can't look at him and remain angry with him. It breaks my heart to see him like this, so callous, so regardless of all I have suffered on his account. I don't blame him. He is not himself. His brain is weakened by his poor body. No. The person I do blame is that accursed woman who allowed him to suffer for her, who skulked behind him for two endless years, who let him sacrifice his life for hers, who never had the courage to say the word, and take her crime upon herself, and get him out of his living grave."

Fay became cold as death in the May sunshine. What ghost was this which was taking form before her? What voice was this, how could it be Wentworth's voice, which was saying at last aloud with passion what that other accusing voice within had so hoarsely, so persistently whispered from its cell, during the long years? Her brain reeled.

"The Marchesa did repent," said Magdalen.

Wentworth laughed harshly.

"Oh, yes. On her deathbed, in order to save her soul. She wanted to be right with the next world. But how could she go on, year in year out, letting him burn and freeze alternately in that vile cell? She must have known, someone must have told her, what his life was like. How well I remember, Fay, your saying: 'Why does not the real murderer confess? How can he go on letting an innocent man wear out his life in prison, bearing the punishment of his horrible crime?' How little we both knew. I always supposed the assassin was a man, a common criminal of the lowest order. Yet it seems there are women in the world, educated, refined women, who can remorselessly pinch a man's life out of him with their white hands. The Marchesa has murdered two people, first her husband, and then my boy, my foolish, quixotic, generous Michael. May God forgive her! I never will!"

CHAPTER XXXII

But one man loved the pilgrim soul in you.

—W. B. YEATS.

Je veux aimer, mais je ne veux pas souffrir.

—A. DE MUSSET.

In the days that followed the Bishop's visit Michael's mind showed signs of reasserting itself. He was as quickly exhausted as ever, and with fatigue came the old apathy and helpless confusion of ideas. But his languid intelligence had intervals of increasing clearness. His face took on at these times a strained expression, as if he dimly saw something with which he felt powerless to cope. We see such a look sometimes, very piteous in its impotence, in the faces of the old, when an echo reaches them of the anguish of the world in which they once lived, which they have well nigh forgotten.

Michael's body, which had so far profited by the inertness of his faculties, resented the change, and gave unmistakable signs of relinquishing the slight degree of strength it had regained.

Wentworth became suddenly frantically anxious once more, and in a moment the wrongs on which he was brooding were forgotten. He decided to go to London the same day under the guise of business, and to consult the great doctor privately about Michael, perhaps arrange to bring him back with him.

"I wish you would drive oftener," he said to Michael before he left. "It's much better for you than walking up and down. Why not, if you feel inclined, as you will be alone all day, drive over to Priesthope this afternoon. I said you would come the first day you could. It's only four miles, just an easy little drive."

An indefinable change passed over Michael's vacant face at the mention of Priesthope. His eyes became fixed. He looked gravely at his brother, as if the latter had solved some difficult problem.

"It's a good idea," he said slowly. "I ought to have gone before, but——"

"The Bishop stopped you most inconsiderately last time."

"Did he? I don't remember being stopped. Oh! yes, yes, I do. But if I *had* gone that day—— But anyhow I will go to-day."

Fay was sitting alone in the morning-room at Priesthope, pretending to read, when Michael was announced.

When he had been conveyed to a chair and had overcome the breathlessness and semi-blindness that any exertion caused him he saw that she looked ill, and as if she had not slept.

"I ought to have come before," he said mechanically, making a great mental effort and putting his hand to his head. "I meant to come, but——" he looked hopelessly at her. He had evidently forgotten what he intended to say.

"The day you were coming with Wentworth the Bishop stopped you," said Fay drearily. Every word that Wentworth had said that afternoon was still echoing discordantly in her brain.

"That's it. The Bishop," said Michael with relief. "He told me, we had a long talk"—his mind was clearing rapidly—"how you meant to save me."

"Yes, I meant to do it," said Fay, looking at him with miserable eyes. "But the Marchesa, the same day—it was in the papers."

"I know, I know. The Bishop told me. He said I ought to know that you had been willing to make the sacrifice. I have come to thank you, Fay, and to ask you to forgive me for misjudging you. You see I was not aware you—had thought of it."

"It's for you to forgive me, Michael, not me you. And you don't bear me a grudge, do you? I somehow don't feel as if you did. And—oh, Michael, you never, never will say anything or do anything, will you—you *could*, you know—to stop my marrying Wentworth?"

Michael's eyes turned on her almost with scorn.

"When first we met again, that second time in Italy," he said gently, "do you remember it by the tomb in the gardens? There were roses all over it. I never saw such roses. Perhaps there were none like them. Then I had no faintest thought or hope of marrying you, though I had not forgotten you, Fay. I had put it all away, buried it. You were another man's wife. Now that we meet again—*the position is the same.*"

Fay looked at Michael.

The impersonal detached look which she had set herself to extinguish that day amid the roses, which had been in his face when she saw him first as a lad, which she had *twice* extinguished, was in his eyes again. There was no pain in them now, any more than there had been when they leaned together beside the tomb: only the shadow of something exceeding sharp, endured, accepted, outlived. Michael looked through her, beyond her.

"And yet the position is not quite the same," he said tranquilly, "for then you were married to a man you did not love, and now you are to marry a man you—Oh! Fay, you *do* care for Wentworth, don't you?"

"I would not have kept *him* in prison for a day," she said, and hid her face in her hands.

If only it might have been Wentworth who had sacrificed himself for her with what desperate rapidity she would have rescued him. How calm her agonised heart would be now. Fay was beginning to learn that it is ill to take a service save from the hand we love. And perhaps, too, in her heart she knew that Wentworth would never have sacrificed himself for her, for Michael possibly, but not for her.

"Wentworth is worth caring for," said Michael. "Not worth caring for in part, a bit here and a bit there, who is? but worth caring for *altogether*. I have loved him all my life. I love him more than anyone in the world. You asked me just now not to say anything to stop his marrying you. But that is just what I've come about. I am so afraid of his marriage with you being stopped."

Fay raised her face out of her hands, and stared at him.

"It's the only thing I've ever known him really wish for, almost keen about. He can't care much about things, not as other men care. He has always waited to see whether things will come to him of themselves, and then if they didn't he thought it was a wise Providence taking them away, showing him the vanity of setting his heart on anything, while all the time it's his own nature really that makes things somehow slip away from him. People slip away from him. I've seen it happen over and over again. He can't take hold like other men. He does not put himself out for any one, you know, and he doesn't realise that other people *do*; he has no idea how men like the Bishop and Grenfell and the Archbishop stand by each other, and hold together through thick and thin. Wentworth has no friends, but he doesn't know it. He has only you and me. The Bishop said we must remember that, and that if—anything happened to shake his—his feeling for either of us, his belief in either of us, it would be cruelly hard on him."

"Why should anything happen," said Fay faintly, "if you don't tell him?"

"I shan't tell him on purpose, you may be sure of that, but since—since the Bishop came over I'm certain he suspects something, I don't know what, and I have to be careful all the time. Fay, I've grown so stupid and muddle-headed since I've been in—in *Italy* that I *can't* remember what I may say and what I mayn't about that time. My only safety is in absolute silence, and lately that has begun to vex him. And he asks such odd questions, which I don't see the meaning of at first, like traps. He often tells me he never asks any questions, but he does, indirect ones, all the time. I'm getting afraid of being alone with him. Sometimes I think if I stay much longer at Barford I'm so idiotic he'll get it out of me. Has he asked you any leading questions?"

"No. Once he asked if you showed any gratitude for what I had done for you in the past. And I said no. It was the first time I had told him a lie, for it was a lie except in the actual words."

"Aren't you afraid," said Michael gently, "that it may not be the only one, that perhaps there may be some more?"

There was a long pause.

"I think Wentworth will find out some day," he went on. "I'm *sure* he will. Then, Fay, it might be too late for you and me to save him from a great pain. He might feel that we had both betrayed him."

Fay turned her quivering face towards him.

"Oh, no. I haven't done that. It's you I betrayed, Michael. I'm so thankful it was *you*, and not him."

"I was yours to keep or to throw away. You could do what you liked with your own. But it is not the same for Wentworth. Wentworth belongs—to *himself*."

In her heart she knew it. Love had shown even her certain things about the man she loved.

"And I am afraid he might feel it if he found out that you had let me stay—in Italy."

"I'd give anything I have," she said with a sob; "I'd give both my hands, I'd give my being pretty, which I think so much of, and he thinks so much of, I'd give anything if only I had not—done that, if I could only undo that. Sometimes I wake in the morning and think I haven't done it, that it's only a dream. And it's like Heaven! I cry for joy. And then the knowledge comes. I did not know, Michael, what I was doing. But since you came back I've *seen*; since I loved Wentworth I've *seen*—what I've done to you; just brushed you aside when you got in the way, and left you to die."

He looked at her in silence. It had come, the moment of anguished realisation that he had foreseen for her, but it had come to her through love for another. That to which his great love would fain have drawn her, she had reached at last by a lesser love than his.

"I have been cruel to Wentworth. I might have tried to get you out for his sake if not for yours. He never had a moment's happiness while you were shut up. But I didn't. I didn't really care for him then. I only tried at last to get you out, because I could not bear the misery of it any longer. I have never cared for anyone but myself—till now. I see now that I have been hard and cruel. I have always thought myself gentle and loving and tender-hearted, like you thought me, poor, poor Michael. You have paid for that. Like Wentworth thinks me now. Oh, Michael, *must Wentworth pay too*?"

Michael looked at her with compassion. "I am afraid he must. But do not let him pay a penny more than is necessary. You still have it in your power to save him part of the—the expense. Let him pay the lesser price instead of the greater. Tell him, instead of letting him find out."

Silence.

"It is the only thing to do, Fay."

No answer.

"I am afraid you do not love him after all," said the inexorable voice.

Again silence.

Michael dragged himself feebly from his chair, and took her clenched hands between both of his.

"Love him a little more," he said. "Take the risk and tell him everything—while there is still time. Listen, Fay, and try to forgive me if I seem cruel. You thought you loved me once. But it was not enough to risk anything for me. You threw me away by your silence because you found the truth too difficult. Don't, don't throw Wentworth away too, because the truth is difficult. Fay, believe me," Michael's voice shook, "it's hard to find out you've been deceived. It's hard to be betrayed." His voice had sunk to a broken whisper. "Don't put him through it. You wouldn't if you—if you knew what it was like."

Magdalen, coming in half an hour later found Fay lying on her face on the sofa alone. She looked, poor little creature, with her outstretched arms, not unlike a cross on which Love might very well be crucified anew. It does not matter much whether it is on a cross of wood, or of fear, or of egotism, that we nail Love to his slow death.

Fay loved for the first time. Was she going to crucify that love, to pierce its upholding hands, to betray that benign saviour, come so late but come at last, to help her in her sore need?

CHAPTER XXXIII

His own thought drove him like a goad.—TENNYSON.

"Now," said the great doctor to Michael next day, "I have been hustled down here against my will by Mr. Maine. I'm wanted elsewhere. I calculate my time at a pound a minute. Out with it. What is it that's worrying you?"

Michael did not answer.

The great man groaned. But his eyes were kindly.

"You want something you have not got, eh? like the rest of us. We are all in the same steam launch."

"I don't want anything, thanks."

"In love?"

"No."

"Quite sure? I have always observed that people who are in love are desperately offended at the bare supposition that such a thing is possible. Things might be arranged, you know. Young women aren't intended by nature to live single any more than you are. Would a few weeks in London meet the case? The season's just beginning. No theatres, of course, and no late hours. Your brother here seems made of money, though he will soon be ruined if he goes on sending for me. For I always charge double if I'm sent for unnecessarily. Come, sir, what *do* you want?"

"I don't know," said Michael, half amused. He was still exhausted by his expedition to Priesthope of the previous day. "I don't want anything, thanks. I'm—all right."

"What do you say to a change?"

"I had not thought of that," said Michael with a flicker of interest. "Now you mention it—yes. That's the very thing. I should like—a change."

Wentworth came forward at once.

"Norway?" he said eagerly, "or Switzerland. We must be guided by you, doctor. Or a yacht? You used to be fond of yachting, Michael. We will go anywhere you like."

Michael's face fell.

The doctor leaned back and examined his finger tips. He had seen what he wanted.

"The yacht won't do," he said with decision. "And Norway's out of the question. Much too far. In fact, there's only one place that will do."

"Where is that?" said Wentworth.

"I don't know yet. Where is it, Mr. Carstairs?"

"I should like," said Michael, colouring painfully, for he knew he was going to hurt Wentworth, "I should like to go to Lostford; not for long, just for a little bit."

"Lostford!" exclaimed Wentworth, amazed. "Lostford, down in that hole. Oh! no."

"Well, and why not Lostford?" said the doctor with asperity. "Mr. Carstairs shows his sense. He is not up to a long journey. Quite near. Interesting cathedral. Cultivated society. I should have suggested Lostford myself if he had not."

"I will ride over and take rooms at the 'Prince Consort' to-day," said Wentworth meekly.

"You will do no such thing. Are you taking leave of your senses. Your brother is not fit to stay in a rackety hotel."

"The Bishop has asked me," said Michael faintly, "to spend a week or two with him whenever I like. I believe—it's very quiet there."

"The Bishop!" said Wentworth. "It would be far from quiet at the Palace. Worse than an hotel. The Bishop lives in a perpetual turmoil."

Then he suddenly stopped short, and became very red. Michael preferred the Bishop to himself.

"It's a good idea," said the doctor. "I know the Bishop. Splendid man. The best of company." He got up with decision. "My orders are, Mr. Carstairs, that you proceed to Lostford without delay. How far is it? Six miles. Go to-morrow." Then he turned to Wentworth. "You will go over and see him in a week's time, and report to me."

"You think him worse," said Wentworth nervously to the doctor in the hall.

"No," said the doctor emphatically, watching his motor sliding to the door, "but he is not better. He is anxious about something, and he can't afford to be anxious. He is not in a fit state to have a finger ache with impunity."

"He has nothing to be anxious about," said Wentworth. "And if he had a trouble I should be the first to hear of it. I have his entire confidence—at least, I had till lately. I must own he has become very changed of late. Of course, I never appear to notice it, but——"

"Quite right. Quite right. I wish others were as sagacious as you are. Let him go to Lostford for a week or two—and get you off his nerves," the doctor added to himself as the motor shot down the beech avenue.

A few days later Wentworth was sitting idly watching the stream of Piccadilly from the windows of his club. The same day that Michael had gone to Lostford he had discovered that he had business in London. He would have found it difficult to say what his business there was. But one of Wentworth's many theories about himself was that he was a very busy man. He had so constantly given "urgent business" as a reason for evading uncongenial social engagements that he had finished by believing himself to be overwhelmed with arduous affairs. So he went to London, and visited a publisher anent his forthcoming history of Sussex, and dined with a man whom he met at Lord's, whom he had not seen for years, and wrote daily to Fay, expressing ardent but vague hopes that he might be able to "get away" from London by the end of the week.

He was in no hurry to return.

A vague fear of something grievously amiss with Michael, he knew not what; an unformulated anxiety weighed upon him. And he was jealous. Jealousy had brought him up to London. He was not going to remain deserted at Barford. Jealousy was keeping him there now. He had seen that Michael was glad to get away from him, that he had caught at the doctor's suggestion of a change. His sullen heart was very sore about Michael. Why did he *want* to leave him? Where would he meet anyone more devoted to him than himself? What could any man do for another that he had not done for Michael? Was it true then, after all, what he had so often heard was the fate of men of deep affections like himself, that they give all, and are given nothing in return.

A sudden exclamation made him look up.

"Why, Maine, is it you?"

A tall, bald man was holding out his hand to him. For a moment Wentworth did not recognise him. Then he remembered him. Lord John Alington.

He shook hands with tepid civility, but Lord John always mistook a pained recognition for an enthusiastic welcome. He drew up a chair at once.

"Now this is what I call luck," he said, his red face beaming. "And so your brother is freed at last. Only heard the news when I landed from Norway a week ago. I congratulate you with my whole heart. I never was so glad about anything before." And Lord John sawed Wentworth's limp hand up and down.

"I was present, you know," he went on. "Made a great impression on me. Sobered me for a long time I can tell you. I saw Carstairs come forward and give himself up. Never had such a shock in my life."

"I remember now you were there."

"Rather. And I was dead certain from the first that he had never done it. I always said so. And now at last the mystery is cleared up. And I was proved right. He hadn't. But fancy shielding that old Marchesa with her long teeth. Why, she was forty if she was a day. Who would ever have thought of it!"

"No one did," said Wentworth.

"*I* didn't. I may tell you frankly that I did *not*. The Marchesa! I knew her. But it never so much as crossed my mind that she had massacred her old hubby. 'Good God! The Marchesa!' Those were my exact words when I heard a week ago. Is Carstairs in London? I should like just to shake him by the hand."

"He is not in town. He is still feeling the effects of his imprisonment."

"I should like to have seen him. It was my fault he was found you know. I said 'Perhaps he's behind the screen.' Dreadfully sorry. Wish I hadn't. Only my fun. Never thought he was there, or anyone. I've never forgotten his coming out from behind the screen. But what I want to know is," Lord John tapped Wentworth on the arm with his eyeglass, and lowered his voice confidentially, "*why he ever went behind it.* That's what has been puzzling me ever since I read the Marchesa's confession. If he wanted to shield her, why the deuce did he hide at all? Why not strike a noble attitude bang in the middle of the room—from the first?"

Wentworth looked at him astonished. The vague suspicion of the last weeks that Michael was concealing something from him was taking shape at last.

There was no doubt that Lord John had got hold of a listener.

"No, no, Maine. When Carstairs was hiding behind the screen he was not dying with anxiety to take the Marchesa's crime on his white shoulders—not at that moment. That explanation don't wash. I believe I know a better one."

Wentworth became very red.

"The Duchess's maid! Did you ever see her? No, evidently not. You've no time for looking at young maids. Taken up with contemplating an old maid in the glass. You miss a lot, I can tell you. She was the prettiest little baggage I've set eyes on for years. And she was not of an iron virtue. But she wouldn't look at a little thing like me. Can't think why. Come, now, don't look so demure. We aren't all plaister saints like you. *I'm* not, in spite of my Madonna face. Wasn't that the truth? The Marchesa story is for the gallery. But you and I are behind the scenes. Mum's the word. But wasn't that why Carstairs was hanging about the house after everyone else had gone just for the same reason that I was—to get a word with that little hussy?"

At that moment a tall, middle-aged man came into the room, and Lord John's roving eye fell upon him. He sprang to his feet.

"Lossiemouth," he said, seizing the latter's unwilling hand. "Why, you're the very man I wanted to see. Congratulations, my dear chap. All my heart. Ship come in, and ancestral halls, and going to be married too, all in one fell swoop. Know Miss Bellairs a little. Jumped with her in the same skipping rope in childhood's happy hours, danced with her at her first ball. Madly in love with her. Never seen her since."

Wentworth escaped.

The chamber of his soul had been long in readiness, swept and garnished for the restless spirit that had returned to it—not alone.

CHAPTER XXXIV

Est-il indispensable, qu'on s'élève à un point d'où le devoir n'apparaisse plus comme un choix de nos sentiments les plus nobles, mais comme une silencieuse nécessité de toute notre nature.

The following afternoon Fay was sitting in the little morning-room at Priesthope, trying to write a letter, a long, long letter. Wentworth's last note to her, just arrived by the second post, was open before her, telling her that he could not return for two days. And then the door opened gently and he was before her.

She turned a white, miserable face towards the door. Then as she suddenly recognised him the colour rushed to her face, and she flew to him with a cry and locked him in her arms, kissing his shoulder, his coat, his hands.

He was thunderstruck. Could a few days' absence so profoundly move these delicate, emotional creatures, whom an all-wise Providence had made almost too susceptible to masculine charm! He had never seen Fay like this. But then, he had never seen anything like anything. She withdrew herself suddenly, and stood a little apart, her face and neck one carnation of soft shame.

"But you are in London," she said, her lip quivering, her eyes falling before his. "I have your own word for it that you are still in London." And she pointed at his letter. "I was not expecting to see you."

A joy so great that it was akin to pain laid its awakening hand on him.

"I am glad you were not expecting me," he said, in a voice that he hardly recognised as his own. "I'm thankful."

And he drew her back into his arms more moved than he had ever been.

Yes. He was loved. He loved and was loved. He had not known the world contained anything as great as this. He had always thought that life at its best was a solitary thing, that passion was a momentary madness with which he did not care to tamper, that celibacy was a cheap price to pay for his independence. But he and this woman were one. This was rest and peace and joy and freedom. This was what he had always wanted, without knowing he wanted it. One of the many barriers between them went down. He thought it was the only one.

They sat a long time in silence, his head against her breast. Her face had become pinched and sharp, the lovely colour had faded. All its beauty and youth had gone out of it. Her terrified eyes stared at the wall.

"Speak! Speak now," said the inner voice. "You were too late last time. Speak now."

"I am very miserable, Fay," in a whisper against her cheek.

Her arms tightened round him.

"Not so miserable now I am with you, but——"

It seemed to Fay that she was holding to her breast the point of the sword that was to stab her to death.

He raised his head, and she saw that there were tears in his eyes. Twice she had seen tears in those narrow grey eyes before: once when he had talked to her of Michael in prison, and once when Michael was exonerated.

They had drawn a little apart.

"When I came here I had not meant to tell you anything about it, I had decided not to, but—Fay, I can't believe it, I haven't slept all night, I have known for two days, I only found it out by the merest accident that that has happened which I never thought could happen, something impossible." Wentworth's lip quivered. "Michael has deceived me, not by mistake, not just for a moment, but systematically, purposely—for years."

There was anger as well as pain in his voice.

"It was about the murder of the Marchese," he said hoarsely, "but I don't care what it was about. That is not the point. He has deceived me for reasons of his own. I don't know what they were. And I am afraid, my darling, he has not stopped there. I am afraid he has deceived you too. I am afraid he hoodwinked you when he persuaded you to let him hide in your room. Why did he hide if he wanted to shield the Marchesa? Don't you see that there was no sense in his hiding, though I never thought of it till—lately? I always believed in him implicitly, as you have done. I thought him just the kind of person who *would* sacrifice himself for a woman. I can understand doing it. It appeals to a nature like mine. I was deeply hurt by his reserve about it, since he came home, but I never thought, it never struck me for one single second that it concealed anything discreditable."

"It does not," said Fay suddenly.

"My dearest, I am afraid there is no doubt it *does*. What was Michael doing in the garden at that time of night. You forget that. I am the last person in the world to think him capable of anything disgraceful, but I can't resist the conclusion that he was waiting—Oh! Fay, your ears ought not to be polluted by such things—was waiting about in the garden because he was attracted by someone in the house."

He felt her hand quiver in his.

How womanly she was, how pure. How could any man have had the heart to throw dust in those innocent eyes. He kissed the cold hand reverently.

"I hate to speak of such a thing to you, and it somehow seems out of the question when I think of Michael's character. I had brought him up so carefully. I had impressed on him my own high code of morals from the first. And yet—and yet—I am afraid, dearest, that Michael must have been hanging about to have a word with—don't start so, why do you tremble?—with your maid."

There was a moment's silence. Fay shook her head. She was unable to articulate.

"Then why was he there? You must have been very much surprised and alarmed at his coming to your room so late. And unless he had given you some reason, you would not have tried to hide him. We always come back to that. Fay, why *did* Michael hide?"

Fay struggled to speak. Her white lips moved, but no sound came forth.

"You and the Duke tried to save him from being discovered. We all know that. The Duke told me so himself."

Another silence. Fay's face became convulsed.

"You are no diplomatist, Fay, thank God. I see very well, my darling, that you know more than you will say. It is plain to me that in the goodness of your soul you are trying to shield Michael—*for the second time*."

He kissed her on the forehead and rose to go.

"Stop!" said Fay, almost inarticulately. "It isn't the second time. I didn't shield him last time. I let him slide. But I will now ... I want to tell you ... I must tell you ... Michael has been here, he came when you were away in London. And he has begged me,—Oh, Wentworth, he has implored me to—tell you everything."

Wentworth became very red. His face hardened.

"*He* has begged you to tell me! He has gone behind my back and tried to depute you to do it, to plead his cause for him. He has not even the courage to come to me himself. No, Fay, I am going. It is no use imploring me to stay. I'm not going to listen to you making excuses for him. I don't blame you, but you ought not to have agreed to do it. Whatever I ought to know I must hear from Michael himself. I shall go over and see him to-morrow morning. Even you, dearest, must not come between—Michael and me."

CHAPTER XXXV

Aimer quelqu'un, c'est à la fois lui ôter le droit, et lui donner la puissance de nous faire souffrir.

The following morning the Bishop and Michael were sitting in the library at Lostford Palace. The Bishop was reading a letter, while Michael watched him, sunk in an arm-chair.

Presently the Bishop thrust out his under lip, and gave back the letter to Michael.

"Wentworth has dipped his pen in gall instead of in his inkpot," he said. "For real quality and strength give me the venom of a virtuous person. The ordinary sinner can't compete with him. Evil doers are out of the running in this world as well as in the next. I often tell them so. That is why I took orders. What do you suppose Wentworth suspects when he says Alington has suggested a discreditable reason for your being in the di Collo Alto villa that night, and that he is not going to allow you to skulk behind a woman any longer? He will be here directly to extort what he is pleased to call 'the truth.' What are you going to say?"

"I don't know," said Michael. "That is the worst of me. I never know."

The Bishop frowned and rubbed his chin.

"I see one thing," continued Michael, "and that is that it's all important that he should not break with Fay."

"That will be his first step—if he knows the truth."

"I am afraid it will, and yet—that's the pity of it, she will last longer than I shall, and he does like her—a little—which is a great deal for him. You don't believe it, but he really does. And he'll want her more than ever—when I'm gone."

The Bishop looked keenly at his godson.

Michael had never before alluded to his precarious hold on life. It was obvious that he was only considering it now in its bearings on Wentworth's future.

"Can a man who has grown grey looking at himself in the glass, and recording his own microscopic experiences in a diary, can such a man *forgive*?" said the Bishop. "Forgiveness is tough work. It needs knowledge of human nature. It needs humility. I forgave somebody once long ago. And it nearly was the death of me. I've never been the same man since."

"Wentworth will have his chance," said Michael. "It's about all we can do for him."

"We all know he says he can, but then he says such a lot of things. He dares to say he loves his fellow men. But I've never yet found that assertion coincide with any real *working* regard for them. There are certain things which those who care for others never say, and that is one of them. The egoist on the contrary is always asserting of himself what he ought in common decency to leave others to say of him,—only they never do. Wentworth actually told me not so long ago that he was intent on the service of others. I told him it was for those others to mention that interesting fact, and that nobody had lied about him to that extent so far in my diocese."

"He always says that there is perfect confidence between us," said Michael. "I've heard him say so ever since I can remember, and I've heard him tell people that I always brought him my boyish troubles. But I never did, even as a boy, even when I got into a scrape at Eton. My tutor stood by me in that. Wentworth never could endure him. He said he was such a snob. But snob or not, he was a firm friend to me. And I never told him even at the first of my love for Fay. I somehow could not. You simply can't tell Wentworth things. But he has got it into his head that I always have, and that this is the first time I have kept anything from him. If I had only Fay's leave to tell him! It is the only thing to do."

The door opened, and to the astonishment of both men, Fay and Magdalen came in. Fay looked as exhausted, as hopeless, as she had done three months ago when Magdalen had brought her to make her confession to the Bishop in this very room.

She evidently remembered it. She turned her lustreless eyes on him and said, "Magdalen did not make me come this time. I have come myself. Do you think, is there any chance, Uncle John, that God will have mercy on me again, like He did before?"

"Do you mean by God having mercy, that Wentworth will still marry you if he knows the truth?"

She did not answer. That was of course what she meant.

She looked from one to the other of her three friends with a mute imploring gaze. Their eyes fell before hers.

"I have not slept all night," she said to the Bishop. "Magdalen stayed with me. And we came quite early because I had to come. Wentworth must be told. It isn't because Magdalen says so. She hasn't said so, though I know she felt he ought to be told from the first. And it isn't because he's sure to find out. And oh! Michael, it isn't for your sake, to put you right with him. It ought to be, but it isn't. But I can't let him kiss me any more, and not say. It makes a kind of pain I can't bear. It has been getting worse and worse ever since Michael came back, only I did not know what it was at first, and yesterday——" she stopped short, shuddering. "He came to see me yesterday," she said in a strangled voice. "He was so dear and good, so wonderful. There never was anyone like him. It is in my heart that he will forgive me. And he trusts me entirely. I can't deceive him any more."

The eyes of Michael and Magdalen met in a kind of shame. Those two who had loved her as no one else had loved her, who had understood her as no one else had understood her, saw that they had misjudged her. They had judged her by her actions, identified her with them. And all the time the little trembling "pilgrim soul" in her was shrinking from the pain of those very actions, was growing imperceptibly apart from them, was beginning to regard them with horror, not because they had caused suffering to others, but because they had ended by inflicting anguish upon herself. The red-hot iron of our selfishness with which we brand others becomes in time hot at both ends. We don't know at first what it is that is hurting us, why it burns us. But our blistered hands, cling as they will, must needs drop it at last. Fay's cruel little white hand had let go.

Michael took it in his and kissed it.

"Wentworth is coming here this morning," said the Bishop gently. "He may arrive at any moment. Stay here and speak to him. And ask him to forgive you, Fay. You need his forgiveness."

"I don't know how to tell him," gasped Fay. "I tried yesterday, and I couldn't."

"Let me tell him," said Michael, and as he spoke, the door opened once more, and Wentworth was announced.

He had got ready what he meant to say. The venomous sentences which he had concocted during a sleepless night were all in order in his mind.

Who shall say what grovelling suspicions, what sordid conjectures, had blocked his inflamed mind as he drove swiftly across the downs in the still June morning? He meant to extort an explanation from his brother, to have the whole subject out with him once for all. He should not be suffered to make Fay his accomplice for another hour. His tepid spirit burned within him when he thought of Michael's behaviour to Fay. He said to himself that he could forgive that least of all.

He had expected to find Michael alone, or possibly the Bishop only with him, the Bishop who *knew.* He was disconcerted at finding Fay and Magdalen there before him.

A horrible suspicion that Magdalen also knew darted across his mind.

It was obvious to him that he had broken up a conference, a conspiracy. His bitter face darkened still more.

"I don't know what you are all plotting about so early in the morning," he said. "I must apologise for interrupting you. I seem to be always in the way now-a-days. People are always whispering behind my back. But I have come over to see Michael. I want a few plain words with him without delay, and I intend to have them."

"That is well," said the Bishop, "because you are about to have them. We were speaking of you when you came in."

"I wish to see Michael alone," said Wentworth, stung by the Bishop's instant admission of being in his brother's confidence.

He looked only at Michael, who, his eyes on the ground, was leaning white as death against the mantelpiece.

"Do you wish us to go, Michael?" said the Bishop.

"I wish you all to stay," he said, raising his eyes for a moment. His hand shook so violently that he knocked over a little ornament on the mantelpiece, and it fell with a crash into the fireplace. His voice shook, too, but his eyes were steady. His great physical weakness, poignantly apparent though it was, seemed a thing apart from him, like a cloak which he might discard at any moment.

"I cannot say all I have to say before others," said Wentworth fiercely, "even if they are all his confederates in trying to keep me in the dark, all, that is, except Fay. We know by experience that she can shield a man who has something to hide even from his best friends. We know by experience that dust can be thrown in her unsuspecting eyes."

"You have been kept in the dark," said the Bishop with compassion; "you have not been fairly treated, Wentworth, you have much to forgive."

In spite of himself Wentworth was awed. He had a sudden sense of impending calamity. He looked again at Michael.

Michael's hand shook. His whole body shook. His lips trembled impotently.

Wentworth sickened with shame. His love was wounded to the very depths to see his brother like this, as it had never been wounded even by the first sight of him in his convict's blouse.

"I always trusted you," he said with a groan, putting up his hand so as to shut out that tottering figure. "I don't know what miserable secret you're keeping from me, and I don't care. It isn't *that* I mind. It is that—whatever it was, however disgraceful it was, you should have kept it from me. God knows I only wanted to help you. Surely, surely, Michael, you might have trusted me. What have I done that you should treat me as if I were an enemy? I thought I was your friend."

No one spoke.

"After all, I don't know that I care to hear. Why should I care. It's rather late in the day to hear now what everyone knows except me, what I've been breaking my heart over, racking my brains over as you well know for these two endless years, what you aren't even now telling me of your own accord, what you have been persuaded to by this—this"—Wentworth looked at the Bishop—"this outsider, this middle man."

A great jealousy and bitterness were compressed into the words "middle man."

"You have got to hear," said Michael, and the trembling left him.

He turned towards his brother, still supporting himself with one hand on the mantelpiece. The two stern faces confronted each other, and Magdalen for the first time saw a likeness between them.

"I have kept things from you. You are right there," said Michael, speaking in a low, difficult voice. "But I never intentionally deceived you till the Marchese was murdered. Long before that, four years before that, I fell in love."

Wentworth's heart contracted. He had always feared that moment for Michael, had always awaited it with a little store of remedial maxims. He had felt confident that Michael had never even been slightly attracted by any woman. How often he had said to himself that if there had been any attraction he should have been the first to know of it. Yet the incredible truth was being thrust at him that Michael had struggled through his first love without drawing upon the deep wells of Wentworth's knowledge.

"The woman I fell in love with was Fay. She was seventeen. I was nineteen."

The room went round with Wentworth.

"Fay," he said, in blank astonishment, "Fay!" Then a glare of light broke in on him.

"Then it was she," he stammered, "not her maid, as that brute Alington said—it was she—she herself that——"

"It was her I went to see the night I was arrested. I was deeply in love with her."

Michael paused a moment, and then added gently, "She never cared for me. I did not see that clearly at the time, because I was blinded by my own passion. I have seen it since."

Wentworth made no movement.

"I decided to leave Rome. Fay wrote to me that I ought to go. I went to say good-bye to her in the garden the night the Marchese was murdered. While I was in the garden, the murder was discovered and the place was surrounded, and I could not get away. I hid in Fay's boudoir. The Duke came in and explained to Fay what had happened. It was the first I knew of it. Then, when they searched the house and I saw that I must be discovered in another moment, I came out and gave myself up as the murderer, because I could not be found hiding in Fay's rooms at night. It was the only thing to do."

Fay took a long breath. What a simple explanation it seemed after all. Why had she been so terrified? Wentworth could not blame her seriously now.

"I never tried to shield the Marchesa," Michael went on. "That was her own idea. I only wanted to shield Fay from being—misconstrued. The Duke understood. He saw me hiding behind the screen, and tried to save me. He told me so next day. The Duke was good to me from first to last."

Wentworth turned a fierce, livid face towards his brother.

"Have I really got at the truth at last?" he said. "How can I tell? The Duke could have told me, but he is dead. Did he really connive at your romantic passion for his wife? If I may venture to offer an opinion, that part of the story is not quite so well thought out as the rest, though it is excessively modern. Anyhow he is dead. You tell me he saw you behind the screen in his wife's rooms at midnight, and felt no need of an explanation. How like an Italian. But he is dead. And you forced your love on another man's wife, though you own she did not return it, wormed yourself into her rooms at night, and then—*then*—yes, I begin to see a grain of truth among these heaps of lies—then when by an evil chance, an extraordinary stroke of bad luck, there was danger of your being discovered, then you persuaded her, the innocent, inexperienced creature whom you would have wronged if you could—you worked upon her feelings, you made her into your accomplice, you persuaded her to hide you.... You mean cur!... You only sneaked out of your hole when escape was absolutely impossible. And so the truth, or some garbled part of it, is choked out of you at last. No wonder you were silent all these years. No wonder you would not speak. No wonder you let your poor dupe of a brother break his heart over your silence. Credulous fool that I have been from first to last. So help me God, I will never speak to you again."

The violent, stammering voice ceased at last.

Fay shivered from head to foot, and looked at her lover.

Both men had forgotten her. Their eyes never left each other. Wentworth's fierce face was turned with deadly hatred upon his brother. Michael met his eye, but he did not speak.

There was death in the air.

Suddenly as in a glass she saw that Michael was saving her again, was sacrificing himself for a second time at enormous cost, the cost of his brother's love.

"Michael!" said Fay with a sob, "Michael, I can't bear it. You are trying to save me again, but I can't bear to be saved any more. I have had enough of being saved. I won't be saved. It hurts too much. I won't let you do it a second time. I have had enough of being silent when I ought to speak, I have had enough of hiding things, and pretending, and being frightened."

Fay saw at last that the truth was her only refuge from that unendurable horror which was getting up out of its grave again. She fled to it for very life, and flung herself upon it.

She took Michael's hand, and turning to Wentworth began to speak rapidly, with a clearness and directness which amazed Magdalen and the Bishop.

It all came out, the naked truth; her loveless marriage, the great kindness of her husband towards her, her determination bred of idleness and vanity to enslave Michael anew when he came to Rome, his resistance, his decision to leave Italy, her inveigling him under plea of urgency to come to the garden at night, his refusal to enter the house, her frantic desire to keep him, his determination to part from her.

There was no doubt in the minds of those who listened in awed silence that here was the whole truth at last.

Fay looked full at Wentworth and then said: "He asked me why I had sent for him, what it was that he could do for me. And I said—I said—'Take me with you.'"

"No," said Michael, wincing as under a lash, "No, you did not. Fay, you never said that."

"You did not hear it, but I said it."

Michael staggered against the mantelpiece.

Wentworth had not moved. His face had become frightful, distorted.

"I am a wicked woman, Wentworth," said Fay. "I tried to make him in love with me. I tried to tempt him. I could make him love me, but not do wrong. And then I let him take the blame when he was trapped. I had trapped him there first. He did not want to come. I forced him to come. I let him spoil his life to save my wretched good name. He is right when he told you just now that I never loved him. The love was all on his side. He gave it all. I took it all, and I went on taking it. It was I who kept him in prison quite as much as the Marchesa. It was I who let him burn and freeze in his cell. A word from me would have got him out."

Wentworth laughed suddenly, a horrible, discordant laugh.

They had rotted down before his eyes to loathsome unrecognisable corpses—the man and the woman he had loved.

Fay looked wildly at him.

"But you are good," she said faintly. "You won't, Wentworth, you won't cast me off like—like I did Michael."

He did not look at her.

He took up his gloves and straightened the fingers as his custom was.

"There is no longer anything which need detain me here," he said to the Bishop, and he moved towards the door.

"Nothing except the woman whose fate is in your hands," said the Bishop gently. "What of her? She deserted Michael because her eyes were holden. Now you can make the balance even if you will. But will you? You can repay cruelty with cruelty. You can desert her with inhumanity even greater than hers, because you do it with your eyes open. But will you? Is it to be an eye for an eye, and a tooth for a tooth? She loves you and is at your mercy, even as Michael was once at hers. You can crush her if you will. But will you?"

"Wentworth!" said Fay, and she fell at his feet, clasping his knees.

His face was as flint, as he looked down at her, and tried to push away her hands.

"Let him go, my child," said the Bishop sternly, and he took Fay's hands, and held them. "It is no use trying to keep a man who does not love you. Go, Wentworth. You are right. There is nothing to keep you here. In this room there are two people, one of whom has sinned and has repented, and both of whom love you and have spoken the truth to you. But there is no love and truth in you to rise up and meet theirs. You do not know what love and truth are, even when you see them very close. You had better go."

"I will go," said Wentworth, his eyes blazing. And he went out and shut the door behind him.

Fay's hands slipped out of the Bishop's, her head fell forward, and she sank down on the floor. The Bishop and Magdalen bent over her.

Michael looked a moment at her, and swiftly left the room. He overtook Wentworth in the hall, groping blindly for his hat.

"Come in here," said Michael, "I want a word with you," and he half pushed Wentworth into a room leading out of the hall. It was a dreary little airless apartment with a broken blind, intended for a waiting-room but fallen into disuse, and only partially furnished, the corners piled with great tin boxes containing episcopal correspondence.

Michael closed the door.

"Wentworth," he said breathlessly, "you don't see. You don't understand. Fay loves you." He looked earnestly at Wentworth as if the latter were acting in some woeful ignorance, which one word would set right. He seemed entirely oblivious of Wentworth's insulting words towards himself.

"I see one thing," said Wentworth, "and that is that I'm not inclined to marry your cast-off mistress."

Michael closed with him instantly, but not before Wentworth had seen the lightning in his eyes; and the two men struggled furiously in the dim, airless little room with its broken blind.

Wentworth knew Michael meant to kill him. The long, scarred hands had him by the throat, were twisting themselves in the silk tie Fay had knitted for him. He tore himself out of the grip of those iron fingers. But Michael only sobbed and wound his arms round him. And Wentworth knew he was trying to throw him, and break his back.

Wentworth fought for his life, but he was over-matched. The awful, murderous hands were feeling for his neck again, the sobbing breath was on his face, the glaring eyes staring into his. The hands closed on his throat once more, squeezing his tongue out of his mouth, his eyes out of his head. He made a last frightful struggle to wrench the hands away. But they remained clutched into his flesh, choking his life out of him. There was a thin, guttural, sawing noise mixed in with the sobbing. Then all in a moment the sobbing ceased, he felt the hands relax, and then an avalanche of darkness crashed down on him, and buried him beneath it.

CHAPTER XXXVI

That game of consequences to which we all sit down, the hanger-back not least.

—R. L. STEVENSON.

Down, very deep down. Buried in an abyss of darkness, shrouded tightly in a nameless horror that pressed on eyes and breath and hands and limbs.

At last a faint sound reached Wentworth. Far away in some other world a clock struck. His numbed faculties apprehended the sound, and then forgot it when it ceased.

At last he felt himself stir. He found himself staring at a glimmer of light. He could not look at it, and he could not look away from it. What was it? It had something to do with him. It grew more distinct. It was a window with a broken blind.

Someone close at hand began to tremble. Wentworth sat up suddenly and found it was himself. He was alone, lying crumpled up against the wall where he had been flung down. He knew where he was. He saw the piles of tin boxes. He remembered.

He leaned his leaden throbbing head against the wall, and wave after wave of sickness even unto death shuddered over him. Michael had tried to kill him. His stiff wrenched throat throbbed together with his head. For a long time he did not move.

At last the clock struck again.

He staggered to his feet as if he had been called, and looked with intentness at a fallen book and upset inkstand. There was a quill pen balancing itself in an absurd manner with its nib stuck in the cane bottom of an overturned chair. He took it out and laid it on the table. He saw his hat in a corner, stooped for it, missed it several times, and then got hold of it, and put it on. There was a little glass over the mantelpiece. A ghastly face with a torn collar was watching him furtively through it. He turned fiercely on the spy and found the face was his own. He turned up his coat and buttoned it. Then he went to the half-open door and looked out.

His ear caught a faint sound. Otherwise the house was very still.

A maid servant on her knees with her back to him was washing the white stone floor of the hall at the foot of the staircase. Another servant, also with her back to him, was watching her.

"Then it is early morning," he said. And he walked out of the room, and out of the house, through the wide open doors. A fine rain was falling, but he did not notice it. He passed out through the gates and found himself in the road. He stopped unconsciously, not knowing what to do next.

A fly dawdling back to the town from the station, passed him, and pulled up, as he hesitated.

"Station, sir?" said the driver.

"No, Barford," said Wentworth, and he got in. The fly with its faded cushions and musty atmosphere seemed a kind of refuge. He breathed more freely when he was enclosed in it.

As in the garden of Eden desolation often first makes itself felt as a realisation of nakedness. We must creep away. We must hide. We have no protection, no covering.

Wentworth cowered in the fly. He passed without recognising them all the old familiar landmarks, the twisting white road that branched off to Priesthope, the dew ponds, the half hidden, lonely farms. He was in a strange country.

He looked with momentary curiosity at a weather-worn sign post which pointed forlornly where four roads met. It was falling to pieces with age, but yet it must have been put up there since the morning. He had never seen it before. He shouted to the driver that he had taken the wrong road. The man pointed with his whip to where, a mile away, the smoke of Barford rose among its trees. The landscape suddenly slid into familiar lines again. He recognised it, and sank back, confused and exhausted. The effort of speaking had hurt his throat horribly. Was he going mad? How could his throat hurt him like this—if it wasn't—if Michael had not——

He thrust thought from him. He would wait till he got home, till his own roof was safely over him, the familiar walls round him.

This was his gate. Here was his own door, with his butler looking somewhat surprised, standing on the steps.

He found himself getting out, and giving orders. He listened to himself telling the servant to pay the fly and to send word by it to his dog-cart to return home. Of course he had gone to Lostford in the dog-cart. He had forgotten that.

Then he heard his own voice ordering a whiskey and soda to be brought to him in the library. And he walked there.

The afternoon post had arrived with the newspapers and he took up a paper. But it was printed in some language unknown to him, though he recognised some of the letters.

How long had he been gone, an hour, a day, a year?

He looked at the clock.

Half-past two. But this great shock with which the air was still rocking might have stopped it. He put his ear to it. Strange! It was going. And it always stopped so easily, even if the housemaid dusted it.

Was it half-past two in the afternoon or in the night?

There was a band of sunshine across the floor and outside the gardens and the downs were steeped in it.

Perhaps it was day.

The butler brought in a tray, and placed it near him.

"Have you had luncheon, sir?"

Wentworth thought a moment, and then said "yes."

"And will Mr. Michael return to-day, sir?"

Wentworth remembered some old, old prehistoric arrangement by which Michael was to have come back with him to Barford this afternoon.

"No," he said, the room suddenly darkening till the sunshine on the floor was barely visible. "No. He is not coming back."

The man hesitated a moment, and then left the room.

Wentworth groped for the flagon of whiskey, poured out a quantity, and drank it raw. Then he waited for the nightmare to lift.

His mind cleared gradually. His scattered faculties came sneaking back like defeated soldiers to camp. But they had all one tale of disaster and one only to tell. He must needs believe them.

Michael had tried to kill him. Whatever else shifted that remained true.

Wentworth bowed his stiffening head upon his hands, and the sweat ran down his face.

Michael had tried to kill him, and had all but succeeded. Oh! if only he had quite succeeded. If only his life had not come back to him! He had died and died hard in that little room. And yet here he was still alive and in agony.

Michael first. That thought was torture. Then Fay. That thought was torture. The woman he had so worshipped, on whom he had lavished a wealth of love, far greater than most men have it in them to bestow, had deceived him, had been willing to be his brother's mistress.

Why had he ever believed in Fay and Michael? Had he not tacitly distrusted men and women always from his youth up? Had he not gauged life and love and friendship at their true value years ago? Why had he made an exception of this particular man and woman? They were no worse than the rest.

What was any man or woman worth? They were all false to the core. What was Fay? A pretty piece of pink and white, a sensual lure like other women, not better and not worse. And what was Michael but a man like other men, ready to forget honour, morality, everything, if once his passions were aroused. It was an old story, as old as the hills, that men and women betray each other. It was as old as the psalms of David.

Pah! what a fool he was to allow his heart to be wrung by what was only the ordinary vulgar experience of those who were so silly as to mix themselves up with their fellow creatures.

He had only himself to thank.

Well, at any rate, he was free now. He was awake now. He was not going to put his hand in the fire a second time.

He was going abroad immediately. He would start to-morrow morning. In the meanwhile, he would go and see somebody, call somewhere, be in high spirits somewhere with others. They (they were Fay and Michael) would hear of that afterwards, would see how little he cared.

He seized up his hat and went out. But when he had walked a few hundred yards he sank down exhausted on a wooden seat in the alder coppice overhanging the house, and remained there. The baby pheasants crept in and out, all round him. Their little houses, each with an anxious step-mother in it, were set at regular intervals along the grassy path. Only yesterday he had walked along that path with the keeper, and had thought that in the autumn he and Michael would be shooting together once more.

They would never shoot together again.

As the dusk fell he heard a sound of wheels. His dog-cart returning from Lostford, no doubt. It did not turn into the court-yard, but came on up to the house. Wentworth peered down through the leaves.

It was the Bishop's dog-cart. He recognised the groom who drove it. To his amazement he saw Lord Lossiemouth get out. After some parley he went into the house.

Why should he have come?

Oh! of course, how dense he was. He had been sent over on an embassy by Magdalen and the Bishop. They wanted to hush up the fight, and bring about a reconciliation between him and Fay. He should be told Fay was making herself ill with crying. His magnanimity would be appealed to by that pompous prig. Well, he had had his journey for nothing. Wentworth saw his servants looking for him, and hid himself in the coppice.

A couple of hours later he left the wood, and went down the steep path to the gardens. It was nearly dark now. Lights twinkled in the house. The lamp in the library laid a pale finger of light upon the lawn, through the open glass doors.

Wentworth went up to it, and then as he was about to enter, shrank back astonished.

Lord Lossiemouth was sitting there with his back to the window. Wentworth stood a long time looking at him. He was evidently waiting for him to come in. He sat stolidly on as if he were glued to his chair, smoking one cigarette after another.

At last he got up. Surely he would go now. He walked to the bookshelves that lined the walls, inspected the books, selected one, and settled himself with a voluminous sigh in his arm-chair once more.

Wentworth stole away across the grass as noiselessly as he had come, and disappeared in the darkness.

CHAPTER XXXVII

Age by age, The clay wars with His fingers and pleads hard
For its old, heavy, dull, and shapeless ease.

—W. B. YEATS.

Wentworth never knew how he spent the night, if indeed that interminable tract in which time stopped could have been one night. It was longer than all the rest of his life put together. In later years, in peaceful later years, confused memories came to him of things that he must have seen then, but of which he took no heed at the time; of seeing the breath of animals like steam close to the ground; of stumbling suddenly under a hedgerow on a huddled, sleeping figure with a white face, which struggled up unclean in the clean moonlight, and menaced him in a foul atmosphere of rags.

And once, many years later, when he was taking an unfamiliar short cut across the downs, he came upon a little pool in an old chalk pit, and recognised it. He had never seen it by day, but he knew it. He had wandered to it on a night of moon and mist, and had seen a fox bring down her cubs to drink just where that twisted alder branch made an arch over the water.

Wentworth sat by that chalk pit on the down utterly spent in body and mind hour after hour, till the moon, which had been tangled in the alder stooped to the violet west with one great star to bear her company. Who shall say through what interminable labyrinths, through what sloughs, across what deserts, his tortured mind had dragged itself all night? The sun had gone down upon his wrath. The moon had gone down upon his wrath.

The land was grey. The spectral horses moving slowly in the misty fields were grey. A streak of palest saffron light showed where the dim earth and dim sky met.

A remembrance came to him of a summer dawn such as this, years and years ago, when Michael had been dangerously ill, and how his whole soul had spent itself in one passionate supplication that he might not be taken from him.

A tender green transparent as the light seen through a leaf in May was welling up the sky. Two tiny clouds floated in it like rafts of rose colour upon a sea of glass.

A deep and bitter sense of injustice was growing within him with the growing light.

A hundred times during the night he had recalled in cold anger every word of that final scene in the library, his own speech, his own actions, his great wrongs, his unendurable pain.

And yet again it returned upon him, always with Fay's convulsed face, and clinging hands, always with the Bishop's scathing words of dismissal. Their horrible injustice rankled in his mind, their abominable cruelty to himself revolted him. Hideous crimes had been committed against him, but *he* had done no evil, unless to love and to trust were evil. Why then was he to be thus thrust into the wrong, thus condemned unheard, cast forth with scorn because he had not obediently fallen in with the Bishop's preposterous demand on him to condone everything? *It was not to be expected of him.*

Suddenly the faces of the others watching him after Fay's confession rose before him, the Bishop's, Magdalen's, Michael's. He saw that they had not expected it of him either—not even Michael. Only in Fay's up-raised eyes as she held him by the knees had there been one instant's anguished hope. Only in hers. And that had been quickly extinguished. *He had extinguished it himself.*

The little clouds turned to trembling flame. The whole sky flushed and then paled. A thread of fire showed upon the horizon. It widened. It drew into an arch. The sun rose swiftly, a sudden ball of living fire; and in a moment the smallest shrub upon the down, the grazing horses, the huddled sheep, were casting gigantic shadows across the whole world.

A faint sound of wheels was growing clearer and nearer.

Wentworth saw a dog-cart coming towards him along the great white road. As he looked it pulled up and then stopped. A man got out and came towards him. The raw sunlight caught only his face and shoulders. He seemed to wade towards him waist deep through a grey sea.

Lord Lossiemouth again!

Lord Lossiemouth's heavy tired face showed sharp and white in the garish light.

"I have been looking everywhere for you," he said, not ungently. "I waited half the night at Barford, and then went on to Saundersfoot station, and then to Wrigley. Your servants thought you might possibly have gone there. But you had not been seen there. Magdalen sent me to tell you you must go back to the Palace. Your brother is very ill. He had an attack of hæmorrhage apparently just after you and he parted in the hall. I promised her not to go back without you. Shall we drive on?"

CHAPTER XXXVIII

Alles vergängliche ist nur ein Gleichniss.—GOETHE.

Michael was dying. All night Magdalen and the Bishop, with nurse and doctor, fought for his life, vainly strove to stem the stream of blood with which his life was ebbing away.

He had been found by Lord Lossiemouth and a servant lying unconscious at the foot of the staircase in the hall. He had been carried into a room on the ground floor. Everything had been done, but without avail. Michael was dying, suffocating in anguish, threshing his life out through the awful hours, in wild delirium.

He was in prison once more, beating against the bars of his narrow window looking out over the lagoon. His hoarse strangled voice spoke unceasingly. His hands plucked at his wrists, and then dropped exhausted beneath the weight of the chains which dragged him down.

Magdalen would fain have spared Fay the ordeal of that vigil. But the Bishop was inexorable. He bade her remain. And shrunk away in a corner, shivering to her very soul, Fay listened hour by hour to the wild feeble voice of her victim, back once more in the cell where he had been so silent, where the walls had kept his counsel so well. She saw something—at last—of what he had endured for her, of what he had made so light.

At last the paroxysm passed. Michael pushed back the walls with his hands, and then suddenly gave up the struggle.

"They are closing in on me," he said. "I cannot keep them back any longer."

The contest ceased all in a moment. He lay back motionless with half-closed eyes, his face blue against the white pillows. The blood had ceased at last to flow from his colourless lips. Death was very near.

He knew no one. Not the Bishop, not Magdalen who kept watch beside him, listening ever for Wentworth's step outside.

In the dawn Michael's spirit made as if to depart, but it seemed as if it could not gain permission.

The light grew.

And with the light the laboured breathing became easier. He stirred feebly, and whispered incoherently from time to time. He was still in his cell. Wentworth's name, the Italian doctor's, rose to his lips. Then, after a pause, he said suddenly:

"The Duke is dead. She will come now."

There was a long silence. He was waiting, listening.

The Bishop and Magdalen held their breath. Fay knew at last what it is to fail another. She had failed Michael. Wentworth had failed her.

"Fay!" Michael said, "come soon."

She had to bear it, the waiting, the faltered anguish, the suspense, the faint reiterated call to deaf ears.

The Bishop got up from his knees beside Michael, and motioned Fay to take his place. She went timidly to the low couch and knelt down by it.

"Speak to him," said the Bishop sternly.

"Michael!" she said.

He knew her. All other voices had gone from him, but hers he knew. All other faces had faded from him, but hers he knew. He looked full at her. Love stronger than death shone in his eyes.

"Fay," he said in an awed voice—"at last."

She had come to release him, after the Duke's death, as he knew she would.

She leaned her white cheek a moment against his in speechless self-abasement.

He whispered to her.

"Have I served you?"

She whispered back, "Yes."

He whispered again, "Do you still love me?" The words were quite inaudible.

Again she said, "Yes."

Again a movement of the lips, but no sound.

He looked at her with radiant questioning eyes.

Again she murmured, "Yes."

It had to be like that. He had always known that this moment had to come. Had he not foreseen it in some forgotten dream?

A great trembling laid hold on Michael, and then a stillness of exceeding joy.

In the silence the cathedral bells chimed out suddenly for early service. The sound of the bells came faintly to him as across wide water, the river of death widening as it nears the sea. It was all part of his dream. The bells of Venice were rejoicing with him, in this his blessed hour.

He was freed at last, free as he had never been, free as the seagull seen through the bars that could no longer keep him back. Useless bars, why had he let them hold him so long? He was out and away, sailing over the sheening water in a boat with an orange sail; in a boat like a butterfly with spread wings; sailing away, past the floating islands, past that pale beautiful grief of sea lavender—he laughed to see it shine so beautiful—sailing away into a pearly morning, under a luminous sky.

The prison was far away now. Left behind. There was a great knocking at its gates, hurried steps upon the stairs, and a voice crying urgently through the bars.

But he could not stay to listen. He was too far away to hear. The voice was to him but like the thin harsh cry of the sea-mew wheeling near, blended in with the marvel of his freedom. He took no heed of it. He was afloat on the great sea-faring tide. Far away before him, but nearer, nearer, and yet nearer, the sea gleamed in trembling ecstasy.

"He does not know me. He does not hear me," said Wentworth, on his knees beside Michael, raising a wild, desperate face to Magdalen. Was Michael's last look of deadly hatred to remain with him through life?

"Speak to him again, Fay," said Magdalen. "Tell him Wentworth is here."

Fay was still kneeling on the other side. The two lovers' eyes met across the man they had murdered.

"Michael," the tremulous voice whispered.

"Louder," said Wentworth hoarsely.

"Michael," said Fay again.

But Michael's face was set. He was sunk in a great rest, breathing deep and slow, deeper and slower yet, his long arms faintly rising and falling with each breath.

"Oh, Fay. For God's sake make him hear," said Wentworth with a cry.

The Bishop and Magdalen standing apart looked at each other.

"He has forgiven her, though he does not know it," he said below his breath.

Fay stooped down. She raised Michael in her arms, and laid his head on her breast, turning his fading face to his brother.

"Michael," she whispered into his ear, with a passion which would have cloven death itself. "Come back, come back and say one word to Wentworth."

Very near the sea now. Very near the great peace and light. This was the real life at last. All the rest had been a vain shadow, a prison where he had dwelt a little while, not seeing that this great all-surrounding water, which had seemed to hem him in, was but a highway of light.

Who were these two with him in the boat? Who but the two he loved best! Who but Fay and Wentworth! They were all floating on together in exceeding joy. They were very near him. He felt them one on each side, but the light was so great that he could not see them. His head was on Fay's breast. His hand was in Wentworth's hand. It was all as in dim dreams he had longed for it to be.

Fay's voice reached him, pressed close to his ear, like the sound of the sea, held in its tiniest shell.

He opened his eyes and his brother's white face came to him for a moment, like sea foam, blown in from the sea of love to which he was going, part of the sea.

"Wenty!" he said, and smiled at him.

And like blown foam upon a breaking wave, the face passed.

And like the whisper in the shell under the hush of the surge, the voice passed.

The shadow which we call life—passed.

THE END